"Are you all right?" Nell asked.

Lord Bromwell studied Nell in a way that sent the blood throbbing through her body as even the tipping coach had not.

"I believe I am undamaged. I wonder…?"

"Yes?"

"I wonder if I should attempt an experiment…."

"Experiment?" Nell repeated quizzically, having some difficulty following Lord Bromwell's line of reasoning and, at that particular moment, not really sure what an experiment was.

With no further warning, without even knowing her name, let alone being properly introduced, the gentleman raised his head.

And kissed her.

The pressure of his lips was as light and beguiling as the brush of a moth's wing, as delicious and welcome as warm bread and hot tea on a cold day, and more arousing than anything she'd ever experienced….

* * *

The Viscount's Kiss
Harlequin® Historical #957—August 2009

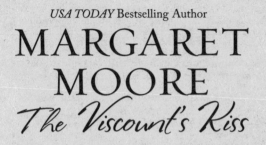

USA TODAY Bestselling Author

MARGARET MOORE

The Viscount's Kiss

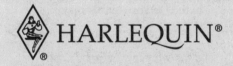

HARLEQUIN®

TORONTO • NEW YORK • LONDON
AMSTERDAM • PARIS • SYDNEY • HAMBURG
STOCKHOLM • ATHENS • TOKYO • MILAN • MADRID
PRAGUE • WARSAW • BUDAPEST • AUCKLAND

Recycling programs
for this product may
not exist in your area.

ISBN-13: 978-0-373-29557-9

THE VISCOUNT'S KISS

For my Dad, Clint Warren,
a hero and father who taught by quiet example

Available from Harlequin® Historical and
MARGARET MOORE

Other works include:

Harlequin Books
Mistletoe Marriages
"Christmas in the Valley"

The Brides of Christmas
"The Vagabond Knight"

HQN
*Bride of Lochbarr
Lord of Dunkeathe
The Unwilling Bride
Hers To Command
Hers To Desire
My Lord's Desire
The Notorious Knight
Knave's Honor
The Warlord's Bride*

Chapter One

It has long been my dream to study these fascinating creatures in their natural habitat, to watch them as they spin their webs and go about the business of living, myself unnoticed save as another species of fauna inhabiting their world.
        —from *The Spider's Web,* by Lord Bromwell

England, 1820

That man does not belong here, Nell Springley thought as she surreptitiously studied the only other occupant in the mail coach headed to Bath. He'd been asleep when she'd boarded in London, and he was still asleep despite the rocking and jostling of the vehicle, his tall beaver hat tipped over his eyes and his arms crossed over his chest.

He was clearly well-to-do, for he wore a fine indigo frock coat of excellent wool and buff trousers that hugged his long legs. His blindingly white cravat, tied in an intricate and complicated knot, fairly shouted a valet's skillful expertise. His slender fingers were likewise encased in superbly fitting kid leather gloves and his Hessian boots were so brightly polished, she could see the reflection of her skirts.

Surely a man who could afford such clothes would have his own carriage.

Maybe he was a gamester who had gambled away his fortune. If he was the sort who frequented outdoor boxing matches, that might explain why what little of his jaw and cheeks she could see had been browned by the sun.

Perhaps he'd been in the Navy. She could easily imagine that figure in a uniform, his broad shoulders topped by an officer's braid, shouting commands and looking very dashing on the quarterdeck.

Or he could be a tosspot sleeping off a night of drunken merriment, having spent the rest of his money on wine. If that were so, she hoped he wouldn't wake up until they arrived in Bath. She had no desire to be engaged in conversation with a sot. Or anyone else.

The coach lurched over a particularly bone-jarring bump that rattled the baggage in the boot and made the guard riding outside the coach curse. Nell, meanwhile, grabbed the seat as her poke bonnet slipped over her eyes.

"Bit of a rough spot," a deep, genial male voice noted.

Shoving her bonnet back into place, Nell raised her eyes—and found herself staring at the most handsome young man she'd ever seen. Not only was he awake, his hat was now properly situated on his head, revealing amiable blue-gray eyes separated by a narrow nose bordered by angular cheekbones. He was young, and yet there were wrinkles at the corners of his eyes that suggested he'd had vastly more experience of the world than she.

But then, most people had more experience of the world than she.

Nell blushed as if she'd been caught eavesdropping and immediately clasped her hands in her lap and lowered her eyes.

As she did, out of the corner of her eye she spotted something moving on the fawn-colored, double crimson-striped seat beside her.

A spider! A big, horrible brown spider—and it was headed right for her!

Gasping, Nell lunged across the coach—and landed on the lap of the young man opposite, knocking his hat from his head.

"Steady!" he warned, his upper-class accent providing more proof he was from a well-to-do household.

Blushing even more, she immediately moved to sit beside him. "I—I beg your pardon," she stammered, feeling hopelessly foolish, while noting that one stray lock of brown hair had tumbled over his forehead, making him look rather boyish and far less intimidating.

"There's no need to be frightened," her companion said. "It's only a *Tegenaria parietina*. They're quite harmless, I assure you."

Now completely humiliated by her childish reaction, Nell didn't know what to say. Instead, she smoothed out her skirts and glanced at the seat she had so abruptly vacated.

The spider was gone.

"Where is it?" she cried, gripping the seat and half rising regardless of the swaying motion of the coach. "Where's the spider?"

The young man held up his hat. "In here."

He had it in his *hat?*

He gave her an apologetic smile. "Spiders are of particular interest to me."

However handsome he was, however gentlemanly, he was definitely eccentric and possibly deranged.

"Please keep it away from me," she said, inching as far away from him and his hat as she could get. "I hate spiders."

The young man heaved a heavy sigh, as if her common aversion was a very serious failing. "That's a pity."

Considering everything she'd done in the past few days, to be condemned for disliking spiders struck Nell as completely ridiculous.

"Most spiders are harmless," the young man continued, peering into his hat as if the spider were a cherished pet. "I'm aware that they aren't as beautiful as some insects can be, like butterflies, but they are as useful in their way as butterflies or bees."

He raised his eyes and smiled, and she was immediately sure he never lacked for partners at a ball. "However you feel about spiders, you must allow me to introduce myself. I'm—"

With a loud crack, the coach flew up as if it were alive before coming down with a thunderous thud that sent Nell tumbling from her seat. Her companion reached for her, pulling her against his body, as horses shrieked and the driver shouted and the coach began to tip sideways.

It fell over, landing with another thud, and Nell found herself sprawled on top of the young gentleman and hemmed in by the seats.

He studied her in a way that sent the blood throbbing through her body as even the tipping coach had not. "Are you all right?"

She didn't feel any pain, only an acute awareness of his

body beneath her and his protective arms around her. "I think so. And you?"

"I believe I am undamaged. I suspect something went wrong with a wheel or an axle."

"Yes, yes, of course," she murmured. She could feel his chest rising and falling with quick breaths, as rapid and ragged as her heartbeat, even though the immediate danger had passed.

"I should investigate and ascertain what has happened."

She nodded.

"Right away," he added, his gaze locked onto hers and his handsome, sun-browned face so very close.

"At once," she whispered, telling herself to move yet making no effort to do so.

"I may be of assistance."

"Yes, of course."

"I wonder…?"

"Yes?"

"If I should attempt an experiment."

"Experiment?" she repeated quizzically, having some difficulty following his line of reasoning and, at that particular moment, not really sure what an experiment was.

With no further warning, without even knowing her name let alone being properly introduced, the young man raised his head.

And kissed her.

The pressure of his lips was as light and beguiling as the brush of a moth's wing, as delicious and welcome as warm bread and hot tea on a cold day, and more arousing than anything she'd ever experienced—completely different from that other unexpected kiss only a few short days ago that had ruined her life.

As he was different from the arrogant, domineering Lord Sturmpole.

This was what a kiss should be like—warm, welcome, exciting, delightful…as *he* was.

Until, with a gasp like a drowning man, he broke the kiss and scrambled backward as far as he could go, so that his back was against what had been the floor of the coach.

"Good God, forgive me!" he cried as if utterly horrified. "I can't think what came over me!"

She just as quickly scrambled backward between his legs, until her back was against the coach's roof.

"Nor I," she replied, flushing with embarrassment and shame, for she *did* know what had come over her—the most inconvenient, ill-timed lust.

This was hardly the way to travel unnoticed and unremarked!

"It must have been the shock of the accident," he offered as he got to his feet, hunching over in the small space and blushing as if sincerely mortified. "If you'll excuse me, I shall inquire as to our circumstances."

He reached for the handle, which was now over his head and without any further ado shoved the door open and hoisted himself up and out as if he were part monkey.

Crouching on the pocket of the door in the side of the coach, Nell straightened her bonnet and took stock of the situation. She was in an overturned coach. She was unhurt. Her clothes were disheveled but not torn or muddy. Her bonnet was mostly unscathed, while the young gentleman's hat had been crushed beneath them, along, no doubt, with the spider inside it.

She had also kissed a handsome stranger who seemed

to feel genuine, heartfelt remorse for that action, despite her obvious—and incredibly foolish—response.

She must be jinxed, born under some kind of ill omen. What else could explain the difficulties that had beset her recently? Her employment as companion to Lady Sturmpole had seemed a stroke of good fortune, then turned into an unmitigated disaster. She had been relieved to catch this coach at the last minute, only to have it overturn. She had been glad she would have to share the journey with only one other traveller, and he was asleep—but look how that had turned out.

As abruptly as he'd departed, the young man's head reappeared in the opening. "It seems the axle has broken. It will have to be fixed before the coach can be righted, so we shall have to find an alternate means of transportation. If you'll raise your hands, I'll pull you out."

She nodded and obeyed. "I'm afraid your hat is ruined and the spider dead."

"Ah," he sighed as he reached down for her. "Poor creature. Perhaps if I had left it alone, it would have survived."

Or perhaps not, she thought as she put her hands in his.

He pulled her up with unexpected ease, proving that he was stronger than he looked. It seemed his apparel, unlike many a fashionable young gentleman's, was not padded to give the appearance of muscles he didn't possess.

Once she was out of the coach, the soft light of the growing dawn illuminated the burly coachman, dressed in the customary coachman's attire of green coat and crimson shawl. He was lying on the verge, a bloody gash in his forehead and his broad-brimmed brown hat a short distance away. His red coat splattered with mud, the guard held the reins of the four nervous horses that had already been unharnessed from the coach. He also held a rather ancient blunderbuss. One of the horses had clearly broken a leg, for its left rear hoof dangled sickeningly. Thankfully, no passengers rode atop the mail coach; if they had been in a crowded stagecoach, people might have been seriously injured or killed.

The young man climbed off the coach painted maroon on the lower half, black above, with a red undercarriage, and the Royal cipher brightly visible on the side, then reached up to help her down.

She had no choice but to put her hands on his shoulders and jump. He placed his hands around her waist to hold her, and again she felt that unaccustomed warmth, that inconvenient lust, invade her body.

He quickly let go of her the moment she was on the ground, suggesting he was no lascivious cad and had been truly distressed by his kiss in the coach.

"Since you're not hurt, I should see to the driver," he said, giving her a short bow that wouldn't have been out of place at Almack's, before going to the driver and kneeling beside him.

After the young gentleman removed his soiled gloves, he brushed back the driver's gray hair and examined the wound in his scalp with a brisk, professional manner.

Perhaps he was a doctor.

"Am I dyin'?" the driver asked anxiously.

"I very much doubt it," the young man replied with calm confidence. "Scalp wounds tend to bleed profusely with very little provocation. Have you any other injuries?"

"Me shoulder. Just about twisted off when I was trying to hold the horses."

The young man nodded, then proceeded to test the area

around the coachman's shoulder, making him wince when he pressed one particular spot.

"Ah," the young man sighed, and the driver's eyes opened wide. "What?"

The young man smiled. "Nothing serious, Thompkins. You've strained it and shouldn't drive a team for a while, but I don't believe there's been any lasting damage."

"Thank God," the driver muttered with relief.

Then he frowned, anger replacing anxiety. "There was a damn dog in the road. I should have just run the bloody thing over, but I tried to turn the horses and hit a rock and—"

"Thompkins, there is a young lady present, so please refrain from profanity," the doctor gently chided as he got to his feet.

The driver glanced her way. "Sorry for my choice o' words, miss."

"Is there anything I can do to help?" she asked, not the least offended by his words, given the circumstances.

The young man untied his cravat and held it out to her. "You can use this to clean the wound, if you will— provided the sight of blood doesn't make you ill?"

"Not at all," she replied, taking the cravat, which smelled of some exotic scent she couldn't name.

"Then I'll see to the horses," the young man said as he absently unbuttoned the collar of his shirt, exposing his neck and some of his chest. Both were as tanned as his face.

Perhaps he was a doctor on a vessel.

The driver started to sit up. "Maybe I'd better—"

"No, you should rest," the young man ordered. "Enjoy having such a charming and pretty nurse, Thompkins, and leave the horses to me. Tell her about the time I tried to drive your team and we wound up in the ditch."

The driver grinned, then grimaced. "Aye, my lord."

My lord? A noble physician? That was very interesting... except that she should be thinking about how they were going to get to Bath and what she should do when they got there.

"First, I need a few words with your nurse," the nobleman said, taking her arm and drawing her a short distance away.

Concerned the driver was more seriously injured than he had implied, she ignored the impropriety of his action and tried to ignore the sensations it engendered, like little flames licking along her skin.

"Is the driver seriously hurt after all?" she asked anxiously.

"No, I don't believe Thompkins has a serious concussion," he said, to her relief. "However, I'm not a doctor."

"You're not?" she blurted in surprise. His examination had certainly looked like that of a medical man.

He gravely shook his head. "Unfortunately, no. I have a little medical training, so I know enough to be aware that he should be kept conscious, if at all possible, until we can fetch a physician. Can you do that while I see to the injured horse and ride to the next inn on one of the others?"

"Yes, I think I can keep him awake."

The young gentleman's lips flicked up into a pleased smile that again sent that unusual warmth thrumming through her body. As she returned to the driver and tried to soothe her nerves, he started toward the guard holding the horses.

She heard the nobleman ask the guard where the pistols were as she began wiping the blood that had slowed to a trickle.

"Under my seat," the man nervously replied, glancing

at the high backseat at the rear of the coach, for mail coach guards generally carried pistols as well as a blunderbuss, to fend off highwaymen.

"I'll hold the horses while you put that poor beast out of its misery," the young gentleman offered.

"What, you want *me* to shoot it? I couldn't!" the guard protested. "I can't be destroyin' government property! It'd be my job. Besides, I'm to look after the mail, not the animals."

"Surely an exception can be made if a horse has broken its leg," the young man replied.

"I tell ya, I'm supposed to guard the mail, not take care o' the horses!"

"I will not allow that poor animal to suffer."

"*You* won't? Who the devil are you?"

"Shut yer gob, Snicks," the driver called out. "Let the viscount do what has to be done."

He was a viscount? A *viscount* had kissed her?

"I'll pay for the horse if need be," the young nobleman said as he marched toward the overturned coach with such a fiercely determined look on his face, he hardly seemed like the same man.

The guard scowled but said no more as the viscount found the pistol which, like the blunderbuss, looked as if it had been made early in the previous century.

With the gun behind his back, murmuring something that sounded like an apology, the viscount approached the injured horse. Then, as the guard moved as far away as he could, the nobleman took his stance, aimed and shot the horse right between its big, brown, limpid eyes.

As the animal fell heavily to the ground, the viscount lowered his arm and bowed his head.

"Couldn't be helped," the driver muttered roughly. "Had to be done."

Yes, it had to be done, Nell thought as she returned to dabbing the driver's wound, but she felt sorry for the poor horse, as well as the man who had to shoot it.

The viscount tucked the pistol into the waist of his trousers before returning to Nell and the driver. Between the pistol, his sun-darkened skin, open shirt and disheveled hair, he looked like a very handsome, elegant pirate.

Pirate. The sea. A viscount who liked spiders who'd gone to sea…

Good heavens! He had to be Lord Bromwell, the naturalist whose book about his voyage around the world had made him the toast of London society and the subject of many articles in the popular press. Like so many others, Lady Sturmpole had bought his book and talked about his remarkable adventures, although she didn't bother to actually read *The Spider's Web.*

No wonder he could be calm in a crisis. Any man who'd survived a shipwreck and attacks by cannibals could surely take an overturned coach in stride. As for that kiss, he must often be the object of female attention and lust. He probably had women throwing themselves at him all the time and assumed she was another who was intrigued and infatuated by his looks and his fame.

And because he was famous, the press might take an even greater interest in a mail coach overturning, perhaps noting that Lord Bromwell had not been the only passenger and asking her name and her destination and why she was in the coach….

With a growing sense of impending doom, wishing she'd never caught the coach, never gone to London, never decided to go to Bath and, most of all, never met *him*, Nell watched as the handsome, renowned naturalist swung himself onto the back of one of the horses and galloped down the road.

Chapter Two

Fortunately, I have been blessed with a practical nature that allows me to take immediate action without the burden of emotion. Thus, I was quite calm as the ship was sinking and my concern was to help as many of my shipmates as possible. It was after the ship had gone down and the storm had abated, after we had managed to retrieve some items necessary to life and found ourselves on that tiny slip of sand seemingly lost in the vast ocean, that I laid my head on my knees, and wept.

—from *The Spider's Web*, by Lord Bromwell

As Lord Bromwell—known as Buggy to his closest friends—had expected, the sight of a dishevelled, hatless, cloakless man mounted on a sweat-slicked coach horse charging into the yard of The Crown and Lion caused quite a stir.

A male servant carrying a bag of flour over his shoulder toward the kitchen stopped and stared, openmouthed. Two slovenly attired men lounging by the door straightened.

The washerwoman, an enormous basket of wet linen in her arms, nearly dropped her burden, while a boy carrying boots paid no heed where he was going and nearly ran into one of the two idlers, earning the curious lad a cuff on the side of the head.

"There's been an accident," Bromwell called out to the hostler as the man ran out of the stables, followed by two grooms, a stable boy and a man in livery.

Bromwell slid off the exhausted horse and, after unwrapping the excess length of the reins from around his hands, gave them to the stable boy. Meanwhile, the grooms, liveried fellows, idlers, bootblack and washerwoman gathered around them. "The mail coach broke an axle about three miles back on the London road."

"No!" the hostler cried, as if such a thing were completely impossible.

"Yes," Bromwell replied as the inn's proprietor, alerted by the hubbub, appeared in the door of the taproom. He wiped his hands on the soiled apron that covered his ample belly and hurried forward at a brisk trot that was impressive for a man of his girth.

"Gad, is that you, Lord Bromwell?" Jenkins exclaimed. "You're not hurt, I hope!"

"I'm perfectly all right, Mr. Jenkins," the viscount replied, slapping the worst of the mud from his trousers. "Unfortunately, others are not. We need a physician and a carriage, as well as a horse for me, for I fear we won't all fit in one vehicle. Naturally I shall pay—"

"My lord!" Mr. Jenkins cried, his red face appalled, his hand to his heart as if mortally offended. "Never!"

Bromwell acknowledged the innkeeper's generosity with a smile and a nod. He'd always liked Mr. Jenkins, which made his father's disparaging treatment of him even more painful to witness.

"You there, Sam," Jenkins called to the hostler, "get my carriage ready and saddle Brown Bessie for his lordship—the good saddle, mind.

"Johnny, leave those at the door and run and fetch the doctor," he said to the bootblack. "Quick as you can, lad."

The boy immediately did as he was told, while the hostler and grooms returned to the stable, taking the coach horse with them. Adjusting her heavy basket on her hip, the washerwoman started back toward the washhouse and the two idlers returned to their places, where they had a good view of incoming riders and vehicles.

"Come in and have a drink o' something while they're getting the horse and carriage ready," Jenkins offered. "I expect you'll want to wash, too."

Bromwell reached up to touch his cheek and discovered he was rather muddy there, too. "Yes, indeed I would," he replied, following the innkeeper toward the main building, a two-storied, half-timbered edifice, with a public taproom and dining room on the lower level and bedrooms above.

Although Bromwell had lost what vanity he'd possessed years ago, believing his looks nothing to boast of especially compared to those of his friends, as he walked behind Jenkins through the muddy, straw-strewn yard, he couldn't help wondering what his female fellow passenger had made of his appearance.

More importantly, though, what the devil had possessed him to act like a degenerate cad? To be sure, she was pretty, with the most remarkable green eyes, and he'd noticed her trim figure clad in a plain gray pelisse when she'd briskly approached the coach before getting on in London. But he'd met pretty young women before. He'd even seen several completely naked during his sojourn in the South Seas. Indeed, while he'd found her pretty, he'd had no trouble at all pretending to be asleep to spare himself any conversation before he really had fallen asleep.

If he hadn't, he might have started to wonder sooner why a woman who spoke with such a refined accent and had such a manner was travelling unaccompanied.

She could be a governess or upper servant, he supposed, going on a visit.

Whoever she was, he should be thoroughly ashamed of himself for kissing her—and he would have been, had that kiss not been the most amazing, exciting kiss he'd ever experienced.

"Look here, Martha, here's Lord Bromwell nearly done to death," the innkeeper announced as he entered the taproom and addressed his wife, who was near the door to the kitchen. "The mail coach overturned."

Mrs. Jenkins, round of face and broad of beam, gasped and bustled forward as if about to examine him for injuries.

"No one has been killed or seriously hurt, as far as I can determine," Bromwell quickly informed her. "Your husband has already sent for the doctor and has offered replacement transportation."

"Well, thank God nobody was badly hurt—and ain't I been sayin' for years them coaches were gettin' too old to be safe?" Mrs. Jenkins declared, coming to an abrupt halt and resting her fists on her hips. She frowned at them as if *they* were personally responsible for the mishap and had the authority to correct everything and anything amiss with the delivery of the Royal Mail.

"Aye, Mother, you have," her husband mournfully agreed, agreement being the best way to react to Mrs. Jenkins's pronouncements, as Bromwell had also learned over the years. "Have Sarah bring some wine to the blue room while Lord Bromwell cleans up a bit—the best, o' course. He'll need it."

"There's clean water there already and fresh linen, my lord," Mrs. Jenkins said briskly as she turned and disappeared into the back of the inn.

"She's right, though," Jenkins said as he continued to lead the way, even though Bromwell was as familiar with this inn as he was with the ancestral hall. "Them coaches are a disgrace, that's what."

Bromwell remained silent as they passed through the taproom, although several customers turned to stare at him and excited whispers followed in his wake.

It was not just because of the accident or his dishevelled appearance, for he heard them uttering his name and, as was all too usual, the words *shipwreck* and *cannibals*.

He was never going to get used to this sort of curious scrutiny and the agitation occasioned by his mere arrival in a room, he thought with an inward sigh. Although he was glad his book was a success and increasing interest in the natural world, it was at times like these that he longed for his former anonymity.

Had the young lady in the coach known or guessed who he was? Did that account for her heart-stopping, passionate response?

And if so, what should he do when he saw her again? How should he behave?

Jenkins opened the door to the best bedchamber.

"There's clean water in the pitcher, although it's cold, and linen there," he said, nodding at the simple white china set and towels on the washing stand.

"Thank you, Jenkins."

"Sing out if you need anything, my lord."

"I shall," Bromwell promised as the innkeeper left the room and closed the door.

The inn's best bedroom was small compared to his room at his father's estate or the London town house, but comfortable and snug under the eaves, with inexpensive, clean blue-and-white cotton draperies, linen and basin set. A colorful rag rug lay on the wooden floor that creaked with every move he made, as would the bed ropes if he lay down.

His friend Drury had complained about that when he'd stopped here on his way to spend some time at Christmas a few years ago, Bromwell recalled as he stripped off his mud-spattered jacket and rolled up his sleeves.

He could just imagine the stunned expressions on his friends' faces if he told them what he'd done today. Not shooting the unfortunate horse—they would expect no less—but that he, good old shy, studious Buggy Bromwell, had kissed a woman whose name he didn't know and whom he'd only just met. They'd probably be even more shocked if he confided that he wanted very much to do it again.

Several times, in fact.

Of course he knew it was man's nature to seek sexual gratification and he was not abnormal in this regard (as certain very willing young women in the South Seas could attest), but he had always behaved with due decorum in England.

Until today.

His equilibrium must have been disturbed by the accident, he decided as he splashed cool water over his face, then picked up a towel and vigorously rubbed his face. Men could act very differently under duress, as he'd seen more than once on his last voyage. Some of the men who could be courageous on land had become whimpering and helpless during a storm at sea and the men he'd been sure would flee at the first sign of trouble had stayed and fought for their companions' safety.

"I've got yer wine, my lord," Mrs. Jenkins declared behind the door, taking him out of his brown study or, as his father would say, "another of your damn daydreams."

"Come in," he called as he rolled down his wrinkled sleeves.

The woman entered the chamber with the force of a strong wind, a wineglass held out to him.

"It's a miracle and a mercy nobody was killed," she declared, her buxom body quivering with indignation while Bromwell downed the excellent wine in a gulp. "I've been telling Jenkins for years some of them coaches weren't fit to be on the road. You ought to get your friend Drury to sue. He never loses, I hear."

"Drury only handles criminal cases," Bromwell replied as he set down the glass and picked up his jacket. "This was an accident, caused by a stray dog and Thompkins's decision not to run it over. I won't go to court over that."

He put on the soiled jacket that his former valet would have wept to see. Not knowing how long he would be at sea, or if he would even return, he'd given Albert a well-earned reference and paid him an extra six months' salary before dismissing him. Since his return, he hadn't bothered to hire another, much to the dismay of Millstone, the butler at his father's London town house, even though Millstone had to admit Bromwell had learned to tie his cravat like an expert, having spent several hours practicing when there was nothing else to do at sea.

What would Millstone make of this latest mishap? Probably he'd just sigh and shake his head and comment that some men led charmed lives, although his lordship really ought to buy a new carriage. He could certainly afford it.

So he could, if he wasn't planning another expedition.

If he told Millstone about kissing the young woman, the poor man would likely drop down in a faint, as shocked and surprised as his friends would be—as shocked and surprised as he had been when it finally dawned on him that he shouldn't be kissing a woman he'd only just met.

Perhaps, as his father complained, he'd been too long away from England.

"Are the horse and carriage ready?" he asked Mrs. Jenkins, who seemed rather keen to linger.

"They should be by now, my lord."

"Good." He looked out the window at the sky gray with thickening clouds. "If you'll excuse me, Mrs. Jenkins, I must be on my way."

She smiled. "Always the perfect gentleman, my lord!"

Not always, he thought as he hurried past her.

Not always.

Bunching the cravat tighter in her hand, Nell glanced up at the sky. The gray clouds were definitely thickening, and moving closer.

"Never fear, lass," the driver said, wincing as he shifted. "Lord Bromwell'll be back with help soon. That lad can ride like the wind."

She gave the driver a smile, but her eyes must have betrayed that she wasn't completely reassured, for he patted her hand as his eyes drifted closed. "I've known him since he was six years old. Might not look like it, but he's the finest horseman I've ever seen. Brave, too."

"But not, perhaps, a competent mail coach driver?" she suggested, trying to keep Thompkins awake.

To her relief, he opened his brown eyes again. "Well, to be sure, that wasn't his finest hour, but he was only fifteen at the time."

"Fifteen? He could have been seriously hurt, or even killed!"

The driver frowned. "Don't you think I knew that? O' course I refused the first time he asked, and lots o' times after that, but he wouldn't let up till I gave in. And he had his reasons all worked out, logical-like, beginning with his skill and how far he'd go—only a mile or so. But that wasn't why I finally gave in. I knew he wanted something to brag about when he got back to school, so his friends would think he was as good as they were—although he's worth the lot of them and always has been and I said so at the time. But he got this look in his eyes, and well, miss, I didn't have the heart to refuse him. We didn't have any passengers that day and if the road hadn't been so slick in that one place, it would have been all right.

"Should have seen him at the start," Thompkins continued, grinning at the memory. "Like one of them Roman charioteers, standing up and working the reins like an old hand until we hit that slick spot and went into the ditch. But no damage to the coach and we was only a little late. Not that it made a mite of difference to his father, though, when he found out what'd happened."

Thompkins sighed, then frowned. "You should have heard the way the earl carried on. Any other man might have been proud of the lad for wanting to try and getting that far, but not him. You'd think young Lord Bromwell'd lost the family estate or murdered somebody.

"The viscount, bless him, told his father he'd forced me to agree to it by saying he'd see I lost my job if I didn't. Well, that was a lie, but he was cool as you please, and damn—pardon me, miss—if his father didn't believe him. And then not another word did young Lord Bromwell say. He just stood there covered in mud from head to toe, and his lip bleeding, too, like the earl was giving a speech in the House of Lords that had nothing to do with him.

"Oh, he's a rum cove, all right, even if he's a nobleman. Have you read his book?"

"I'm sorry to say I haven't," she replied, wishing that she had.

"To be honest, I ain't read it, either, since I can't read at all," the driver admitted, "but I heard all about his narrow escape from them savages and the shipwreck, too. And the tattoo, o' course."

Nell paused in her ministrations. "Lord Bromwell has a tattoo?"

Thompkins grinned and lowered his voice. "Aye, but he ain't never told anybody what it is, or where. Just that he got one. Some of the nobs have made a bet on it and put it in that book at White's, but so far, nobody's collected."

Nell was aware of the famous betting book at that gentlemen's club, and that men who belonged would—and did—wager on almost anything.

Thompkins looked past her and pointed down the road. "Thanks be to God, here he comes."

Nell looked back over her shoulder. There was indeed a horse and rider coming toward them, and it was Lord

Bromwell. He still wore no hat, so his slightly long hair was ruffled by the ride, and his coat was as muddy as his formerly shining boots.

"Mr. Jenkins of The Crown and Lion is sending his carriage and a doctor. They should be here soon," Lord Bromwell said as he drew the brown saddle horse to a halt and dismounted.

Nell discovered she couldn't meet his steadfast gaze as he came toward them. The memory of those moments in his arms and especially of his kiss were too vivid, too fresh, too disturbing. Instead, she continued to wipe Thompkins's forehead, even though the bleeding had stopped.

Lord Bromwell's boots came into her line of sight. "I trust the patient is resting comfortably?"

"Aye, my lord," Thompkins replied, "although my head hurts like the devil."

"You're not dizzy or sleepy?"

"Not a bit, my lord. The young lady and I have been having a fine time."

The toe of Lord Bromwell's boot began to tap. "Have you indeed?"

"Aye. I told her about the time you drove the coach, and we talked about yer book."

She risked a glance upward, to discover that Lord Bromwell looked even more rakish and handsome with his hair windblown and his shirt still open and the hint of whiskers darkening his cheeks. However, his expression was grave, his blue-gray eyes enigmatic, and his full lips that could kiss with such devastating tenderness betrayed no hint of emotion.

She swallowed hard as she looked back to the driver.

"I wasn't aware you were the famous Lord Bromwell,"

she said, determined that he appreciate that, although what kissing him without the excuse of his fame might suggest about her, she didn't want to consider.

"Forgive me for being remiss and not introducing myself sooner. And you are?"

"Eleanor Springford, my lord," she lied, hoping he would mistake her blush for bashfulness and not shame.

The driver's eyes twinkled with mischief. "We were talking about yer tattoo, too."

"It's a common practice among the South Sea islanders," Lord Bromwell gravely replied, as if it was the polite thing to do, like taking tea. "Ah, here comes Jenkins's carriage."

With that, he strode off to meet it, leaving Nell to wonder what such a man would make of her if he ever learned the truth.

Chapter Three

*I believe it is an intense curiosity and an unwill-
ingness to simply accept the world without further
explanation that separates the scientist from the
general population. It is not enough to see a thing;
the scientist seeks to find out the how and why it
works, or in the case of the natural world, how and
why a creature does what it does.*

     — from *The Spider's Web,* by Lord Bromwell

"The supper will be served in half an hour, my lord,"
Jenkins announced from the door of the slightly smaller,
more cramped room Bromwell had taken when they returned from the scene of the accident so that Miss Springford could have the better one. "The wife's glad she killed
that chicken this afternoon, or she'd be in some state now,
I can tell you, what with you here and all."

"I've been here plenty of times before," Bromwell replied as he reached for his brush, determined not to look
a complete mess when he went below. "She should know
I like everything she makes, especially her tarts. When I

was stranded on that strip of sand, I would have sold my soul for one."

"Tush, now, my lord, that's almost blasphemy, that is!" Jenkins cried, although he beamed as proudly as if he made the tarts. "I'll be telling the wife, though. She'll be pleased."

"As I am by her tarts," Bromwell said, bringing his hair into some semblance of order, although it occurred to him that it was in need of a trim.

"Ah, here's Johnny now with your baggage, my lord."

"Thank you," Bromwell said as the boy carried in his small valise.

With another nod, Jenkins left him to change, followed by the gaping Johnny, who paused on the threshold to look back and whisper, eyes wide. "Was you really nearly et by cannibals, my lord?"

"I might have been, if they had caught us," Bromwell replied gravely, and quite truthfully.

The lad's eyes grew even wider.

"If you'll excuse me," Bromwell said, starting to close the door.

The lad nodded and disappeared.

Bromwell shut the door with a sigh. He was seriously beginning to wish he'd left that part of his voyage out of his book. Everybody asked about it, to the exclusion of many other fascinating events and observations.

Well, in mixed company, at any rate, he thought as he took off his soiled shirt, trousers and stockings. When he was with men after suppers or in the clubs, they wanted to know about the women and sexual practices, waiting with avid and salacious curiosity.

They were inevitably disappointed when he began describing the flora and fauna of the islands, including spiders, instead. Sometimes, if they listened and were patient, he would describe a *heiva*, a celebration involving dancing, the *otea* done by men, the *upa upa* by couples, and the *hura*, called hula in Hawaii, danced exclusively by women.

Recalling some of those dances and the dancers who'd performed them, he donned a clean white shirt, woollen trousers and stockings. What would Eleanor Springford think of those dances?

What would she think if she knew he'd participated?

Between that, and his insolent kiss, she'd certainly think he was no gentleman, although her response hadn't been exactly ladylike, either.

He suddenly remembered that he'd heard her name before, and his heart began to pound as if he were again participating in an *otea*. *Lady* Eleanor Springford was the daughter of the Duke of Wymerton. She was also one of the many young ladies his mother had mentioned in hopes he would take a wife and stop chasing after spiders.

What the devil was a lady of her wealth and family doing dressed in such plain, inexpensive clothes and travelling alone in a mail coach headed to Bath?

He had no idea, but he doubted it was a pleasure trip.

If she was in some sort of trouble, it was his duty to help her; it would be his duty whether she was twenty and pretty, or sixty and the homeliest woman he had ever met.

Determined to speak with Lady Eleanor and offer her any assistance he could render without further delay, Bromwell hurried down to the dining room.

But when he entered, he found the room full of people he'd never seen before, and he couldn't see the duke's daughter anywhere.

Everyone fell silent when they realized he had arrived,

so he plastered a weak smile on his face and, as he continued to silently search for Lady Eleanor, again damned the fame he'd never wanted.

"Oh, my lord! What a tragedy!" cried an overdressed, middle-aged woman wearing a silk gown overburdened with ruffles and frills, in a shocking combination of orange and pink that wouldn't have looked out of place in a bordello.

She hurried toward him past a group of silent, brawny men. He suspected they were local farmers or tradesmen dragged here to meet the famous naturalist by their wives, many of whom were equally colorfully dressed in the latest styles.

"Indeed, it was a most unfortunate occurrence," he muttered, unable to look directly at that gown another moment.

"I've been after them to fix that road," a man growled as he ran a puzzled gaze over Bromwell, thinking, no doubt, that the viscount didn't look like a world-famous explorer.

Bromwell had long since given up trying to explain that he was a different sort of explorer, that his journey had been intended to find flora, fauna, insects and especially spiders, not lands to claim, people to conquer or resources to exploit. "May the local government take heed," he said politely.

"They will if you write a letter to the *Times* about it," the man declared as Jenkins appeared, dressed in what was surely his Sunday best.

Bromwell's discomfort increased as Jenkins introduced him to the local gentry like he was some prized possession Jenkins was eager to show off, beginning with the man who'd complained about the roads. Since Bromwell liked Jenkins, he submitted, but he also continued to look for Lady Eleanor, until he decided she must be dining in her room.

This was going to be a long evening, he thought as he stifled a sigh, taking one last survey of the room.

At last he spotted her, crammed into the corner as far as she could get and wearing a flowing gown of pale blue silk like something fairies had cut out of a summer's sky. Unlike the other women's gowns, the cut was simple, with a bodice high in the back, a modest neckline, tight sleeves and only one ruffle at the hem. Her dark brown hair, which had been covered by her simple straw bonnet, proved to be thick and lustrous in the candlelight. It had been done simply, yet elegantly, around her gracefully poised head. In spite of the simplicity of her gown and hair, she was easily the most elegant, best-dressed woman in the room.

Having been blessed with uncommonly good eyesight, however, he immediately noticed something odd. Unlike the clothing she'd been wearing earlier, her gown did not fit properly. It was too large in the bodice, gaping where it should be snug, and tight under the arms. The length wasn't quite right, either, as if it had been made for a slightly taller woman.

Excusing himself from the group surrounding him, he immediately made his way toward her.

"Good evening," he said with a bow when he reached her and kissed her gloved hand, keeping his attention on her solemn face.

It took every ounce of his self-control not to glance down at that gaping bodice.

He'd want to hit any man who did, even if it was one of his friends. *Especially* if it was one of his handsome, charming, interesting friends.

"Good evening, my lord," she said, her expression impassive, her eyes unreadable, as she inclined her head and he realized her gloves didn't fit properly, either.

"How is Thompkins?" she asked as she pulled her hand away.

"Well on the road to recovery," he replied. "He won't be able to drive for a few days, though."

"I'm glad to hear he'll suffer no permanent injuries. We shall require a different driver, though. Perhaps you, my lord?" she suggested, giving him a questioning look that both embarrassed and delighted him.

"I've given up my career as a driver. Much too risky."

Her beautiful eyes widened. "Unlike travelling around the world to all sorts of savage places looking for spiders?"

"Ah, but I don't attempt to captain the vessel. I'm merely a passenger."

She laughed, a lovely, musical sound that went straight to his heart.

For the first time, he understood how his friends had fallen so deeply in love with their wives, and so quickly. He had always found that baffling, for they had all been men of the world who'd had other liaisons with beautiful women before meeting the women they married. Or in Brixton Smythe-Medway's case, realizing the woman who would make him blissfully happy had been his acquaintance from boyhood.

Not that he was lacking similar worldy experience with women, but when Lady Eleanor laughed and her eyes sparkled as she looked at him, he felt as if she was the only woman he would ever want to be with for any length of time. Ever.

He immediately stepped back. She might be in trouble and he would help her if he could, but he had to be free of emotional entanglements.

"Ah, here's the supper!" Jenkins announced, giving him the opportunity to beat a hasty retreat.

"You sit at the head, my lord," the innkeeper invited, "since you're the guest of honor."

Bromwell acknowledged his request with an inclination of his head and took his place, relieved to see that Lady Eleanor was to be seated at the far end of the table covered with a long white cloth and sporting what was no doubt Mrs. Jenkins's best Wedgwood china. He was also asked to say the grace.

Once that was over, he turned his attention to the food.

Or at least he tried to, for despite his wish not to become involved with any woman at this point in his life, as the supper of potato soup, roasted beef, stuffed chicken, boiled vegetables and fresh bread progressed, with wine and ale and fruit, he couldn't ignore Lady Eleanor, even though he was pestered with questions.

They were the same ones he got asked every time he was in company, about the shipwreck and the cannibals. He tried to be patient and emphasize the various new species of plants, animals, insects and spiders they'd found, but nobody seemed very interested in that.

Except Lady Eleanor, whom he caught listening avidly as he described the spiders in Tahiti, although she blushed and looked away when she met his gaze.

He also noticed that Lady Eleanor ate the plain, wholesome, plentiful and delicious food with impeccable manners, as delicately and demurely as a nun, taking tiny bites. Every so often, however, she would lick her soft, full lips, a motion that was more alluring to him than the swaying of a naked Tahitian woman's hips during a *hura.*

What might have happened if they had met in London,

at Almack's, or a ball, or one of Brix and Fanny's parties? Would he have felt the same powerful attraction and found a way to be properly introduced, or would he have thought her simply another rich heiress of the sort his father was forever pestering him to marry, and avoided her completely?

Such speculation was pointless. They had met under very unusual circumstances and he had most insolently and inappropriately kissed her. She must surely think he was a rake, a lascivious libertine.

If he could help her, it might make her think more highly of him and erase the poor first impression he must have made.

Whatever the outcome, he would do all he could to discover if she required his assistance and render any aid he could before he went on to the family estate.

And then he would never see her again.

A few hours later, Nell waited anxiously as the full moon rose and shone in through the mullioned window. She was going to have to leave without paying her bill. She had very little money left in her purse and no idea how long it might be before she could earn more.

The bright moonlight would mean it would be easier for someone to notice her as she absconded, but it also meant she would be better able to see where she was going. Since the only mode of transportation she could afford was her feet, she didn't want to fall and injure herself.

What would her parents say if they knew what she'd done today, and yesterday and the day before that? They had tried to raise a good woman, sacrificing much to send her to an excellent school, to learn manners and deportment and etiquette, to be the equal of any well-born gentlewoman.

All for nothing. It was a mercy they were dead, so they would never know what had happened to her, and what she'd done.

Hoping everyone was asleep at last, she rose and, taking her valise in her hand, eased open the door and listened again. She heard nothing, save for the occasional creak of bed ropes from Lord Bromwell's room.

Perhaps he wasn't alone. It had sounded as if he'd come up the stairs by himself after she had retired; nevertheless, she wouldn't be surprised to learn that he had a woman with him—some comely serving maid or one of the women at supper who had been gawking at him. She could well believe women had vied for his favors even before he'd become famous, and he must practically have to beat them off with a stick since his book had been published.

If he had come to expect such a reaction, it was no wonder he'd kissed her and then sought her out before dinner, even though it should have been obvious she didn't want to have anything more to do with him. She couldn't.

Sighing, Nell crept cautiously into the hall and closed the door behind her. The hall was as dark as pitch. Putting her hand to the wall, she carefully made her way toward the stairs.

"The coach isn't due to depart for some hours yet."

There was no mistaking Lord Bromwell's voice.

Nell turned. Although she couldn't see his face clearly in the dark, his body was as close as it had been in the coach, and if she could only see the vague outline of his body, she could feel his warmth as if he were embracing her.

Fighting to calm her racing heart, she gave him the excuse she had prepared. "I couldn't sleep, so I thought I'd see if I could find some wine."

"You felt it necessary to wear your pelisse and bonnet, as well as take your baggage, to get a nocturnal beverage?"

"I was afraid I might be robbed if I left my valuables in my room."

He stepped closer and she could see him better now, although it was still dark. He wore only his boots, buff trousers and shirt open at the neck. "You must have a lot of valuables."

"No, but I can't afford to lose what little I have. I'm sorry if I disturbed you," she said, continuing toward the stairs.

He put his hand on the wall ahead of her, so that he blocked her way. "Something is wrong," he said, his voice gentle but firm. "I wish to be of service, if I can."

He wanted to help her? He sounded genuinely sincere, yet how could she trust him? How could she trust anyone?

Besides, she'd lied to him about who she was. "The only thing amiss, my lord, is that you won't let me pass. Let me go or I shall call for help."

His voice dropped even lower. "No, you won't."

Sweet heavens, had she completely misjudged him? Was he a man to be feared after all?

But she didn't dare rouse the innkeeper or other guests, either, so she kept her voice low as she commanded him again to let her pass.

A door opened below and heavy footfalls sounded on the wooden floor of the taproom, then started toward the stairs.

She mustn't be found here, especially with him, especially dressed as he was.

She turned and ran back to her room. He followed and before she could get the door shut, he was inside the room, closing it behind him.

Chapter Four

Someday, we may learn what forces move the salmon to make that dangerous journey upstream to spawn, or why a dog will sit for hours by the bed of its deceased master. Yet for now, there remain instincts and emotions, reactions and defensive intuitions, unknown and mysterious, that govern every living creature upon the earth.

—from *The Spider's Web,* by Lord Bromwell

Panting, aghast, Nell's whole body shook as she faced him. Yet in spite of her distress, she stayed silent, for the footsteps came up the stairs, then past the room. Another door opened farther along the corridor. Mrs. Jenkins's voice mumbled a sleepy greeting to her husband, who muttered something about a sick horse before the door shut again.

"Get away from the door," Nell ordered with quiet ferocity, gripping the handle of her valise, prepared to swing it at Lord Bromwell's head. She had been trapped by a man before and fought her way free, and she would do it again if necessary.

Unlike Lord Sturmpole, however, the viscount addressed her not with arrogant outrage, but as calmly as if they were conversing in a park on a summer's day. "Are you planning to walk to Bath in the dead of night?"

His tone and his distance were a little reassuring, but she wasn't willing to trust him. "I've told you what I'm doing. Now let me pass!"

"There's no need to be frightened," he said, still not moving any closer. "I won't hurt you. I'm hoping I can be of service to you."

Service? What kind of service did he have in mind? Lord Sturmpole had claimed she would benefit from his attentions—and suffer if she refused.

Yet there was one important difference between her situation in Sturmpole's study and this. She had been horrified by Lord Sturmpole's advances; she had not been by Lord Bromwell's.

Nevertheless, she wasn't about to let him know that, or to have anything more to do with him. "Perhaps my impulsive reaction to your impertinent embrace has given you the wrong idea, my lord. I assure you that I do not go around kissing men to whom I've not been introduced. Or those to whom I *have* been introduced, either," she added.

"I'm delighted to hear it, but the service I wish to offer is not the sort you seem to be assuming. Despite my lapse of manners earlier today, I'm not a cad or scoundrel who seeks to take advantage of a woman. It's obvious something is amiss here, and my only intention is to find out what it is and help you if I can."

"By holding me prisoner?"

He ignored her question. "If all is quite well, why are

you travelling alone, wearing gowns that don't fit properly and neglecting to use your title? And why, my lady, are you attempting to leave this inn in the middle of the night?"

It felt as if the room had grown very cold. "I am not a lady."

"You're not Lady Eleanor Springford?"

Nell struggled to hide her growing panic. She wasn't Lady Eleanor, or any kind of lady. She'd heard that name in school, from one of her fellow students who was forever bragging about her lofty, if distant, relations. Nell had thought it wise to use a name similar to her own because it would be easy to remember.

That seemed the most ridiculous of reasons now.

But surely if he had met Lady Eleanor, he would have known at once that she was an impostor and said something before this, or summoned the law.

"No, I'm not and I never said I was," she replied, wary and determined to reply with more care. "Nor am I running away. I'm going to visit my uncle in Bath. As for my gown, I thought you were an expert on spiders, my lord, not ladies' fashions."

"It is my nature to be observant."

"My *modiste* had a terrible seamstress in her employ. Unfortunately, there was no time to find or hire a better one before my departure."

She crossed to the window and turned with an indignant huff, despite her trembling legs and the trickle of perspiration down her back. "There is the door, my lord. Now that I've explained, please use it."

He planted his feet and crossed his arms. "Not until I'm sure you're not in trouble."

Oh, God help her. She believed he meant that, and that he had no selfish, licentious motive—but why did she have to encounter a chivalrous gentleman here, and now? "Your aid is quite misguided, my lord. I am in no trouble."

"Then, unfortunately, I must assume you're attempting to renege on the payment of your night's accommodation."

She stared at him, aghast, her mind working quickly. He was right, after all, but of course she couldn't admit that.

She thought of one excuse he might accept. "There may be another explanation for my wish to leave this room, my lord."

He raised a querying brow.

"Has it not occurred to you that I might be afraid to be sleeping so near the man who so impertinently kissed me? Who can say what else you might be capable of, as your presence in this chamber attests?"

His eyes widened. "You fear I would *attack* you?"

"Why should I not believe you are capable of such an act? You did, after all, embrace me without my consent or invitation, accost me in the corridor, follow me into this bedroom and you refuse to leave."

"I'm a gentleman, as my friends and associates will tell you, or the Jenkinses."

"I don't call your behavior today very gentlemanly."

He ran his hand through his hair before he answered. "Nor can I," he admitted. "However, it is not unknown for people to behave under duress as they never would otherwise. I believe it was so in my case. I was not quite myself after the carriage overturned."

Neither was she.

Still, she wasn't going to let him think he could behave any way he would, and she would accept it. "The women on that island you were describing at supper—would they consider you a proper gentleman, if they knew what behavior was expected of one?"

"Yes, they would," he firmly replied. "I acted in complete accordance with their customs and beliefs."

"As *I* have done nothing wrong."

"Perhaps not," he replied, "but either you are some kind of cheat or criminal, or you're running from someone or something. If it is the former, I am duty-bound to hold you here. If it is the latter, I ask you again to allow me to be of assistance. But whatever your answer, I'm not going to allow you to go wandering about the countryside at night. It's too dangerous and I would never forgive myself if something happened to you."

Whether he was genuinely concerned for her safety or not, she could see his determined resolve and realized he wouldn't leave until she gave him an explanation that was both feasible and believable.

She would have to come up with one.

Remembering what the driver had told her about Lord Bromwell's father and the way he'd chastised his son, she put down her valise, which contained her clothes, her toilet articles and three of Lady Sturmpole's gowns.

Spreading her arms in a gesture of surrender, she spoke as if reluctantly revealing the truth. "Very well, my lord. You are quite right. I *am* Lady Eleanor Springford and I *am* running from someone—my parents and the Italian nobleman they're trying to force me to marry. The count is rich and has three castles, but he's old enough to be a grandfather and lecherous into the bargain. He has twice as many mistresses as manors and, despite his age, gives no sign of wishing to be loyal to a wife. That's why I ran away and have no maid or servant to accompany me."

"This is the nineteenth century, not the Dark Ages," Lord Bromwell said, his brow furrowed. "Surely you could simply refuse the betrothal rather than running away alone and putting yourself in danger."

She walked to the washstand and toyed with the end of a towel. "I suppose one can't expect a man who's been free to travel the world to understand the pressure than can be brought to bear upon a woman to marry, especially if the groom is a very wealthy aristocrat and her family not as rich as people believe."

"Actually, I can," Lord Bromwell said from where he still stood by the door. "My parents were far from pleased with my choice of career and my mother begged me not to go on my last expedition, so I do know something about parental expectations and coercion. Yet surely they would have relented in time. I daresay they're frantic with worry about you now."

"Perhaps. I'm unfortunately certain they're searching for me, although I hope they're still looking in Italy."

"You've come all the way from Italy *by yourself?*" he asked with undisguised awe.

She'd really come all the way from Yorkshire, but she couldn't admit that, either. "Yes, our family went there for my father's health."

That was what Letitia Applesmith had told them and Lady Sturmpole had confirmed during an afternoon of gossip with a friend that Nell had dutifully endured.

Lord Bromwell's frown deepened and she wondered if he knew something she didn't about the Duke of Wymerton or his family, until he said, "Yes, I believe my mother mentioned that."

"Travelling alone wasn't as difficult as I feared," Nell

said, relieved. "Most people were very kind, especially the women, who guessed, I think, that I was fleeing an unhappy domestic situation. Sometimes a man made an unwelcome remark, but no one touched me until…well, until you, my lord."

He blushed like a bashful boy, and she hurried on, not wishing to dwell on that encounter. "It must have been the shock of the accident that made me tell you my real name and I beg you not to reveal it. You're so famous, the press is bound to hear about the coach overturning, and perhaps learn who was with you. I'm hoping to get to the home of my godfather, Lord Ruttles, in Bath as quickly as possible. He will take my side and protect me, I'm sure."

"I see," the viscount said, regarding her with such genuine, kind sympathy, she felt like the worst, most degenerate criminal in the world. "Do you have any money? Or is the lack of it the reason that you're sneaking out?"

Trying to ignore his sympathetic expression, she said, "I have a little money left, but not enough to pay for this room."

"I shall gladly assume that cost."

She was sure he could afford it, so she didn't protest. "Thank you, my lord."

"Despite your success thus far, I am not comfortable allowing you to continue your journey alone and short of funds. Would you consider accepting an invitation to my family's estate? It's a few miles outside Bath. You'll be safe from pursuit there, and you can send a message to your godfather to come to you there."

His cheeks colored and his gaze drifted to the floor. "You need not fear that I shall attempt to take advantage of the situation, or of you."

Recognizing his generosity for the disinterested kindness it was, she was grateful, even if she couldn't accept his offer. "Thank you, but I couldn't impose and I think it would be better if I don't involve you or your family in my troubles, my lord."

"As you wish," he replied, his disappointment obvious, although his tone was still kind and concerned. "However, you must allow me to pay for your room tonight and provide you with sufficient funds for the rest of your journey."

He reached into his trouser pocket and produced a wallet of thin, soft leather. He opened it and drew out several ten-pound banknotes.

She didn't want to accept, but she needed the money. "Thank you, my lord," she said, taking the bills he held out to her and folding them in her hand. "I shall never forget your generosity."

Or your kiss.

"I shall repay you as soon as I can."

Whenever, if ever, that might be possible, and provided she wanted him to learn that she had deceived him.

He smiled, looking incredibly handsome and virile in the moonlight. "I must say I didn't expect to have such an exciting, eventful coach ride to Bath."

"Neither did I. I don't know what we would have done after the coach overturned if you hadn't been there."

"I'm sure you would have managed. You're obviously an intelligent, resourceful woman."

Coming from another man, that might not have seemed a compliment. Coming from him, however, she was sure it was. "As you are a most courageous, chivalrous man."

He began to walk closer. She waited, holding her breath, expecting—hoping for—another kiss.

Until he immediately halted a few feet away. "I had

best get back to my room before I'm discovered here and explanations are required. I wouldn't want our reputations to be ruined, although mine is already subject to some speculation."

Tucking the notes into her bodice, she followed him to the door, sorry for the lies, wanting him to know she was truly grateful, because she would never be able to repay him. After tomorrow, she would never see him again. "I really do appreciate your kindness and generosity, my lord."

A cock crowed in the yard below and he gave her a wry little smile as he eased open the door. "Good *day,* my lady."

"Wait!" she cried softly.

He turned back, his blue-gray eyes wide with query.

She couldn't help it. She had to do it.

She grabbed the front of his shirt, pulled him forward and kissed him. Not lightly and tenderly, as he had kissed her in the coach, but passionately, fervently, as her desire demanded.

Lord Bromwell stiffened, motionless with either shock or dismay. For a terrible instant, she thought he was going to push her away—but then his arms went around her and he held her close, deepening the kiss, his tongue probing until she parted her lips. She relaxed against him, her knees soft as pudding, her breasts pressed against his hard, muscular chest.

How he could kiss! Excitement ran along her veins, her flesh, setting it tingling with need. She had recoiled from her former employers' unwelcome embrace with all the force of her outrage, but she wanted nothing more than for Lord Bromwell to pick her up in his strong arms and carry her to the bed and lay her down and…

As if he could read her mind, Lord Bromwell moved farther into the room, taking her with him and shoving the door closed so that her back was against it. Still kissing her, he slid his hand around her side to cup her breast through her pelisse and gown.

Her breathing quickening, her body warming, she slipped her hand under his shirt, feeling his heated skin, the muscles bunching beneath. She had never been this intimate with a man, had never wanted to be, but every part of her mind urged her to tear off his shirt and press her lips to his naked skin.

She began to bunch the tail of his shirt in her hands and lift it until, with a gasp, he broke the kiss and stepped back, his eyes wide in the dawning light.

His chest heaving, his brow furrowed with scholarly concentration. "Once again, forgive me. Being a civilized human being, I should be able to overcome my primal urges."

His primal urges? This time, she had been the one to act upon hers.

He put his hand on the latch. "I wish you well, my lady."

"And I, you, my lord," she whispered as he slipped out of the room.

Nell moved away from the door toward the bed. She had never been more ashamed, not even when she was stealing from Lord Sturmpole.

What came over her when she was with Lord Bromwell? How could she behave with such wanton disregard for the risk she was taking, and that his fame engendered?

She had barely sat on the end of the bed before Mrs.

Jenkins blew into the room carrying a steaming pitcher of hot water.

"Good morning," she said as she set it on the washstand. "All ready for an early start, I see. It's a fine day for travelling, I must say. Breakfast will be ready shortly. I'll just make up the bed, if you don't mind."

Nell quickly went to wash.

"Quite a fine fellow, isn't he?" Mrs. Jenkins asked.

"Who?" Nell asked, although she was sure she knew to whom Mrs. Jenkins referred.

"Why, Lord Bromwell, o' course," the woman replied as she plumped the pillow. "You're a very lucky woman, my dear."

"We were fortunate he was with us with the coach overturned. We might have worsened Thompkins's injuries if he'd not been there to tell us not to move him."

"That's not what I meant. I wasn't born yesterday, my dear," the innkeeper's wife replied.

"He's never brought a woman here before, though, nor have any of his friends," she continued as she worked, "and a fine lot of scoundrels they can be, or so I've heard, all but the lawyer. He's as grim as a ghost, that one. Hard to believe he's married now, but then, I'd have said I'd never see the day Lord Bromwell would bring his—"

"I fear you're under a misapprehension, Mrs. Jenkins," Nell interjected, wondering why she'd let the woman go on for so long. "Lord Bromwell didn't *bring* me and I am not his anything. I was merely a passenger in the same coach."

Again, Mrs. Jenkins straightened, but this time she frowned. "Say what you like, my girl, but the floors creak something fierce. You weren't alone in this room."

"I was upset after the accident and couldn't sleep. You simply heard me moving about. By myself."

Mrs. Jenkins shook her head. "There's no point lying to me. I've never seen Lord Bromwell look at anything the way he looked at you last night, 'cept the time he caught the biggest spider I ever laid eyes on in the stable."

"I hardly think it's a compliment or a sign of affection if he regards me as he would a spider," Nell retorted in her best imitation of a haughty young lady. "If indeed, he does regard me with anything more than mild interest."

"You sound just like him, too, when he's going on about his spiders," Mrs. Jenkins said with a sigh, apparently not the least put off by Nell's imperious manner. "Can't follow the half of it. He's got a lovely voice, though, ain't he?"

He did, but Nell wasn't going to agree in case the woman took that for additional confirmation of her suspicions.

The innkeeper's wife fixed her with a worldly-wise eye. "And then, I saw him leaving your room."

That wasn't so easy to explain. Nevertheless, she tried. "He merely wished to ascertain if I had been able to sleep despite the accident."

"You're a smooth one, I must say," Mrs. Jenkins replied with a wry shake of her capped head as she wrestled the featherbed back into place. "But there's no need to lie to me. I don't blame you a bit, even if others might. Why, if I was twenty years younger and unmarried, I'd be the first to…"

She cleared her throat and her broad cheeks pinked. "Well, I'm not, so never mind. I just wanted to say this before you go. He's a good man, and a kind one, so I hope you won't break his heart."

"I am in no position to do so," Nell firmly assured her, "nor will I ever be and I say again that he came to my room only to ascertain if I was all right."

"Have it your own way then," Mrs. Jenkins replied, clearly still not believing her explanation.

This situation was getting worse and worse, Nell thought with dismay. She was a decent, respectable young woman—or had been until six days ago. Now she could be branded a thief and immoral into the bargain, especially if Lord Bromwell paid for her accommodation.

On the other hand, Lord Sturmpole would never suspect the woman he was chasing was the same woman others believed to be the mistress of the famous Lord Bromwell.

"Have you informed Lord Bromwell of your conclusion?" she asked.

"If it was anybody else," the innkeeper's wife replied, "I'd have thrown them out the minute I realized what was goin' on. Jenkins and I run a respectable inn, we do."

So she had kept her suspicions to herself, which was a relief. "Thank you for your kindness and discretion," Nell said. "Lord Bromwell and I are most grateful, especially if you'll continue to keep our secret."

"Worried about losing sponsors for his next expedition if word gets out, is he?" Mrs. Jenkins asked with triumphant satisfaction.

Nell hadn't known the viscount intended to sail again, but she hid her surprise and nodded, for a scandal would surely hamper such efforts despite his previous success.

"Well, my dear, you can count on me. But mind what I said about breaking his heart, or you'll have me to reckon with!"

"I shall," Nell promised, even as she noted the good

woman didn't seem to care about the state of *her* heart. Perhaps Mrs. Jenkins considered her simply mercenary, with no heart to break. "Do you know where Lord Bromwell is now?"

"In the stables, I think, probably looking for another spider."

Nell suppressed a shiver as she hurried from the room.

It didn't take her long to find Lord Bromwell. He was standing by the stables, talking to one of the grooms.

He still wore no hat, and his hair ruffled slightly in the breeze. He also had on dark trousers, white shirt, light green vest and the same shining boots and well-fitting gloves. He leaned his weight casually on one leg, and she could hear him laughing.

His laugh was as nice as the rest of him.

She hoped he never found out the truth about her. That way, he might remember her with affection, as she would certainly remember him.

Before she could catch his attention, a large black coach with an ornate coat of arms on the lacquered door came barrelling into the yard. The driver, dressed in scarlet and gold livery, shouted and pulled on the reins with all his might to stop the coach, while the footmen at the back held on for dear life as it came to a rocking halt.

No one in the inn's yard moved—not even the dogs— or spoke as one of the livered footmen leapt down, staggering a bit as he went to open the door of the coach and lower the step.

A tall, imposing gentleman appeared, wearing an indigo greatcoat with four capes and large brass buttons. As he stood on the step, his gaze swept over the yard until it came to rest upon Lord Bromwell.

As if announcing the end was nigh, the man threw out his arms and cried, "My son!"

Chapter Five

Of course Drury won the case, as expected. We're having a little dinner party to celebrate, but nothing that you should mourn to miss.

I trust you're handing your pater *and* mater *with your usual savoir faire when you're not taking refuge in your sanctuary, although how you can concentrate in such surroundings is beyond the limited powers of my comprehension.*

—from a letter to Lord Bromwell
from the Honorable Brixton Smythe-Medway

There had been many times in his life that Bromwell had craved his father's attention.

This was not one of them.

"My lord," he said, dreading what this sudden, unexpected advent signified as he walked quickly toward the Earl of Granshire, who actually deigned to alight in the yard in spite of the gawking servants, other travellers and the mud.

Normally his father only left his estate for the opening of Parliament, or if some important business matter made a visit to his banker or solicitor in Bath necessary. Even then, more often than not, such men came to him.

He hadn't even gone to Dover when his son had returned after two years at sea.

"I came to bring you home to your mother," the earl announced.

As if he were a child who'd run away after a fit of pique, Bromwell thought, his jaw clenching, very aware that Lady Eleanor was watching from the taproom door.

He'd noticed her at once, of course, drawn to her presence like a migrating swallow to Capistrano, feeling her proximity before he saw her. Like his ability to know what time it was without consulting a watch or clock, he couldn't explain the phenomenon; it simply was.

As she was simply lovely, and exciting, and the most desirable women he'd ever met.

"Your poor mother was beside herself when we received your message about the accident," his father declared, making Bromwell instantly wish he hadn't sent it, even if his delayed arrival might cause her to worry.

"Never fear, my dear, I said," his father continued, raising his hand as if calling upon supernatural powers, "I shall retrieve him!"

Bromwell doubted any actor currently appearing at the Theatre Royal could deliver those lines better. Indeed, at this precise moment, he could well believe his father had missed his true calling.

"I regret giving Mother any cause to worry," he said. "There really was no need for you to come. I'm quite all right."

"Perhaps, but it could have been otherwise. That's what comes of selling your carriage and travelling in a mail coach!"

"Plenty of people travel in mail coaches without mishaps," Bromwell said, although he suspected it was useless to try to make his father appreciate that such accidents weren't common.

"*Plenty of people* are not the heirs of the Earl of Granshire," his father retorted. "Fortunately, I have come to spare you any further indignities."

It took a mighty effort for Bromwell not to roll his eyes. "Naturally, I'm grateful. If you'll wait in the taproom, I'll settle the bill with Mrs. Jenkins and then we can be on our way."

The earl's lip curled at the corner, as if his son had suggested he wait in a cesspool. At nearly the same time, however, a cool breeze blew through the yard and the door of the kitchen opened, sending forth the aroma of fresh bread.

"Very well," the earl agreed. "Quickly, though, Bromwell. Your mother is prostrate with worry."

That was likely true, Bromwell thought as he followed his father across the yard. She was probably lying in her chaise longue with a maid hovering nearby.

The earl halted in mid-step at the sight of Lady Eleanor. "Who is that charming creature?" he asked, not bothering to subdue his stentorian voice.

God give me strength! Bromwell thought as he hurried forward to make the introductions, wondering if he should omit the mention of her title, as she had before.

She spoke first, saving him that decision. "I am Lady Eleanor Springford," she said with a bow of her head, "and I owe my life to your son."

Bromwell was torn between wanting to admit the situation hadn't been as dire as Lady Eleanor painted it and kneeling at her feet.

The earl drew himself up and placed one hand on his hip. "I would expect no less of my son."

"Her ladyship was quite an angel of mercy to the poor coachman," Mrs. Jenkins interjected, coming up behind her like a large and vibrant acolyte. "They make a lovely couple, don't you think?"

Bromwell's heart nearly stopped beating. What the devil had prompted Mrs. Jenkins to make such an observation— and to his father, of all people! It could only have been worse if she'd said it to his mother.

"Indeed," his father replied, running a measuring, arrogant gaze over Lady Eleanor, who endured his scrutiny with amazing aplomb.

"Perhaps we'd all be more comfortable inside," she suggested.

"Yes, of course," the earl agreed. "Justinian, you may attend to your business while I share some refreshments with Lady Eleanor. Come along, my lady."

With that, he swept her inside, calling for wine as he went, and left Bromwell standing in the yard.

Fearing what his father might say about him in his absence, Bromwell immediately followed them inside and paid Mrs. Jenkins what both he and the lady owed for their night's accommodation.

It struck him as a little odd that the innkeeper's wife didn't make any comment about his payment of both bills, but he was in too extreme a state of agitation to dwell upon it. No doubt she thought he was merely being a gentleman.

That done, he hurried to join his father and Lady Eleanor by the hearth, taking note that there were only two glasses of wine and his father had already finished his.

"Ah, Bromwell, here you are!" the earl exclaimed as if

his son had been miles away instead of across the room. "Were you aware that Lady Eleanor's father is the Duke of Wymerton? I went to school with him, you know."

No, he hadn't known that his father and the Duke of Wymerton had been at the same school, although perhaps he should have guessed. His father seemed to have gone to school with eighty percent of the nobility. That might explain why so many were, like his father, woefully ignorant of anything except the classics. Even then, their grasp of those subjects was often rudimentary at best.

"Did you indeed, Lord Granshire?" she asked. "He's never mentioned it."

That didn't please his father, but at least he didn't accuse her of lying. "What brings you to Bath at this time of year, my lady?"

"I'm going to visit my godfather, Lord Ruttles."

"I don't think so."

Lady Eleanor started, as well she might, at his father's firm response.

"He's hunting grouse in Scotland and won't be back for at least a month," his father continued.

Unfortunately for Lady Eleanor, that was probably true. His mother had a prodigious correspondence and kept abreast of all the nobility's comings and goings.

"Rutty always was absentminded," the earl remarked, then he smiled as if he'd just solved all the world's ills. "You must come and stay at Granshire Hall until he returns, Lady Eleanor. My wife and I would be delighted to have you."

Bromwell didn't quite know how to react. On the one hand, as he himself had said, that would be the safest place for Lady Eleanor. On the other hand, perhaps that wasn't the best idea after all.

Unfortunately, and despite his best efforts, he seemed incapable of maintaining a due sense of propriety and decorum in her presence. It was as if he imbibed some sort of potent brew that took away all restraint when she was nearby—and it seemed she had a similar reaction to his presence. How else to explain that second passionate kiss? That had certainly been at her instigation, not his, even if he'd been too thrilled and aroused to end it at once.

As he should have.

Lady Eleanor looked equally confused and hesitant. "Oh, my lord, I don't think I should impose—"

"Nonsense! It's no imposition at all," the earl interrupted. "Indeed, you would be doing us a great favor. My son has been too much among sailors and other savages. He needs to spend more time with civilized people and young ladies in particular, or I despair that he'll ever attract a suitable wife."

Bromwell nearly groaned out loud. His father had been told more than once that he wasn't ready to marry and wouldn't be for years. "Father, it may be that Lady Eleanor would prefer to arrange—"

"You see, my lady?" the earl cried. "His manners are distinctly wanting. You must come to Granshire Hall and stay for as long as you like. Summon your maid and have her bring your baggage. Bromwell, see to it, will you?"

As was usually the case, there was no room for discussion, not even for Lady Eleanor.

Giving in to the inevitable, Bromwell dutifully started to stand while the earl hoisted himself to his feet. "On second thought, if I want it done properly, I had better attend to it myself. We wouldn't want my coach to tip."

Bromwell did not point out to his father that he had had

no part in causing the accident, either through the improper storage of baggage or the mail, or by driving. Nor had he damaged the axel, put out the rock, or sent the dog running across the road.

"But I don't…have a maid," Lady Eleanor finished in a murmur as the Earl of Granshire marched out of the taproom like a soldier bound on an errand vital to the government of the realm.

Bromwell let out his breath in a sigh. "As you may have noticed, my father is the sort of fellow who won't take no for an answer. If you don't give in, he's liable to demand why not and attempt to persuade you for the better part of the day."

Lady Eleanor clasped her hands in her lap, looking pretty and vulnerable and uncertain all at once. "Since my godfather is gone from Bath, I'm grateful for his offer and gratefully accept."

She flushed. "I hope you don't think me a sinful wanton because of…because I… When you were leaving the room this morning, I thought we'd never see each other again."

"Of course I excuse you," he said. After all, how could he not, without condemning himself, too? "Just as I hope you don't consider me a rakish cad."

"No, and I'm sorry I said those things to you. Sadly, there are too many bad men in the world, and I was afraid to trust you."

"And now?"

"And now, I believe I can."

Feeling as if he was back on solid ground after being suspended and twisting in the wind, Bromwell smiled with relief. "Then let us assume our unusual behavior was due to the accident and begin anew."

When she smiled in return, his body's immediate and

powerful response made a mockery of his determination to maintain his emotional distance. But he must, so he would, no matter how stimulated he was by her presence.

Her smile drifted away and a vertical line of worry creased her brow. "Unfortunately, there is one other problem, my lord. I don't have a maid, or even proper clothes. Perhaps I should explain my circumstances to your father."

"I think not," Bromwell firmly replied even as he wondered what it would be like to try to kiss away that little wrinkle. "My father would no doubt say it's your duty to obey your parents and write to your father at once. And as it happens, a friend of mine faced a similar situation not long ago, when the lack of a maid could have led to awkward questions and explanations. We shall tell my father that your maid has run off and taken most of your clothes with her."

"You'd lie to your father?"

"In this instance, yes." *For your sake.*

She didn't seem quite convinced. "Won't your father expect the authorities to be summoned if he thinks there's been a robbery?"

"Not if I offer to take charge of the investigation. Even if he doubts my competence, he'll be happy not to be bothered with such matters."

She stared at him with wide-eyed surprise. "Surely he can't doubt your competence after all you've done, the places you've been, the dangers you've faced and survived?"

He was pleased that she was so surprised and thought so highly of him; even so, he answered honestly. "As you heard, he can and he does. However, the important thing is that you'll be safe at Granshire until your godfather returns."

Her green eyes sparkling like emeralds, Lady Eleanor

finally acquiesced. "Very well, my lord. I shall accept your father's generous invitation and—woe is me!—my abigail has run off with my clothes!"

Riding in the earl's fine coach should have been enjoyable, for the weather was fine, the vistas lovely, the coach well sprung and the seats upholstered in thick silk damask and cushioned with horsehair. Nell had a whole side to herself and, with Lord Bromwell across from her, the journey could even have been quite entertaining. She'd always liked to read histories of Britain, and she was sure a learned man like Lord Bromwell could tell her even more about this part of the country, and the Roman settlement and spa so close to Stonehenge.

Unfortunately, Lord Bromwell's father was also in the coach. Worse, he apparently felt silence in a coach some kind of sin, so he talked the whole way while they were forced to listen, trapped like flies in a web. He complained about the sorry state of the roads, the exorbitant cost of building supplies, the inefficiency of the mail, the generally terrible government and the difficulty in finding good servants.

Once she caught Lord Bromwell's eye and gave her companion-in-captivity a sympathetic smile, but that proved to be something of a mistake, for his eyes brightened and his full lips began to lift, instantly reminding her that he was a very attractive man who kissed with passionate, consummate skill.

Blushing yet again, ashamed yet again of her wayward, lascivious thoughts, she turned her attention back to the boastful earl, who had now moved on to the subject of the renovations to his estate and his hall.

"The very finest situation in the county since I've rebuilt

the house," the voluble earl noted, as if he'd personally laid every brick. "The gardens were designed by Humphrey Repton. Cost a fortune, but worth every penny, I think you'll agree.

"Nothing but the best for the earls of Granshire and their heirs, my lady. Yes, it'll be a lucky young woman who marries my son, provided he can be persuaded to stop gallivanting all over the world after those insects."

"As I've explained to you before, Father," Lord Bromwell said with an air of long-suffering patience, "spiders are not insects."

"All right, spiders," the earl said. "Disagreeable things they are, too."

Lord Bromwell opened his mouth, then closed it again and gazed silently out the window.

"While they can be a little unnerving up close," Nell said, coming to their defence for his sake, "I understand most of them are harmless—and I'd rather come upon a spider than a wasp."

She had her reward when Lord Bromwell looked at her as if she'd just announced she was Mother Nature and going to provide him with a sample of every spider in existence.

His father's expression was only slightly less impressed. "So, you like spiders, my lady?"

While she was happy to help Lord Bromwell, or at least defend his interest, there was a significance in his father's look and manner that was all too easy to understand, and that ought to be nipped in the bud.

"I can't say I like them as much as your son," she admitted with a bland smile, "but I suppose most people don't like them as much as your son."

"No, they do not," the earl replied, as if Lord Bromwell

wasn't there. "He'd spend hours staring at them spinning webs in the stable or outbuildings when he was a boy. His mother and I thought he'd ruin his eyes."

"Obviously he didn't," she said.

"And then he just about gets himself killed sailing off around the world looking for bu…spiders."

"As I've also explained, Father," Lord Bromwell said, and it was clear his patience was wearing thin, "there are things to be learned from nature and I want—"

His father waved his hand dismissively. "I'm not saying discovery isn't all well and good, but leave it to those better suited to such deprivations, I say."

Lord Bromwell's ears turned red. "Perhaps we can discuss this later, Father. In private."

The earl once more addressed Nell rather than his son. "He's no doubt going to try to convince me to give him more money for his next expedition. We'll just have to try to persuade him to stay in England, though, won't we, my dear?"

As if she could, she thought.

And now, having met his father, she could more easily understand why Lord Bromwell might want to sail to the far ends of the earth.

"Father, why don't you tell Lady Eleanor about the grotto?" Lord Bromwell suggested.

"Ah, yes, the grotto!" the earl exclaimed. "The latest thing, you see. Very charming and rustic. I've got a hermit, too. You'll have to go and see him. Plays the pipes. Infernal noise, really, but very picturesque."

Nell glanced at Lord Bromwell, who was looking out the window the way a prisoner in a dank cell might gaze at the sky through the bars, longing for freedom.

"I suppose, Lord Bromwell, that spiders like the grotto?"

With the suggestion of a smile on his face, he turned to address her. "As a matter of fact—"

"Spare us another lecture, my son," the earl said as the coach turned off the main road and down a long, sweeping drive. "We aren't the Royal Society—and soon you shall see something worth talking about, my lady."

Lord Bromwell wasn't the only occupant of the coach whose patience was wearing thin. "Many people are talking about your son's book, my lord."

Instead of looking proud or pleased, Lord Granshire frowned darkly. "Some parts of it anyway. Have you read it?"

"I'm sorry to say I have not."

"Nor should you. Why Bromwell put in that nonsense about those savages—"

"*Those savages* are in some ways more civilized and humane than many a supposed gentleman I could name," Lord Bromwell snapped, his tone so brusque and sharp, it was like a slap—something he seemed to realize at once. "Forgive me, my lady, but I fear too many ig—too many people have made similar comments, and I feel I must speak up for the maligned native peoples. Granted some of their customs may be difficult to understand, but many of ours are equally baffling to them. The handkerchief, for instance. They don't understand why one would wish to collect—"

"Bromwell, have the goodness not to discuss bodily functions in mixed company!" his father ordered.

"I only wished to point out that—"

"Never mind that now," his father dismissed. He gestured grandly toward his left and beamed at Nell. "Here is Granshire Hall."

Nell looked out the window to see the drive curve in front

of an imposing mansion of gray stone. It was indeed built in the latest style, with several tall windows and three stories. It had, she guessed, at least thirty bedchambers and who could say how many rooms on the main floor. There was also likely an army of servants to clean and maintain it.

"What do you think of it, my lady?" the earl asked proudly.

She wanted to tell him exactly what she thought of *him,* but instead answered his question. "It's very lovely. I don't think I've ever seen a more splendid home."

The earl fairly purred with satisfaction as the coach rolled to a stop and a footman jumped down to open the door. Lord Bromwell got out first and extended his hand to help her.

The earl got down beside her, then, brushing aside his son, took her arm and led her into the magnificent country house. She managed a quick glance over her shoulder, to see the viscount speaking to the coachman as if he wasn't a bit disturbed by his father's behavior.

He was, she supposed, used to such treatment.

Inside the hall, she discovered more evidence that the earl's boasts had not been empty bragging. The builders had used beautiful materials—Italian marble on the floors, and mahogany inlaid with lighter oak in the grand entrance hall and staircase. Ornate plasterwork on the ceiling surrounded an elaborate painting of a classical scene that quite took her breath away. She'd never seen so many half naked, fighting men depicted anywhere.

"The Battle of Thermopylae," Lord Bromwell explained as he came up behind her. "My father admires the Spartans, although you'd never know it from his hall."

"Fallingbrook!" the earl bellowed just as a stout man who had to be the butler came to stand almost at his elbow.

"Welcome home, my lord," the butler said, after nodding a greeting at Lord Bromwell and giving him a grin that disappeared the instant the earl turned to him.

"See to my son's baggage, Fallingbrook, and that of our guest, Lady Eleanor Springford, the daughter of the Duke of Wymerton. Tell Mrs. Fallingbrook her ladyship will be staying and requires the services of a maid, her own having absconded with most of her baggage."

The middle-aged butler's sandy brows rose. "Indeed, my lord?"

"Indeed. Servants are going to the dogs in this country, just like the government." Lord Granshire turned to Nell and was just as suddenly all sweetness and light. "Fallingbrook will show you to your room."

He turned back to the butler. "The green room for Lady Eleanor. Where's the countess?"

"In her sitting room, my lord. She asked that Lord Bromwell come up as soon as possible."

The younger man nodded and bowed to Nell and his father before trotting up the staircase and disappearing from view.

Nell tried not to feel abandoned, or afraid. After all, thanks to her education, she need have no fear she wouldn't know how to conduct herself in a stately home or among the nobility.

"If her ladyship will follow me," the butler said, "I'll take you to the green room."

"She'll need clothes, Fallingbrook," the earl called out as he hurried up the stairs ahead of her. "Tell your wife to find her something in my wife's dressing room. The countess has scads of gowns she never wears."

"As you wish, my lord. Please, follow me, my lady."

* * *

"Justinian, my boy!" the Countess of Granshire cried, holding out her arms as her son entered her sitting room.

It was a small chamber, well-appointed and comfortable, beside her bedroom on the main floor that opened onto the terrace and formal garden—or as Bromwell always thought of it, nature made unnatural.

As he'd expected, his mother was reclining on the chaise longue, with a gilt pedestal table close at hand bearing a lamp and what was clearly pages of correspondence.

Bromwell knew enough of medicine to realize his mother wasn't seriously ill. He'd tried to tell her so many times, until he realized that his mother used poor health as a means to get and keep his father's attention, as well as his own.

He embraced her and sat on a delicate harp-back chair beside the chaise. "You're looking rather better, Mother," he said, as he always did.

"A bit, perhaps. Dr. Heathfield has given me some marvelous new medicine."

"Oh? What is it?"

She waved her hand feebly. "I don't know. I didn't ask. But it doesn't taste bad."

Bromwell clenched his jaw and said no more about her medicine, although he would try to find out what it was as soon as possible. Dr. Heathfield wasn't a quack, but he wasn't the most learned man of medicine either, and his mother might be better off without his latest potion.

"It's so good to see you," his mother said with a sorrowful smile. "I was so worried when we got the message about the accident."

"Didn't Father tell you that I was quite all right? I said so in my note."

"Oh, yes, of course, but a mother always worries, even when her son's in the same county."

He understood exactly what she was *not* saying—that she worried even more when he was at sea. However, since she hadn't raised the subject of his next voyage directly, neither would he.

His father burst into the room and came to a halt, feet planted, arms akimbo, as if he were a military man, which he was not and never had been.

"So, has he told you?" he demanded of his wife. "He's been travelling with a *woman*."

Chapter Six

In nature's kingdom, nurturing is primarily the responsibility of the female of the species. The male may possess the finer plumage or coloring and may be the larger, heavier and more muscular sex, but over and over again I saw that it was the mothers who were the fiercest when their offspring were threatened. At such times, the fine plumage, size and weight of the males counted for very little against the determination of the protective females.

—from The Spider's Web, by Lord Bromwell

His father made it sound as if his association with Lady Eleanor was illicit, not merely coincidental, and the earl wasn't so much scandalized as shocked and, beneath that, proud.

Bromwell wasn't overly surprised by his father's reaction. He suspected his father was even rather relieved to think his son had a mistress. It was no secret to Bromwell that his father had doubted his inclinations when it came to his sexual proclivities. Certain passages in his book should have reassured him in that regard, if his father had ever read it.

He doubted his father had done more than glance at the title page.

"She's Lady Eleanor Springford, the daughter of the Duke of Wymerton," he clarified, "and we aren't travelling together as you imply. We happened to be in the same coach, that's all. We are mere acquaintances."

The earl's eyes narrowed. "Mere acquaintances, eh?"

"Yes, Father, mere acquaintances," he confirmed, even if she was an acquaintance he'd kissed more than once, that activity arousing such a primal passion in him, he could still hardly believe it.

"What's a duke's daughter doing travelling in a mail coach?"

"I was in a mail coach."

"Because you sold your carriage. Her father has at least two coaches and twice as many carriages."

Trust his father to remember a detail like that about another nobleman. "Perhaps she prefers to travel with people of another class. One can have some very interesting discussions with people of different backgrounds."

His father looked at him as if he had just announced that he believed himself the king of Tahiti, while his mother murmured something about contagious diseases.

"Mail coaches are faster than a post chaise," he truthfully added, hoping his father would find that simple statement of fact enough of an explanation.

"If she'd been in one of the duke's coaches, her maid probably wouldn't have run off with her clothes," his father said.

"She has no clothes?" his mother asked, looking as if

she thought they meant Lady Eleanor was wandering about as naked as a newborn babe.

"A few," Bromwell quickly assured her.

He then repeated the lie he'd suggested to Lady Eleanor. His parents hadn't been staying at the London town house when that excuse had been used before.

"Oh, the poor woman, to have so many catastrophes at once!" his mother cried, moving as if she were going to get up, until his father threw himself into the nearest chair covered in emerald-green and gold brocade.

"That's why I invited her here," his father said. "Your son would have had her going to some hotel in Bath, despite the riffraff she might meet there. Besides, her father was one of my best friends at school."

"Really?" Bromwell said, not able to hide his skepticism. "I've never heard you speak of him."

"Maybe if you paid attention to dinner conversation once in a while, you would have," his father retorted.

Maybe if you conversed about something interesting, I would, Bromwell thought. Instead of voicing that thought aloud, however, he said, "I didn't realize we had a connection to the family. I've never met them, have I?"

That question didn't increase his father's opinion of his son's intelligence. "You probably had your nose in a book the last time they were here. They've been in Italy for the past five years. I thought they were still there."

Bromwell racked his brain, but for the life of him, he couldn't remember meeting Lady Eleanor.

"She must make free of my wardrobe, if my clothes will fit," his mother offered, "or they can be made over if they don't."

"Thank you," Bromwell said, pleased by her generosity.

"I've already directed Mrs. Fallingbrook to select some garments for our guest," her husband said. "I'm sure the duke will be grateful for any assistance we can render his daughter."

Bromwell was quite sure the duke's response would not be favorable if he ever learned they'd given sanctuary to his daughter as she fled a marriage they were keen to promote. Unlike his father, however, he didn't care what the Duke of Wymerton—or anyone else—thought of him for helping her.

All that mattered was that she was safe, and free.

"Her looks have improved considerably, I must say. She's grown into quite a beauty," his father noted with an unmistakable significance that made Bromwell want to roll his eyes with frustration. "I've told you, Father, that I've no intention of taking a wife anytime soon."

"Well, you should!" his father growled, glaring at him. "I'm not going to live forever, you know, and it's your duty to provide an heir, or this house, this estate—all that I and your ancestors have worked for—will go to that tosspot second cousin of mine in Jamaica. I won't stand for it, Bromwell!"

"Now Frederic, must you quarrel?" the countess pleaded. "Justinian's only just arrived and—"

"No, Mother, we shan't quarrel," Bromwell said as he got to his feet. No doubt this visit had been a colossal waste of time and effort, except that he'd made his mother happy, and met Lady Eleanor. "I'm well aware of Father's opinions, as he should be of mine. I know my duty, as you call it, but I also have a calling that I consider at least as important."

"You call studying bugs a *calling?*" his father demanded.

Bromwell ignored that question and addressed his mother as well as his father. "I'm not opposed to the idea of marriage, but I won't leave a wife behind in England while I'm on my expedition. Now if you'll excuse me, I'd like to rest before supper, provided you'll allow me to stay even though I have no interest in Lady Eleanor as a prospective bride."

His mother reached out and took hold of his hand, then looked beseechingly at her husband.

"Of course you can stay," his father muttered.

"Thank you, my lord," Bromwell said with formal politeness and a bow before he turned and left the room.

Nell looked out the window at the beautiful gardens laid out below and wondered how soon she could get away.

To be sure, this bedroom, with its lovely flowered wallpaper of roses and vines and delicate mahogany furnishings, was absolutely charming and more comfortable than she would have expected. Given the grand entrance hall, she'd been anticipating a vast, chilly chamber with a huge curtained bed from the Elizabethan age. Instead, because it faced south, the room was bright and warm and even cozy. Everything was spotless, from the linen on the washstand to the silk draperies. There wasn't a speck of dust, not even in the crevices of the ornately carved wardrobe, suggesting that the chamber was cleaned daily whether anyone was using it or not. A thick Aubusson carpet covered the floor and a gilded cheval glass stood near a screen painted with an oriental scene that hid the washstand.

A knock sounded on the door, and in the next moment, a tall, thin, middle-aged maid glided into the room with some gowns over her arm. "Mrs. Fallingbrook said you were to have these, my lady," the maid intoned, her voice as sepulchral as her manner.

"Thank you," Nell replied, thinking it was a relief that a lady didn't owe a servant any explanations for anything, whether it was her presence or apparently missing garments, while wondering how Lord Bromwell's meeting with his mother had gone.

Surely better than any encounter with his father, who clearly didn't appreciate his son's intelligence or accomplishments.

"I'm to be your maid while you're here. My name is Dena. Shall I help you change, my lady?" the woman asked as she laid the gowns on the bed.

There was a light green one of silk that was very pretty, a scarlet one of soft wool with gray trim that was more suitable for an older woman, and a pretty sprigged muslin with a square neckline she could hardly wait to try on. "The muslin, I think, please."

The maid didn't reply as she took Nell's pelisse, then helped her change her simple gown of light brown wool for the muslin.

Fortunately, Nell had no cause to be ashamed of her chemise or pantelettes. Although it had been an extravagance, she'd purchased new ones before she'd gone to the Sturmpole estate in Yorkshire, suspecting that life as a lady's companion was going to permit few luxuries.

She had not expected it to be dangerous.

Soon enough Nell was dressed in a gown that, if it didn't fit perfectly, fit as well as the blue silk she'd worn the night before. She had no jewellery, so she tied a ribbon she retrieved from her valise around her neck.

Looking at herself in the cheval glass, she was pleased

with the effect. She didn't study her reflection long; she knew she was a pretty girl thanks to the features she'd gotten from her mother—large, bright eyes and delicately arched brows over a slender nose. From her father she had inherited her chestnut hair, excellent teeth, full lips and a jaw that was a bit too strong, perhaps.

"How shall I do your hair, my lady?" Dena asked without any enthusiasm.

Nell fetched another ribbon and suggested a simple style, with the ribbon woven through it. "Do you think you can do that?"

"Yes," the maid said curtly, taking the ribbon as Nell, subduing a sigh, sat at the dressing table.

"I didn't mean to imply you were incapable," she said.

The maid didn't reply.

"Have you been with the family long?" Nell asked amicably, hoping to mend the apparent breach as the maid began to brush her hair with brisk, hard strokes.

"Twenty years, my lady."

"So you've known Lord Bromwell from boyhood."

The maid didn't respond.

Undeterred, Nell asked, "Was he an adventurous sort of child?"

"I can't say, my lady. I wasn't the nursery maid."

"Surely you would have heard if he was."

"He got into trouble now and then," Dena conceded. "But how he could be so thoughtless and sail off and worry his poor mother half to death after she spent all those sleepless nights nursing him when he was sick so often…"

Dena fell silent, her lips so compressed it was as if they were locked together to prohibit another word from escaping.

"I suppose all spirited boys get into mischief now and then."

When Dena didn't reply, Nell tried a different tack. "You must be proud to work for the family of such a famous naturalist."

Dena's dark brows drew even closer together.

"His book was very well received," Nell prompted.

The maid's expression grew yet more disapproving.

"I take it, Dena," Nell said, "that you aren't impressed by Lord Bromwell or his field of study?"

At last the woman spoke, and it was as if a dam had broken—or she finally felt she'd been given the opportunity to voice opinions too long held in check. "Spiders, of all things! Nasty, creeping creatures! I can't think what God was about creating them.

"As for the viscount, he used to be a fine young gentleman but then he went on that voyage and what he did when he was with those heathens, walking about nearly naked, dancing those disgusting dances and drinking their foul brews, and no doubt doing who knows what with the native women…well, it's enough to make a Christian woman sick!"

However Dena felt about his adventures, Nell's reaction was quite different. She immediately envisioned Lord Bromwell nearly naked, dancing with wild abandon in torchlit shadows under a palm tree, then slipping off into the bushes with an equally half naked woman.

Who looked a lot like her.

She shoved that disturbing yet exciting vision out of her mind and wished more than ever that she'd read Lady Sturmpole's copy when she'd had the chance. "You've read his book?"

"Mrs. Fallingbrook took it upon herself to read it aloud in the servant's hall during dinner, until I asked her to stop," Dena replied. "It ruined my appetite to hear about an English gentleman, the son of our employer, behaving like that. *I* think he ought to be ashamed of himself.

"It nearly killed his poor mother, him going off like that, despite her pleading for him to stay," Dena continued. "She took to her bed for weeks after he sailed and we were all afraid it would be the death of her and then there he is, acting like a heathen himself!"

"But he returned," Nell noted, "and his book is a great success. His mother must be pleased about that."

"She would be if he'd settle down and marry and not go sailing off again for who knows how long."

Nell was sure Lord Bromwell didn't plan his expeditions as a means to upset his mother; his zeal for his chosen field and his belief in the necessity of learning about the natural world made that quite clear.

And after all, he wasn't the only man who travelled far from home. Mothers, sisters and wives of whalers and other seamen must get used to their sons and brothers, fathers and husbands being gone for years at a time.

Or perhaps, she silently acknowledged, they had merely learned to hide their fears beneath a mask of stoic acceptance.

She couldn't fault the countess for being worried or Dena for her sympathy for her mistress, especially when she recalled how her own mother had cried before leaving her at school. She, on the other hand, had been too excited by the possibility of making friends to be sad, as Lord Bromwell was no doubt excited by the possibility of making new discoveries.

"He's advancing the cause of science and our understanding of the natural world," she pointed out in his defence.

The maid's only response was a loud and scornful sniff. Fortunately, Dena had also finished dressing her hair.

"I'll be here to help you when you retire, my lady," she said, stepping back.

That wasn't exactly cheerful news, but there was no way to refuse, Nell supposed. "Thank you," she said, rising and leaving the room, heading for the drawing room where, she assumed, the family would be assembled prior to proceeding to the dining room.

This must be how prisoners being taken to the Old Bailey must feel, she thought as she went down the stairs. Afraid, uncertain, worried that every past transgression was going to be used against you…

She hesitated on the threshold of the drawing room and slowly surveyed the grand chamber dominated by an ornate fireplace of marble, wide and with a mantel the height of a man's shoulders. Two figures of women in Greek garments were on either side of the opening, and a large pier glass hung above it. The walls were painted a pea-green, with white plasterwork of Grecian urns and vines around the ceiling. The furnishings were of various gleaming woods, and included several Hepplewhite chairs and a Grecian couch upholstered in green silk, with curving gilded arms and feet. The heavy velvet draperies were still pulled back to allow the last of the daylight to shine into the room, although candles in shining silver holders had also been lit, and a fire kindled in the fireplace. A painted screen stood near it, and there were more paintings on the walls, of men, women and children in sober family groups dressed in the fashions of years gone by. Huge oriental vases full of roses and hothouse flowers stood on side tables, their scent mingling with beeswax and burning coal from the fire.

It was a lavish, expensively decorated chamber, if not an overly pleasant one.

Nor was it unoccupied.

In evening dress and with his hands behind his back, Lord Bromwell stood by the window, looking rather like a beetle among the butterflies as he stared up at the moon as if contemplating its composition.

Chapter Seven

So much remains to be learned about the natural world, including human beings. Are we subject to the same needs and instincts as the lesser orders, or can our impulses be controlled by reason and rational discourse, as we would like to believe?
—from *The Spider's Web,* by Lord Bromwell

What a will of iron must be concealed beneath that handsome, studious, civilized exterior, Nell thought as she studied him, noting his well-cut and immaculate evening attire of dark cutaway coat, gray vest, white shirt and cravat, breeches and silk stockings that proved his calves were as muscular as the rest of him. How dedicated he must be to his chosen field to continue his studies despite his disapproving, critical father and his fearful, anxious mother. She doubted she would have the strength to do what he had done in the face of such resistance. Her parents had always been kind and loving, seeking the best for her, wanting her to be happy.

Which made her crime that much heavier to bear.

She went farther into the room, treading on a dark green carpet that must have cost hundreds of pounds. Looking at him now, in this room and in those clothes, she found it almost impossible to believe that he had danced with wild abandon among heathens.

She might have found it completely impossible to believe if she hadn't felt the unbridled passion in his kiss. Having experienced that primitive desire, feeling her own aroused by his touch, she knew there was a wild, untamed, virile male beneath those expensive, civilized clothes.

Lord Bromwell turned. That lock of hair had fallen over his forehead again, bringing a boyish charm to his otherwise elegant appearance.

He smiled, yet made no move to come any closer. She smiled, too, longing to tell him that, having met his parents, she admired him even more. That he looked breathtakingly handsome in his evening dress. That she wished with all her heart she really was a lady and his equal. That he would kiss her again, and not stop with kissing.

Instead, she seated herself on the edge of the Grecian couch and folded her hands in her lap. "I regret that I haven't yet had the pleasure of reading your book. I was wondering if I could borrow a copy from your father's library to read while I'm here."

Instead of looking pleased by her request, Lord Bromwell's expression grew decidedly uncomfortable. "Of course, if we can find one. He's probably given away all the ones I gave him."

Surely a man who could brag for hours about his house and grounds would keep a copy of his own son's bestselling work. "He must have one, at least. Where is the library?"

"This way," Lord Bromwell said, walking to the door, "but I fear you're going to be disappointed."

As he must be, if he was right.

Nevertheless, and hoping he was wrong, she followed him out of the drawing room to the library a short distance down the wide, marble-floored corridor with brisk, eager steps.

What if she was wrong, and there was no copy there? What should she do? Console Lord Bromwell? Vilify his father?

She put any thought of comforting him from her mind as they entered a large room with long, narrow windows on the south side and shelves of dark oak on the others. Lord Bromwell went to the hearth and got a brimstone match which he used to light an oil lamp on one of the side tables by the windows.

In the brighter light, she noted one was a chess table, the pieces lined up ready for a game. A picture of a bucolic country scene populated by people clothed in the fashions of the previous century hung over the black marble fireplace. Busts of long dead Romans and Greeks stood on top of the shelves, like so many spirits watching over them. The several volumes on the shelves were leather-covered, and all appeared of recent manufacture.

There was a large Pembroke table in the center of the room, with a single book upon it. Surely if any book deserved pride of place...

She went there at once and soon Lord Bromwell was beside her. He set the lamp on the table, illuminating the cover and title of the book: *Peerage of England, Scotland and Ireland*.

Nell didn't dare look at Lord Bromwell and didn't know what to say. *I'm sorry* seemed hardly adequate.

Instead, she set her mind to figuring out where a man as vain and proud as the earl would put his son's book.

"Perhaps it's over here," she said, heading toward the nearest shelf.

"We shouldn't waste our time," Lord Bromwell said with quiet resignation. "I'll have one sent to you via your godfather, with my compliments."

Which meant she would never receive it and he would find out that she'd been deceiving him. Yet what else could she say except, "Thank you."

"It's no trouble. I have several. Not that I go sending them out to everybody I meet…"

His voice trailed off into an embarrassed silence.

She risked a swift glance at his face, to see that he was blushing from his collar to his hairline and said, "I think you're a very remarkable man, Lord Bromwell."

"I think you're a rather remarkable woman, to have travelled so far by yourself," he replied, not meeting her gaze. "For a young woman to even decide to do such a thing, and in the face of parental disapproval, is astonishing."

"It seems we both have had to disappoint our parents in order to be free."

Except, in her case, her parents were dead, and she was all alone.

As he was, at least in one way. Even here in the family home, no one understood him or the forces that drove him. The desire to learn. The zeal to discover. The willingness to risk everything in the advancement of science. She didn't fully comprehend what compelled him, either, but she could easily admire him for his dedication and devotion.

As she stood beside him close enough to touch, the glow of the lamp surrounded them, a circle of enveloping light in the encompassing darkness, as if they were all alone in this vast mansion, this county, this country, the world. An island of sanctuary in a hostile world.

Only the two of them, separate, but not alone. Not anymore.

She could have no hope for any kind of future with him. She was a thief, a fugitive and a liar. She was here under the most false of pretences, taking advantage of his kindness and generosity, and her only hope should be that he never found out the truth.

She parted her lips, ready to say something, anything, to break the spell cast by the lamplight and her admiration and sympathy.

He leaned closer, as if to listen.

Or to kiss her.

"My lord, dinner is served," the butler announced from the doorway.

At Fallingbrook's announcement, Bromwell immediately moved away from the beautiful and far-too-tempting Lady Eleanor.

If she knew the thoughts and images that swirled in his head about her, she would think him the most lascivious libertine in England. She must never know, and he must and would master his desire. He must and would behave as he should, no matter how enticing she was.

She needed his help, not his unwelcome advances.

"Shall we?" he said, politely offering her his arm.

She duly laid her hand upon it and they dutifully and silently proceeded to the dining room.

"Ah, here you are!" his father cried as they entered and his triumphant smile was almost too much to bear in silence.

Almost, for what could he say to his parent that wouldn't alert Lady Eleanor to his father's persistent wishes regarding his future?

Surprisingly, his mother was there, too, looking more alert and healthy than she had in a long time. She had always enjoyed the company of younger women, and he had more than once suggested she have a companion, but that proposal had always been met with her own kind of stubborn resistance. She would say she wouldn't need a companion if her son would visit more often and stay longer.

Since the countess was already seated and made no effort to stand, her son brought Lady Eleanor to her. "Mother, this is Lady Eleanor Springford. Lady Eleanor, my mother, Lady Granshire."

"Delighted," his mother murmured as Lady Eleanor dropped her hand from his arm and dipped a curtsy.

His father, meanwhile, nodded at the liveried, bewigged footman, who pulled out a chair that would be to his right at the table.

"My lady," the earl said, nodding toward the chair.

Again demonstrating her admirable, amiable poise, Lady Eleanor gave her host a pleasant smile, then did as she was ordered and took her seat.

After the earl delivered a grandiose grace as if it were the Sermon on the Mount, supper was served.

Bromwell was well aware he need not be ashamed of any meal in his father's household; unfortunately, the price for such sumptuous fare as turtle soup, turbot with lobster, lamb cutlets, venison, beef, goose, peas, salad, meringues à la crème and chocolate cream was having to listen to his father, who had an opinion, however ignorant and ill formed, on everything.

Lady Eleanor ate as delicately as before and listened politely. She never ventured a remark unless the earl asked her a direct question, an opportunity that came precisely once, when he asked her about the condition of Italian roads compared to English ones. Even then, he didn't really listen to her response. He simply continued to assert his opinion that English roads were in a disastrous state and all those convicts being shipped off to Australia could be put to better use fixing the roads and verges in England.

Having witnessed the disembarkation of men, women and children from a convict ship in Australia, Bromwell didn't disagree. "It might mean more of them survive," he noted. "The conditions on those vessels—"

"I'm not saying we should keep them here to do them good," his father cried as if Bromwell had suggested putting them up in hotels, "but as a means of saving the government money."

"To make them slaves," Bromwell said. "You've never been to a sugar plantation, or you would realize that slavery—"

"Is not what we're discussing. We were talking about roads—the very roads that nearly got you killed."

"The accident wasn't that bad," Bromwell replied, trying to be patient. "We were not in danger of dying."

"If there had been passengers on top of the coach, though," Lady Eleanor ventured, "they might have been seriously injured or killed."

"Ah! There!" his father cried triumphantly. "Exactly my point!"

Bromwell tried not to feel betrayed. "I admit that's true, especially if we'd been going at a faster rate of speed. Nevertheless, I think there's a vast difference between saying that the roads should be kept in good repair and using slave labor to ensure it."

"This is what comes of an expensive education," his father complained to Lady Eleanor. "Theory over practicality every time. Maybe if my son stayed in England instead of haring off after bugs, he'd realize the state this country is in."

"When you have seen as much of the world as I have," Bromwell said quietly, thinking of certain images that would be forever burned into his brain, "you can appreciate how fortunate we are, although there is much that could be done to improve England, and the English."

His father's brows lowered. "Now you sound like one of those damned Frenchmen, spouting off about *liberté* and *equalité*. Look what happened there. Turned the country into a bloody mess."

Lady Eleanor shifted uneasily in her chair, and his mother looked equally uncomfortable.

"Perhaps we should refrain from political discussion until the ladies have retired to the drawing room," Bromwell suggested, hurrying on before his father took that as an indication that his son was admitting he was wrong. "Did I not see a new horse in the stables, a very fine black hunter?"

"Yes, you did," his father replied. "Got it for the new season. Wonderful animal."

His father proceeded to describe not just the qualities of his latest purchase, but every other horse and hound he possessed. Although changing the subject was precisely the goal Bromwell had hoped to achieve, he subdued yet another sigh as he wondered what Lady Eleanor made of his family.

At last the final course of fruit and chocolate crème had been served, and the ladies left him alone with his father. Instead of returning to politics, however, Bromwell was forced to endure another lecture on his duties as an Englishman, a nobleman and especially the heir of the Earl of Granshire.

Having been subjected to this harangue several times before, Bromwell allowed his mind to drift to Lady Eleanor, although that proved to be something of a mistake. His imagination immediately conjured the picture of her lithe, graceful body engaged in a *hura,* the dance done by the women of Tahiti, which was as different from a measured, genteel English ballroom dance as it was possible for a dance to be.

"Well, Bromwell? What do you intend to do?" his father demanded, tugging his mind back to cold reality.

"For now, join the ladies," his son replied as he rose and headed for the door.

Nell had thought the dinner at the inn had been like trying to make her way through a maze, but that was nothing compared to the tension she experienced in the Earl of Granshire's dining room. Thanks to her education— which the earl would likely consider a waste of money— she knew what glass to drink from and how to manage the fish bones; otherwise, she felt like the unwilling spectator at a trial, with Lord Bromwell as the defendant and his father both judge and jury. His mother, for all her apparent concern for her son, said nothing in his defence. Instead, she sat as silent as a spirit and picked at her food like a bird.

No, that wasn't right, she thought as she sat across from Lady Granshire, who was reclining on the Grecian couch in the drawing room while they waited for the tea. A ghost might have groaned or tipped over a chair to reveal its presence. Lady Granshire simply ate her food, sipped her wine and ignored the conversation around her.

Perhaps she was used to such conversations between her husband and son, which surely meant they weren't uncommon. Poor Lord Bromwell! How difficult it must be for him here!

"You're shivering," the countess said with maternal concern. "Shall I have a footman fetch you a shawl?"

"No, I'm quite all right, thank you," Nell replied. If anything, the room was rather too warm, for the fire had been built up while they'd been in the dining room, probably for Lady Granshire's benefit.

Lord Bromwell and his father would no doubt find the room almost unbearably warm. Of course, having been in such hot climes during his voyage, Lord Bromwell might not find such temperatures uncomfortable, although he might be tempted to remove his coat…

"I do hope you're not coming down with something. Perhaps I should have Dr. Heathfield see you when he comes for his weekly visit."

"No, I'm sure I'll all right. I must thank you for the loan of this gown and the others."

The countess gave her a shy smile that was very like her son's. "Think nothing of it. I have too many to wear." She leaned forward and took hold of Nell's hand with unexpected strength. "You mustn't mind my husband, Lady Eleanor. He is arrogant and stubborn and easily agitated, but he can be kind and generous, too."

"It's hardly for me to judge him," Nell protested, taken aback by her fervor.

Lady Granshire let go of her hand and lay back. "It's just that he had certain aspirations for his son and Justinian has ignored them and gone his own way."

"To great acclaim," Nell observed.

"Yes," the countess agreed, "but—"

She fell silent when Lord Bromwell appeared in the door. He nodded a greeting, then went to stand by the window in the same attitude as before, feet planted, hands behind his back, but this time, it looked as if he was preparing himself for a rigorous dressing down, not studying the moon or stars.

His father entered and posed by the hearth, his elbow on the mantel, shoulders back, chest out, in an attitude that, she suspected, he thought made him look imperial and impressive.

"What a charming picture!" the earl declared as he regarded them with a condescending smile. "To think I have two of the loveliest women in England in my drawing room!"

His wife blushed, while Nell gave the supercilious, boastful earl a meaningless smile. At least he wasn't criticizing his son.

"And of course, I wish to have two of the loveliest women in England at our hunt ball. You will stay for that, won't you, Lady Eleanor?"

She avoided looking at Lord Bromwell. She shouldn't care what he thought of that suggestion, because she didn't dare attend. Any such gathering might mean an introduction to someone who knew the real Lady Eleanor.

"When is it?" Lord Bromwell inquired.

"Gad, Justinian, you should know. It's always the first Saturday of November," his father replied.

"I was asking for Lady Eleanor's benefit," he calmly explained.

A month. She didn't dare to remain here a whole month.

"I suppose you've invited the usual set?" Lord Bromwell asked his mother.

"Of course."

"Will Lady Jemisina be attending?"

Whoever Lady Jemisina was, Nell hated her instantly.

His mother's eyes brightened and she darted a swift, thrilled look at her husband. "I've already had her acceptance."

"And her father?"

That question doused the happy light in Lady Granshire's eyes, while Nell felt as if she'd unfairly maligned the harmless Lady Jamesina. "Yes, but Justinian, you must promise me you won't—"

"Gad!" his father cried. "Do you hear *nothing* that I say to you? You will *not* pester our guests with requests for sponsoring another ridiculous expedition!"

Nell looked swiftly at Lord Bromwell, expecting him to flush or frown or even leave the room. Instead, he merely raised a brow as he replied, "How do you know that I don't have something of a more personal matter to discuss with Lady Jemisina's father?"

His mother clasped her hands as if she was about to receive her heart's desire. "You *do?*"

In spite of her rational realization that there could be nothing between Lord Bromwell and her, Nell suddenly felt disappointed and dismayed—until Lord Bromwell gave her a swift, inscrutable glance and said, "I may—or I may not. I was merely pointing out to my esteemed parent that since he cannot read my mind, he can only guess at my intentions.

"Now if I might make a suggestion, I think Lady Eleanor is rather fatigued. Perhaps, my lady, you'd like to retire?"

"Yes, I would," she quickly agreed, thinking it best to get away from them all, but especially from Lord Bromwell, before she did something really foolish.

Like fall in love with him.

Early the next morning, Nell slipped out onto the terrace and continued into the garden. Wrapping the cashmere shawl Lady Granshire had provided about her shoulders, she kept to the paved walks, for the dew was still sparkling on the grass.

The yew hedges, shrubs and edges of the walks were all neatly and precisely trimmed. The flower beds were pristine, the plants evenly spaced, the roses expertly pruned. Every portion was formal and clearly planned to the last detail.

Instead of being impressed, however, as the earl would no doubt expect, the formality and man-made arrangement made her yearn for wild, open country or a forest, where plants and trees grew untended and free.

Perhaps that was another reason Lord Bromwell had gone to sea, to get away from the constraining regulation of his family's estate.

She encountered a ha-ha at the far end of the garden. The sunken fence was in a shallow moat and beyond it she could see a path leading into a wood. Determined to reach that bit of natural nature, she stepped back a few paces, took a deep breath, ran and jumped.

She almost fell and spent a few frightening moments teetering on the brink of the opposite side before she got her balance. Once she did, she walked briskly along the path into the shadows of the oaks, beeches and alders, feeling triumphant and happy to be away from the stifling formality of Granshire Hall. Large royal ferns, browning with the season, lined the path and carpeted the wood floor, along with wild garlic and campion. Lichen clung to the tree trunks, and years of fallen leaves made her progress silent. She spotted two chaffinches on a branch overhead, their slightly red breasts a bright spot among the yellowing leaves.

The way was uneven and a little rocky, and she wasn't exactly dressed for a long walk, but after a little while, it was as if she'd left the Earl of Granshire's estate far behind and entered a mysterious, enchanted wood. She wouldn't have been surprised to come upon a fairy ring, or a centaur, or a unicorn.

Or a knight on horseback, clad in chain mail and looking like Lord Bromwell.

She supposed she was running away again, albeit in a less drastic manner. She probably ought to leave Granshire Hall and the viscount and his family—but where exactly was she going to go? Where would she be safe from the law and Lord Sturmpole?

The memory of that terrible night invaded the peace of the wood. She felt the same horror as she had when she realized Lord Sturmpole had no intention of paying her wages unless she submitted. The struggle that ensued. The locked door. Her escape and fear and flight…

She paused beneath a willow beside a babbling stream, the leaves a canopy made by Mother Nature, the grass a natural carpet. If only she could stay here forever…

Something that was most definitely not the stream, or a bird, or the call of an animal, broke the silence.

Somebody was singing. Or rather, chanting, followed by rhythmic clapping.

Keeping to the edge of the stream, she slowly followed the sound until she reached an opening where the stream formed a deep pool. There, at the edge, she could see the singer, who was also dancing, or so she supposed the rhythmic steps and arm movements must be.

It was Lord Bromwell, clad only in dark trousers and boots, chanting in a foreign language and moving his body as she'd never seen a body move, in a dance like no dance she'd ever seen and a very far cry from a quadrille or a waltz.

Chapter Eight

The process is both time-consuming and somewhat painful, as I can personally attest. I declined the full tattoo given to adult males, which caused much hilarity among the women, who clearly thought I was admitting I was but a child despite my years and certain other evidence that I was not.

—from *The Spider's Web,* by Lord Bromwell

Nell stared in complete fascination, marvelling at the lithe ease and grace with which Lord Bromwell moved, the undulations of his body, the deep bends and the way he moved his knees back and forth like the wings of a butterfly. She had never seen anything like it, and likely never would again.

He turned, so that he was facing away from her, and she spotted something on his back, slightly visible above the waistband of his trousers. It was a dark mark, like a large birthmark…or a tattoo?

It had to be, she thought as she inched her way forward. What was it supposed to depict? She was too far away to tell and too much of it was covered by his trousers to guess what it was with any accuracy—and she really shouldn't linger here. Surely he would be mortified if he found her there, as she would be to have him know that she'd been watching him.

Nevertheless, she hesitated, then decided it was worth the risk to listen to his chant and watch him dance like some sort of warrior from long ago calling on his gods.

Until a dog bayed nearby. Loudly.

Lord Bromwell instantly stopped dancing while, with a gasp, Nell began a hasty retreat.

A huge black dog burst through the bushes nearby, growling and baring its teeth as if it was about to attack.

Nell stopped dead, too panicked to scream. The dog stood where it was and began to bark as if to summon an army.

"Quiet, Brutus! Sit!"

Relief flooded through Nell as the dog did as Lord Bromwell commanded, abruptly settling on its haunches, silent and panting, as Lord Bromwell appeared from the trees. He had hastily donned a white shirt that was still half undone and open nearly to his navel, as well as a blue frock coat.

"I'm sorry if he frightened you," he said, walking up to the huge, slavering dog and patting its head. "The game-keeper must be nearby. I suspect Brutus thought you were a poacher, but even so, he's all bark, which is why he's an excellent guard dog."

She sidled closer to the animal and put out a hand to pat him. The dog's tail began to thump as he looked up at her with mild brown eyes.

"See? Now he's a friend for life," Lord Bromwell assured her, while she tried not to glance at the opening in his shirt and that expanse of sun-browned naked chest. "What brings you this far from the house, and so early?"

Before she could answer, an elderly man in leather gaiters and a heavy black coat, with a felt hat pulled low on his forehead, stepped out of the trees. His face was nearly as brown as his hat, much wrinkled, and he had the widest mouth she'd ever seen. He also had a shotgun cradled in the crook of his arm.

Although he bobbed his head in greeting, his eyes, shaded by the hat, narrowed when he saw her.

"This is Billings, the gamekeeper, my lady," Lord Bromwell said before turning to address him. "I'm afraid poor Brutus gave Lady Eleanor quite a scare."

"He was only doin' his job, my lady," the gamekeeper said gruffly.

"He has a very loud bark."

"Aye, like his father—and a good thing Castor were loud, or his lordship here would be nothing but bones."

"There are some caves nearby and when I was about ten, I decided to go exploring," Lord Bromwell explained with a rueful grin, reminding her that he was not as old as his fame and accomplishments might lead one to believe. "I got stuck trying to squeeze into an opening and couldn't get out. Brutus's sire found me and the rescue party was able to follow the sound of his barking to get me out.

"It was not," Lord Bromwell added self-deprecatingly, "my finest hour."

"Oh, now, I dunno," Billings replied, tipping back his hat and revealing sparse gray hair. "Come out of it laughing, he did, like it was all just a lark to him."

"Because I had every faith you'd find me."

Billings shook his head. "After hours alone trapped in the dark? Enough to give grown men the willies."

"It wasn't dark the whole time," Lord Bromwell corrected, leaning his weight on one leg and speaking as if they were at a dinner party. "My candle lasted for most of it and there was a *Meta menardi* to keep me company."

"That'd be some kind of spider, I suppose," Billings said.

"The common name is the orb-weaving cave spider," Lord Bromwell replied.

Billings shook his head as if perturbed, but there was a glint of pride in his dark eyes and the hint of a smile at the corner of his wide mouth. "Most boys go for puppies or ponies. The viscount here goes for spiders. Has he shown you where he keeps 'em? It's not far."

Nell glanced at Lord Bromwell, who was swiftly buttoning up his shirt as if he'd suddenly realized he'd been exposing a rather vast amount of skin. "I don't think she'd be interested in my specimens, Billings."

"Oh? Scared of spiders, are you?"

"Not unless they're very close to me," she replied.

"They're all dead," Billings assured her.

"Except for the harmless sort who usually inhabit such buildings," Lord Bromwell amended.

"Not that we let folks know that," the gamekeeper said with a wink. "Haven't had a poacher on the place since his lordship come back because they think he might have brought some poisonous ones back with him and let 'em loose."

"I'd very much like to see Lord Bromwell's collection," Nell said honestly. After all, they would be dead.

"Well, then, since I've already seen 'em, Brutus and me'll be off," Billings said.

He slapped his hand against his thigh, and the dog rose

and trotted toward him. Then, giving the viscount a nod of farewell, and Nell a grin, the gamekeeper disappeared back into the trees with his dog.

"Do you really want to see my collection?" Lord Bromwell asked shyly when they were alone. "I won't be offended if you'd rather not."

Suddenly, the risk of being alone with him seemed far less important than learning about the subject that interested him so much that he would take such risks to collect specimens and bring them home. "Yes, I do."

He smiled with delight and the warmth of it seemed to heat her down to her toes before he turned and pointed at a brown stone building a little way in the distance. She hadn't seen it before because it was half-hidden by shrubs and ferns and surrounded by thick trees, and she had been too busy watching him dance.

"Billings started that rumor about poisonous spiders himself, to keep poachers away," the viscount said as he led the way. "He thought it would be more effective than laying traps."

"Apparently it works."

"Apparently," Lord Bromwell said, sliding her another boyish grin, and her heartbeat seemed to skip.

Reaching the small stone structure, he leaned forward and pushed down on the latch, then shoved open the rough wooden door before stepping back to let her enter ahead of him. "Welcome to my idea of heaven, Lady Eleanor."

She moved past Lord Bromwell into the dim building that was about twenty feet wide and thirty feet long. The only illumination came from two wide, square windows that were half-shuttered and a small fire in the hearth at the other end of the room. There were shelves to her right bearing several glass jars with objects floating in them and a large, cluttered table of scarred oak in the center. On the table were the remains of a candle in a simple pewter holder in addition to an oil lamp, as well as some papers and what might be a box of pencils of the sort artists used. Beside the rough stone fireplace was a wooden cabinet with wide, narrow drawers. Shelves above it held a few books. There was also an assortment of what looked like cooking utensils, a kettle, plates, cups and cutlery, along with some other things she couldn't begin to name, on an ancient sideboard on the other side of the hearth. A cabriole sofa with a sagging seat was along the wall to her left, with a pillow and rumpled blanket at one end.

Lord Bromwell squeezed past her and went to fold the blanket. "Forgive the disarray. Normally nobody comes here except me. The servants won't set foot in the place. Sometimes I sleep here when I'm working on a paper, as I was last night."

The blanket folded, he hurried to the hearth and took a brimstone match from a container on the unfinished wooden mantel. He put it into the fire, then used it to light the oil lamp. As it glowed into life, she could see what floated in the jars.

Spiders. Large ones, small ones and several sizes in between. Some were dark, some colourful, one or two were completely black.

No wonder the servants wouldn't come here, she thought as she wrapped her arms around herself. "I didn't realize they could get so big," she murmured, staring at one particularly enormous specimen.

"Oh, they can," Lord Bromwell replied. "I have other specimens, too, in the drawers."

He nodded at the cabinet. "It pains me to have to kill

them, but there is no other way to bring them home for further study."

He reached for one of the bottles. "This fellow is the same kind that gave you such a turn in the coach, *Tegenaria parietina,* also known as the cardinal spider because Cardinal Wolsey apparently shared your reaction to them."

"It's a common reaction to spiders, of course," he continued as he regarded his collection. "Even the daughter of one of the first men to write well of them seemed to have had a similar response. Her name was Patience."

He slid Nell a sidelong glance. "Perhaps you've heard of her? Her father was Dr. Thomas Moufet."

"Little Miss Muffet?" Nell cried. "She was a real person?"

"So it seems," he said, grinning, "although I don't know who came up with the rhyme."

He moved further down the shelf and pointed at another specimen. "And this beauty is a tarantula from Italy. Its poisonous bite is supposedly cured by music and wild dancing."

She thought of *his* wild dancing, the memory so vivid and exhilarating she doubted she would ever forget it. "You don't believe that?" she asked, for his expression was decidedly amused.

How would he look if he'd known she'd seen him when he thought he was alone?

"No," he replied with a shake of his head, "although it's an interesting notion. Inhabitants of the same regions where this spider dwells used to hold rites dedicated to Bacchus. I suspect the bite of the tarantula is merely an excuse to continue similar unbridled excess and all manner of…"

He cleared his throat and immediately went to the next species. "This is a spider that I found near Kealakekua Bay, in Hawaii, where Captain Cook was killed."

As he continued describing his collection, he became more enthused and entertaining, and less the serious scholar.

She'd never met a man so keen on his profession, so thrilled by his work, so excited by his studies. So handsome and charming, so modest and yet so heroic. So lean and yet so muscular....

"Am I boring you? I can get quite carried away, I know," Lord Bromwell asked, obviously misinterpreting the far-off look in her eyes.

"Not at all," she answered. What would he think or do if she confessed she'd just been imagining him without any clothes on?

"Would you like some tea? I have some, and there's water in the kettle. Unfortunately, I don't have any milk or sugar."

"A cup of tea would be lovely," she said, "if you think we can spare the time."

He stepped briskly toward the fireplace. "My mother never comes down to breakfast and my father's never been an early riser."

"Then please, let's have some tea."

Nodding, he hung the kettle from a pot crane and moved it over the flame. He fed more wood into the fire and got two cups and spoons and a tin from the sideboard. "I'm aware spiders aren't as attractive as butterflies or flowers, but they're still worthy of study. For instance, their webs are amazingly strong for their size and weight. Just think what we could do if we could figure out how to imitate the properties of spiders' silk! Unfortunately, not many share my opinion. Mostly they, like my father, consider my devotion to the study of spiders a waste of time."

"Which makes your dedication that much more impressive."

"Do you really think so?" he asked eagerly, turning so quickly toward her that the stray lock of hair fell over his forehead again.

"I do," she confirmed, moving closer to the table and leafing through some sketches there. They were very good, proving that Lord Bromwell was a man of many talents.

"My father has never understood me at all," Lord Bromwell said with a sigh. "I was a great disappointment to him as a child. I wasn't a particularly robust boy, and I preferred reading to riding and hunting.

"I became interested in spiders when I was recovering from scarlet fever. A cardinal spider inhabited a corner of my room across from my bed and when I had no new books to read, I would watch it.

"The maids kept destroying its web, but the spider always returned and built another. I was fascinated by both the web, and the creature's persistence."

She imagined him as a lonely little boy with only a spider for company. And yet…"Thompkins said you're an expert horseman."

"Practice, over many years, aided by the instruction of my friends who all ride better than I," Lord Bromwell replied.

"You seem to have outgrown any tendency to sickliness," she noted as she studied a particularly fine drawing of a plant she'd never seen before.

"Not completely," he said, coming closer as she picked up another picture, this one of a hairy-legged spider. "I became very ill during my last voyage. Measles, of all things. Fortunately, I didn't lose my eyesight."

"Or the world would have lost a talented artist as well as naturalist."

"I'm competent enough to draw from life, but I'm hardly an artist," he demurred.

Acutely aware of his proximity, she tried to focus her attention on the sketches of insects and plants. "These are very realistic."

She was nearly at the bottom of the pile when a very different picture caught her eye. She drew it out and found a charcoal sketch of herself, looking pensive and plaintively out of the window of the coach.

It was startling to see herself so accurately rendered with a few strokes of charcoal. "I thought you were asleep for most of the journey," she murmured. "The next time I share a coach with someone I think is sleeping, I might have to kick him to make sure."

His lips curved up in a rueful smile. "If I had known how much I would enjoy your company, I would have stayed awake."

The kettle began to whistle and she let out her breath as he went to make the tea, trying to calm her rushing heartbeat. "I don't blame you for preferring to spend time here, but it must get a little lonely sometimes, just you and the spiders."

"Billings and Brutus join me sometimes, and bring a rabbit to stew. Then we have quite a little party," he said, pouring boiling water through the tea strainer into a pot. "I did miss Granshire when I was at sea, more than I thought I would. I even missed Father, although there was a certain chieftain in Tahiti who reminded me of him a great deal. Obuamarea had a daughter he was particularly keen I marry. Of course I had to refuse."

"Was she pretty?" Nell asked.

"Very, once one got used to the tattoos."

She remembered the black mark on his back and wondered again what it depicted.

He handed her the cup, which she rested on her knees. "I probably shouldn't have gotten one myself, but I was curious about the process. I do wish, however, that I'd kept that particular experience out of my book."

She wrapped her hands around the warm cup. "Is there really a bet about it at White's?"

"Sadly, yes, there is. My friend Brix—the Honorable Brixton Smythe-Medway—made it. He called the wager repayment for a certain bet some friends and I made that caused him some grief—but if you knew Brix, you'd believe as I do that he would have done it anyway, just to make mischief."

"He doesn't sound like the sort of friend I'd like."

"Oh, he's really a fine fellow," Lord Bromwell said as he leaned back against the sideboard, holding a chipped teacup. "He's a bit of a comedian, that's all. We met at school and he was the first boy to speak to me. That's how I met Edmond and Charlie and Drury, and we've been friends ever since, although they can't quite understand my interest in spiders, either.

"But I could never be an attorney like Drury, or write poetry and novels like Edmond. Brix is helping to improve his father's estate and Charlie's in the navy, so I suppose I have the most in common with him." He gave her another rueful smile. "But listen to me going on about myself! Tell me about your interests, my lady."

"I—I don't have any," she admitted, feeling woefully ignorant and boring.

"Surely there must be something?" he prompted. "You can rest assured I shall be open-minded."

She truly believed he would be, even if she expressed an interest in something scandalous, like a career upon the stage.

There *was* one thing she wanted, one dream she'd always harboured that seemed safe enough to mention. "I've always wanted to have children."

And a home, and plenty of money, but she didn't add those things.

"So have I," he said as he put his empty teacup on the sideboard. "Someday, when I'm no longer able to go on expeditions, I hope to be so blessed. But until then, I won't ask a woman to marry me only to make her wait for me to return, always wondering if I'm safe or if the ship's gone down."

As his mother waited. As she would wait now, for word of him. "You could take her with you, couldn't you?"

"I would never subject a wife to the crowded conditions and deprivations of such a voyage."

"What if a woman were willing to wait for you?"

He spoke firmly and unequivocally. "I would tell her not to."

"Whoever you choose to marry, whenever you choose her, she will be a very lucky woman," Nell said as she got to her feet.

"I doubt that," he said, reaching out to take her cup and setting it beside his on the sideboard. "I am a titled man with a mania for spiders who happened to write a book that, for now, is popular. Next year, next month, someone else will be the toast of London, and I'll merely be an eccentric nobleman, the same as I was before."

"You are more than that," she protested, upset that he so obviously believed what he'd just said, no doubt the legacy of the censure and ignorance of others, especially his father. "You're a kind, generous, heroic man any woman would be proud to marry."

He tilted his head and studied her as if she were one of his specimens. "Would *you* marry me if I asked?"

He wasn't really proposing and even if he did, she could never be his wife. He deserved a rich, titled woman who could support his scientific endeavors as much as he deserved the respect and praise of his family and peers. She knew it as surely as she drew breath and he liked spiders, no matter how much she wished it could be otherwise.

Nevertheless, she answered honestly. "I believe any woman would be happy to be your wife."

"Any woman?" he asked quietly, moving closer.

"Any woman," she confirmed.

It was time to leave, before she said or did something she would regret. "We should go, my lord."

He nodded and didn't move.

She waited, scarcely breathing.

He took a step closer.

So did she.

For she could bear it no longer. Although it would be wrong and foolish and might lead to more trouble, she couldn't help it. She had to give in to her longing.

So she rose up on her toes, and kissed him.

Chapter Nine

❦

Every culture and every species has its own unique mating rituals, but all lead to the same end: procreation. It is one of nature's strongest urges, as great as the need for food and water, shelter and warmth.
—from *The Spider's Web*, by Lord Bromwell

For a horrible moment, Nell feared that she'd made another terrible mistake, until Lord Bromwell put his arms around and responded with passionate fervor as if he'd been waiting for this since that other kiss. Angling himself closer, he pressed his tongue against her closed lips and it seemed the most natural thing in the world to part them.

Yet even that close contact was not enough. She wanted to be more intimate, to feel his skin beneath her hands, to let him feel hers.

Leaning into him, she pulled his shirt free of his trousers and slipped her hands beneath, revelling in the sensation of his hot flesh beneath her fingertips as she tentatively, gently, slid her hands upward. She laid a palm over his taut nipple while his own hands glided up her back. Her knees seemed soft as melting butter, and in one swift, fluid motion, he picked her up and carried her to the worn sofa where he laid her upon it as if she were Sleeping Beauty.

Then he stood back and looked at her. At that moment, he was no restrained Englishman, his actions ruled by man-made rules of etiquette. He was a hero, a warrior, a man who had been tested and proven by trials she could scarcely imagine.

Yet he was also a man of flesh and blood, whose storm-gray eyes bespoke the needs of that longing flesh, that heated blood.

His chest rose and fell rapidly as he tore off his jacket and tossed it aside before joining her on the sofa, covering her body with his.

She rejoiced in the weight of him, the length and strength of his body, as she hurried to undo his shirt. He kissed her cheek, her jaw, and then her neck, his mouth working its way lower and lower, until he reached the rounded softness of her breasts.

Here, for now, she no longer cared that he was a lord who thought she was a lady. That he was as far beyond her as the moon was from the earth. That he had seen and done so much, and she had done so little, and not all of it good.

When she had all the buttons undone, she pushed him back a little and he laughed deep in his throat as she shoved his shirt from his shoulders, revealing his chest completely. He was leanly muscular, more like a young farmhand than the half-naked prizefighter she had once seen at a fair.

Kneeling, he put his arms around her and pulled her so that she was sitting up, her breasts against his chest as he began to undo the hooks at the back of her gown.

Society would say she should be appalled and demand

that he stop. Her heart and her body said otherwise, and to them she listened, kissing his shoulder as her hands ventured to the waistband of his trousers.

The back of her gown opened and his hand slithered inside, loosening her bodice still more. "Let me," she murmured, lying back and tugging the sleeves down. Her bodice followed, until only her thin chemise covered her breasts.

"You're so beautiful," he murmured, gazing at her with desire-darkened eyes.

"So are you," she whispered, reaching for him again.

"I should stop now, before—"

She raised herself and silenced him with another passionate kiss. He said no more, but kissed with swift, fierce passion, as if his desire had finally escaped. Or been set free.

His hands moved over her, gliding, stroking, caressing, arousing. She reached for the buttons of his trousers, but he caught her hand. "Not yet," he whispered as he kissed her earlobe. "Not yet."

She gasped when he sucked her earlobe into his mouth and stroked it with his tongue. Where had he…in the South Seas…?

Soon she neither knew nor cared where he'd learned what he did as his lips and tongue moved elsewhere on her body. He teased her nipples, the pleasure unlike anything she'd ever known, and her desire bloomed like a flower after a drought, unfurling and yet there was a tightness, too, like a piece of yarn being stretched nearly to breaking.

She raised her knees and brought her hips closer to his. Her skirts were between them, but she could feel his hot arousal. She knew what that boded, and was eager, not afraid.

She reached for his buttons again, and this time, he didn't stop her. His breathing grew more erratic, more rushed, as she felt his hand on her leg, raising her skirt, feeling for the drawstring of her pantelettes, pulling it until the knot was undone and he could insinuate his hand inside.

She gasped when he touched the moist hair and moaned when he pressed the heel of his hand against her, while his fingers moved with delicate determination.

She had no idea that…that she…

She tugged down his trousers, freeing him, boldly running her hand over his smooth, hardened length.

"I want you," she whispered. "I want you to make love with me."

"I want you, too," he panted as his finger slid inside her.

That wasn't what she meant…but it felt so good….

She instinctively grasped him a little tighter and ran her hand over him. A low groan escaped his lips, encouraging her, exciting her.

He pressed the heel of his hand against her again and a second finger joined the first, making her gasp. And the tightness grew.

"Please…" she murmured, shifting, trying to make him see that she really did want to love him. That she was anxious to love him.

He pushed once more with his hand and the tension snapped. Crying out, she half rose with the strength of her release, gasping and grabbing his shoulders, her toes clenching.

As the powerful throbbing passed, she fell back and heard his hoarse breathing. She had had relief, but he had not. She raised her arms and pulled him down to kiss, sliding her body toward him, wanting to give him the only thing of value she possessed—her body.

"No," he gasped, abruptly pulling away and tucking himself back into his trousers. "As tempted as I am, I won't. No matter how I feel. I won't marry or ask for a promise of marriage before I sail, and there mustn't be a child."

His words were like a bucket of cold water on her head. And yet how could she blame him? He was both right and wise.

As he got off the sofa and reached for his jacket, she pulled her bodice back up and her skirts down. "I understand, my lord," she said, his title a fitting reminder that whatever their feelings, they could never share a future.

"I—I'm sorry," he stammered, walking across the room toward the shelves before he turned to face her. "I have not behaved like a gentleman."

"Nor I like a lady," she said quietly, reaching back to try to hook her gown.

"I was planning to go to London today and I believe it would be best if I stayed there until I must return for the ball. My self-control is not what I thought it was."

Neither was hers and no doubt he was right to stay away, for if she felt so dismayed by this parting, how much worse would she feel if they'd given in to their desire?

Perhaps it was time she left Granshire, too.

As if he'd read her mind, he said, "You should stay here until your godfather returns to Bath."

In response to the letter she hadn't written, and never would, although she'd say she had. "I don't want to impose upon your parents."

"Trust me, my lady, it would be no imposition. Indeed, you would be doing them a kindness. My father is happy to entertain the daughter of a duke, and my mother will be better for the company."

Since he put it that way, and because she had little money and would be safe from Lord Sturmpole here, she said, "Very well, my lord, and thank you."

"There's no need for thanks," he replied brusquely.

"If you don't mind, I require your assistance on another matter," she said, determined to be calm and composed.

He raised his brows.

She turned her back to him. "I cannot hook my gown."

"Ah."

He came behind her and she could hear his soft breathing as he did up the hooks he had so recently unclasped. She wouldn't think about his lean, deft fingers that had stroked and caressed her and aroused her, or the end of that act. She wouldn't imagine what it would be like to be with him without it being wrong and a mistake.

Because it was, and there was nothing that could change that.

"Now you had best return to the hall," he said when he was finished. "I'll follow in a little while."

A few minutes later, Bromwell watched as she hurried away along the path. Then he closed the door and leaned back against it, his eyes closed.

He had always sought knowledge, craved it as other men did wine or wagering, never minding hardship or difficulty if it was in service of that goal. But here, at last, he had found something that threatened, as nothing else ever had, the course he had been so determined to tread since he'd watched that single spider spin its web in the corner by his bed when he was six years old.

* * *

"Back so soon, my lord?" Mrs. Jenkins cried later that afternoon when Lord Bromwell strolled into the nearly empty taproom of The Crown and Lion.

The only other inhabitants at that hour of the day were two farmers quaffing some ale near the kitchen, and another traveller sitting on the settle near the hearth.

"I'm going back to London for a few days," Bromwell replied. "How's Thompkins? Doing well, I hope?"

"Well enough. He went to London the day after you left—the doctor thought he could and he wanted to rest in his own bed."

"As long as the doctor approved," Bromwell said, not worried if that was the case. The driver hadn't seemed that badly hurt to him, either. "He didn't try to drive, though, did he?"

"Lord love you, no! He went inside the coach."

Smiling at the mental image of Thompkins seated inside the coach instead of atop it, no doubt criticizing the other driver the whole way back to London, Bromwell rubbed his hands, which were still a little chilly from the ride. "Now that my mind is at ease about his health, I'll have one of your tarts while the hostler saddles a fresh horse for me."

"O' course! Moll, one of the apple tarts for his lordship! And tea. Be quick, girl!" Mrs. Jenkins called as she hurried off to the kitchen.

Meanwhile Bromwell sat at a table beside one of the windows overlooking the yard.

Although the interior of the inn was relatively calm and quiet, the yard was busy with grooms and stable boys and servants going about preparing to receive the next stage. It was due at any moment, Bromwell knew from his own particular interior timepiece, but whether it would actually arrive at the appointed hour was subject to conjecture. That was one reason he preferred the mail coach when he didn't ride.

A harried-looking female servant with cap askew appeared with a tray bearing the aforementioned tart, as well as a teapot, cup and saucer. Mrs. Jenkins took the tray from the woman's hands and carried it toward the viscount as if bearing a gift to Caesar.

"Here you are, my lord. Just baked this morning," Mrs. Jenkins said, placing the tray before him. "All by yourself, are ye, then?"

"Yes," he replied, distracted by the aroma of the sweet-smelling tart. When he'd been shipwrecked, he would have sold his soul to have one bite of a tart like this.

"The young lady's well, I hope? Not suffering any troubles after the accident?"

The tone with which Mrs. Jenkins asked her question and the sly inquisition in her friendly eyes caused Bromwell to leap to a conclusion he should have considered before, and for some reason had not.

"She was quite well the last time I saw her," he replied, making it sound as if that was days ago, before he finished the last of the excellent tart.

Wiping his mouth with the napkin, he got to his feet. "Good day to you, Mrs. Jenkins. Commend me to your husband, will you?"

"I will, my lord," she said, her brow furrowing as she picked up the tray and watched him stroll out again.

"Tell me, Mrs. Jenkins, who was that fine young fellow?" the stranger sitting on the settle asked, nodding at the door through which the viscount had exited.

"That's Lord Bromwell, the naturalist," Mrs. Jenkins replied.

"The one who was nearly eaten by cannibals?"

"Aye, that's him," she replied proudly. "He always stops here when he's going between his family's estate and London."

"But not always alone, eh?" the man asked with a knowing smile.

"He's a *gentleman,* the viscount is," Mrs. Jenkins huffed like an irate mother hen. "The young woman we was referring to came in the same coach as him the last time, that's all."

"The mail coach that overturned? I heard about that at the inn I stopped at last night. It was quite fortunate no one was injured. Who was the young woman? A friend of the viscount's?"

Mrs. Jenkins frowned. "She's a lovely, modest young lady, that's what," she snapped before she bustled off to the kitchen as if something of great import required her attention.

"Pardon me, I'm sure," the traveller muttered insincerely as he rose and went to the window, where he watched the famous Lord Bromwell ride out of the yard.

Chapter Ten

*What could I say to him? That he should give her up
and let her go? That if he loved her, he should try to
win her heart, even if it meant forgoing his expedition?*

*What if he listened and then his decision proved
to be a mistake? I nearly destroyed my own chance
for happiness; I wouldn't wish to be responsible for
destroying his.*

—from the journal of Sir Douglas Drury

"Drury!"

Sir Douglas Drury, baronet and barrister, gowned and
bewigged, came to a startled halt outside the Old Bailey.
Spotting Bromwell's familiar face in a hackney cab, he
smiled and, with his ruined hands clasped behind his back,
made his way across the busy street.

"I must protest being accosted in that insolent manner,
my lord," Drury said with mock severity as Bromwell
pushed open the door for him to enter. "I am not a peddler."

"I most humbly beg your pardon," Bromwell replied
with equally feigned remorse. "However, I feared a silent

wave of my hand would fail to capture your notice. Deep in thought over a case, were you?"

"Actually, no," Drury admitted. "Juliette's been a little unwell."

"Nothing serious, I hope?" Bromwell asked, his own dilemma momentarily forgotten in his concern for his friend's wife.

"No, I don't believe so," Drury replied with an expression that assuaged Bromwell's dread. "What brings you back to London? Business, pleasure or spiders?"

"Spiders, mostly. I'm presenting a paper to the Linnean Society on the Brazilian wandering spider," Bromwell said. "However, I'd also like to ask your advice on a legal matter."

Drury regarded his friend with genuine surprise. "Don't tell me you've done something illegal?"

"It's nothing of a criminal nature."

"Thank God. But if it's not criminal, you would likely be better off consulting a solicitor. I'm sure Jamie St. Claire would be happy to help you," Drury said as he settled back against the squabs and hit the roof to signal the cabbie to drive on.

"If you think that best," Bromwell replied, "although I'd like to keep it as private as possible."

Drury's eyes flared with surprise, which he quickly and effectively masked. "If you tell me, I can present the facts to Jamie without involving you or mentioning any specific names."

"I'd prefer that," Bromwell said, thinking Lady Eleanor would probably prefer that, too.

"There was a woman in the mail coach with me on the way to Bath," he began as the cab lurched over a rut in the street, "and there was an accident. The coach overturned—

nobody was seriously injured," he hurried to assure his startled friend.

"Thank God," Drury muttered. "Continue."

"We were quite literally thrown together, and…"

This was likely not a good time to mention the kiss. If there ever would be a good time.

"Afterward, I discovered she's in some difficulty, so I invited her to stay at Granshire Hall. She's there now, enduring my parents. It's her situation that requires legal advice."

"Ah." Drury steepled his fingers that, while better than they'd been when he'd first returned from France, were still misshapen. "Was this woman an elderly grandmother or a middle-aged matron?"

"No. She's young."

"Pretty?"

"Very."

Drury raised a dark brow. "Does she like spiders?"

"Sadly, no. But at least she didn't run out of my laboratory when she saw my collection."

Drury's other brow rose. "You invited her into your laboratory?"

"She, um, was walking in the woods and I met her near it, so yes, I did."

Bromwell saw no need to explain that he'd spent the night in the lab so he wouldn't have to see her, or think about her sleeping a short distance down the corridor in Granshire Hall.

Drury held up his hand. "Perhaps this should wait until we're home. Otherwise, you'll just have to repeat these details to Juliette—or would you rather this was strictly between us?"

Bromwell thought a moment. It wasn't a situation he

was eager to share. On the other hand, Juliette was a kind, bold, clever woman who'd had her share of troubles, so she might have some valuable advice. And although he had every faith that Drury would keep this discussion private if he requested it, he wasn't keen to put secrets between a man and his wife. "No. I think Juliette's opinion might prove helpful, too. Brix and Fanny are still visiting with Edmond and Diana in Lincolnshire?"

"Yes. You'd want their advice, as well?"

He shook his head. "Gad, no!"

He could just imagine Brix's merry interrogation regarding the circumstances of his first encounter with Lady Eleanor and Diana would probably want to use it in the opening of a novel. Even worse, Edmond might take it into his head to compose a sentimental poem. He still hadn't gotten over Edmond's *Ode to an Arachnid*. "That is, I don't think the lady in question would care to have too many others know her troubles.

"How is your new house?" he asked, turning the conversation away from Lady Eleanor and to Drury's recent purchase.

On the edge of Mayfair, it wasn't the most prestigious location, but Drury had never cared about the trappings of success. Indeed, he hadn't even owned a town house until he'd gotten married. Until then, he'd lived in his chambers at the Inns of Court. He'd chosen this town house, he'd explained, because it was well built, with the latest in modern conveniences, and sure to increase in value over time.

"Fine, although Juliette is full of plans for painting and curtains and those sorts of things. I confess, old friend, that there are times I seek sanctuary in my study."

Bromwell shared a companionable smile. "As I flee to my laboratory when my parents try my patience to its limit."

That building could be a sanctuary for other reasons, too, as he'd recently discovered.

The cab rolled to a stop and as Bromwell looked at the white Georgian town house, he had to agree that Drury had spent his money wisely. Built across from a small park, it was in excellent condition with tall windows so clean they sparkled.

A young man in butler's attire opened the door as they got out of the cab and went up the steps.

"Good God, that's not Mr. Edgar, surely?" Bromwell cried, for the fellow was the spitting image of Drury's longtime servant, although at least twenty years younger.

"It's his son," Drury replied. "We call him Edgar Minor."

They had barely crossed the threshold and given Edgar Minor their hats when Drury's wife came rushing down the stairs right into her husband's arms.

"If you please, my dear," he chided even as he held her close, "we have company and the door to the street is still open."

Despite his frown, he wasn't fooling Bromwell or Edgar Minor or his wife, either. His eyes were too full of love and laughter.

"Oh, Buggy doesn't mind, do you, my lord?" Juliette asked after giving her husband a hearty kiss.

She left her husband's arms and hurried to Bromwell, kissing both his cheeks in the French manner. "Welcome! Of course you will stay for supper and tell us all about the plans for your expedition."

"Of course," Bromwell agreed with a smile. He had liked Juliette from the moment he'd met her. Although

Drury had never said so, Bromwell had guessed his friend had suspected him of harbouring a *tendre* for the French seamstress.

He hadn't. There hadn't been any woman who'd touched his heart until Lady Eleanor landed in his lap.

"Buggy has a friend with a legal dilemma," Drury said as they entered the comfortably appointed drawing room done in soothing tones of blue and cream. It was much smaller than the drawing room at Granshire Hall, but Bromwell would trade this for the other in a heartbeat.

"Oh? I hope it is not a serious one," Juliette said as she took a seat in a wing chair by the Dutch tiled hearth.

After her husband had joined her and Bromwell was sitting on a brocade-covered chair opposite, she picked up a small item from the sewing basket beside her, set it on her lap and threaded a needle.

Bromwell studied the fabric for a moment before he realized it was a small nightgown. A baby's nightgown.

"That looks a little small for Amelia," he said, referring to the recent addition to the family of the Honorable Brixton Smythe-Medway.

Juliette glanced at her husband and smiled, her brown eyes shining. "It is not for Amelia."

Bromwell followed her gaze to his friend, who was trying to appear nonchalant.

And failing miserably.

It didn't take a genius to realize what that, and Juliette's slight illness, must mean. His friend was going to be a father, too.

At once Bromwell envisioned this house as his, with Lady Eleanor seated by the hearth in the evening, sewing a little garment for their child.

Never before had he imagined a domestic future for himself. When he'd contemplated marriage, he had never thought beyond the ceremony and even that as some distant event, when he was too old to travel.

But now, here, this vision of a future with Eleanor struck him like a blow, a sudden, sharp, powerful pang of longing.

"I thought you would be happy for us," Juliette said, her brows knitting.

Bromwell came to himself with a start and smiled. "Oh, I am!" he said, hurrying to shake Drury's hand and kiss her cheek. "Delighted for you both. I envy you, that's all. That leaves only Charlie and me unmarried and childless."

Juliette resumed her sewing. "Someday, a woman will win your hearts and you will both be as happy as my Drury and me."

"I hope so," he answered, although the vision receded as he remembered his plans for his expedition. "In the present, however, I need your husband's help with my friend's dilemma."

He proceeded to describe Lady Eleanor's recent history and when he was finished, Juliette was wide-eyed with dismay. "Oh, the poor girl! To be forced to marry an old man!"

She looked at her husband, who was equally upset, although a stranger would probably have assumed he wasn't at all affected by what he'd heard. It took long acquaintance to see the subtle changes in the set of Drury's jaw and the glint in his dark eyes to realize he was disturbed.

"British law requires that both parties consent to any marriage," Drury said, "so it's a good thing she returned to England."

"And by herself, too!" Juliette exclaimed. "A brave girl, and clever, too, no doubt."

"Very," Bromwell confirmed.

"Unfortunately, as far as the law is concerned, she is her father's chattel until she's married, and then she becomes her husband's. However, if her parents are in Italy, we might be able to have her godfather declared *in loco parentis*. Jamie will know for sure, but even if that's unlikely to succeed, the legal suit might cause her parents to reconsider their position."

Bromwell felt better already.

"Perhaps if their daughter were to find her own husband, especially a wealthy and titled gentleman, they would relent even faster," Juliette suggested.

Bromwell flushed, but spoke just as firmly to her as he had to his father. "I have no intention of marrying anyone until I'm no longer able to travel, provided Lady Eleanor would even consider it."

"I did not necessarily mean she should marry you," Juliette returned, her hands as steady as her voice. "Maybe she will meet someone at your father's hunt ball. You wish her to be happy, do you not?"

He did—although the thought of her being happy with anyone else wasn't a welcome one.

"The first thing to do," Drury said in his usual logical, businesslike tone, "is to see what Jamie has to say about the law in such matters. Until then, everything is mere speculation, and I would much rather speculate on the subject of Edmond's new book. Apparently he's taken it into his head to write about something called a vampyre."

"Indeed, he has. He wrote to me about them, because they're not unlike spiders in some aspects," Bromwell replied, happy to leave the subject of Lady Eleanor for a while and speak of other things.

Even if she was never far from his thoughts.

The day after Lord Bromwell went to London, Mrs. Fallingbrook took Nell on a tour of Granshire Hall. It was indeed a magnificent house, although it was more like a museum than a home.

She spent another few days wandering about on her own and attempting to avoid the earl, who bored her nearly to death talking about his plans for the house and gardens. He was considering waterworks on a scale to rival Versailles, or so it seemed, and she had to wonder how the cost for such a venture would compare to the cost of his son's proposed expedition.

The countess kept mostly to her room, and the servants were busy and preoccupied preparing for the hunt ball, as well as the guests who would soon arrive in anticipation of that major event.

She walked in the garden and occasionally to the viscount's laboratory, where she dusted the jars and found herself studying the contents not with revulsion, as when she'd first seen them, but with increasing interest. She was surprised to discover how many kinds of spiders there were, and how different they could be from one another. Some of them were even rather beautiful.

Afraid she might disturb Lord Bromwell's work in some way, she hesitated to do more than dust the jars and wash the few dishes. She did open the narrow drawers of the wooden cabinet carefully and slowly, to find even more specimens of spiders, dried and mounted. They were like little jewels, lying so still in their trays.

This morning it was too damp to go to the wood and or the laboratory, so she decided to go to the library and find a book to read. It was one of the more comfortable rooms in the house, and as she strolled around the perimeter she remembered being here with Lord Bromwell, wondering if he was going to kiss her…hoping that he would….

Such thoughts would avail her nothing, she told herself, and she tried to concentrate on finding a book to read for education, if not amusement, since most of the volumes were histories of ancient Rome or Greece, Italy, England and France, or philosophy and religious sermons.

She gave up hope of finding anything appealing after she had gone around the entire room and found herself once again by the door. Sighing, she pushed it half closed and glanced at the shelves behind it.

The Castle of Count Korlovsky by Diana Westover was on the middle shelf, right at eye level. She'd heard of that book, and also the author, the wife of Viscount Adderley. Their marriage had been something of a sensation not so long ago. Indeed, Lady Sturmpole had been so fascinated by the gossip, one would think the author was one of her relatives, although she was not.

Nell pulled out the book and read a little of the first chapter. Then a little more. Taking the volume, she was about to head for a chair to spend the rest of the morning reading when another book, on the far end of the shelf almost completely hidden by the door, caught her eye:

The Spider's Web.

This must be how Lord Bromwell felt when he discovered a new kind of spider, she thought as she eagerly pulled it from the shelf, happy for another reason, as well. This meant his father had kept a copy, after all.

She hurried to one of the large chairs near the window and settled down to read. She would save Diana Westover's book for later; first, she must read Lord Bromwell's.

As she expected, the viscount's book was no dry, scientific report about spiders or the other various species of flora and fauna he encountered and collected.

In spite of the many scholastic elements of *The Spider's Web,* it was also a rousing adventure, full of exciting events and danger, as well as humor and wry observations not just about foreign cultures and habits, but about life aboard ship. Many times Nell could practically smell the salt air and hear the crew's colourful language.

Nor did Lord Bromwell leave out the less attractive facets of life in close quarters. Often she could almost smell the bilge water and taste the hard biscuits, see the rats and hear the snores.

It was no wonder he didn't want to take a wife on such a voyage.

Then there were the dangers, not just the hurricane that had wrecked their ship, killed some of the men and left the others stranded on an island little more than a spit of sand, but the unpredictable inhabitants of the exotic lands who might welcome visitors, or kill and eat them. Lord Bromwell, the captain and the rest of the crew had never been quite sure which sort of encounter it would be until they landed.

Some of their experiences with the natives were of a distinctly pleasant nature. He spoke of their food, their social customs, their tattoos and their dances, and she realized he'd been doing something called the *upa upa* by the pond. As for other, more intimate, activities between the native population and their visitors, Lord Bromwell was discreet and couched his language carefully, but she could read between the lines. She was fairly certain he hadn't kept aloof from the women.

And he had done more than dance.

Yet through it all, running like a thread of spider's silk, were two obvious themes—Lord Bromwell's passionate interest in his subject, and his modesty. And if he hadn't already proven to her that he was a capable, intelligent, admirable man, she would know it now.

A man cleared his throat loudly.

Startled, she looked up, half-expecting to see Lord Bromwell himself, as if reading his book had conjured him all the way from London like a magic spell.

It was not Lord Bromwell; it was his father, who stood with his chest out, his hands behind his back, rocking on his heels and regarding her gravely.

"I've been looking for you, Lady Eleanor," he announced. "There is something I wish to discuss with you."

For a horrible moment, she wondered if he'd discovered she was not who she claimed to be, until she realized he would surely be more angry and direct if he had.

No, it must be something else he wished to talk about, so Nell subdued a sigh and girded herself to hear more about fountains, or water pumps, or the difficulties of shipping Italian marble.

Instead—and what proved even more unnerving—the earl didn't say anything at first.

She shifted uncomfortably, but wasn't about to venture a remark.

"I presume you know that my son is the only living child of my wife and I?" the earl said at last.

"I had assumed so, since no one ever spoke of siblings," she replied.

"Which means that, in due course, he will be the Earl of Granshire, a most noble and ancient title."

Nell inclined her head in silent acknowledgment of that fact.

"He will be a very wealthy man. This estate and the house in London will be his, as well as a considerable fortune. His wife would, therefore, have every luxury and comfort."

"She would also have your son, a not inconsiderable reward," Nell pointed out.

"Provided she could get him to stay in England and not go haring off after more bugs!" the earl said with a frown, clapping his hands behind his back and starting to pace.

Nell didn't know what to say to that, so she didn't reply.

"He could have been anything," Lord Granshire grumbled as he marched back and forth. "A statesman—even Prime Minister. He was the cleverest boy at his school. All the masters said so. Instead he wastes his time and talent on bugs! They even called him Buggy Bromwell at school. My son, the heir of Granshire, a viscount, smartest lad at Harrow—Buggy! It's enough to make a man tear out his hair!"

"Surely you must be proud of him now," she protested, dismayed by his attitude and alarmed by his vehemence.

"How can I be proud of a son who studies bugs? Who dances with savages? Who won't do his duty and marry and get an heir?"

"I'm sure he'll marry some day and hopefully there will be children."

The earl stopped pacing to fix her with a searching gaze that, at the moment, reminded her of the son he seemed to hate. "If my son could be persuaded to marry and especially if he could be persuaded to give up this notion of another voyage, I would be very grateful. His bride could count on a very generous wedding gift from his grateful father."

His meaning was unmistakable. He was offering her a bribe to marry his son.

"And you need not think he'll be lacking in the bedchamber," his father continued. "His book provides ample evidence that—"

She leapt to her feet before he went on. "By God, sir, you should be ashamed of yourself! What kind of a father are you? Are you truly that stupid, that blind to the merits of your son?

"You should be *proud* of him. He could have been a rakehell, a cad, a scoundrel. He could be a gambler or a sot. He could be getting into debt or spending his money on Cyprians. Instead, he's contributing to the sum of human knowledge. He's doing something good and honorable. I'm sure there are many other men who would envy you your son and not belittle his work or consider him lacking, as you so obviously do.

"As for his taking a wife, there will be no need to bribe a woman to seek his hand. He's not only intelligent and brave, capable and clever, he's kind and generous—and there can be no doubt that such a man would be wonderful in every way a woman desires."

The earl flushed as if he was on the verge of an apoplectic fit, but she didn't care. She didn't care if he demanded that she leave at once, or threw her out of Granshire Hall on her ear. At the moment, she didn't even care if he summoned the magistrate.

"How dare you?" he demanded. "How dare you stand there and berate me! I don't care if you are the Duke of Wymerton's daughter, you have no right to speak to the Earl of Granshire that way."

"Perhaps I don't, but *somebody* should," she retorted. She grabbed the two books on the table beside the chair and marched to the door. "If you'd like me to leave in the morning, I shall, and gladly!"

At the door she turned to face him one last time. "And if I am ever so fortunate as to have children, my lord, I hope I shall encourage them and not stifle them. That I shall love them as every child deserves to be loved, even if they like spiders. Or ants. Or snails. I wish—"

That I had any chance at all of being your son's wife.

Tears of rage and indignation and dismay choked her, so she said no more before she fled the library.

Chapter Eleven

❦

The poison of the Phoneutria nigriventer, *while virulent, may not necessarily be deadly. However, if it is not, it may cause priapism, which turns what should be a pleasant state of arousal into an hours-long ordeal and can lead to permanent impotence.*
—from a presentation by Lord Bromwell on the Brazilian wandering spider

At the sound of approaching servants, whom she most certainly didn't want to meet, Nell ran into the nearest room.

She found herself in the huge ballroom with pier glass on the walls, its inlaid, waxed wooden floor gleaming, and French doors leading onto the terrace. She hurried beneath chandeliers shrouded with cheesecloth so they looked like large white nests, then out the doors, across the terrace and into the garden.

Dashing away her tears with the back of her hand, she paid no heed to the threatening skies and chilly breeze; nor did her steps slow when she reached the ha-ha. She leapt across and kept going, heading for Lord Bromwell's laboratory where she would be alone and undisturbed, where she could gather her thoughts and make her plans.

And leave him a note of farewell.

After what she'd said to the earl, he would surely insist that she leave. At once.

She reached the laboratory and went inside. Her hands trembling, she set the books down on the sideboard, lit a fire in the hearth and slumped into one of the chairs. No wonder Lord Bromwell had his working space so far from the hall!

The door creaked open and she turned, expecting to see Billings or perhaps Brutus on the threshold.

Not Lord Bromwell.

His face full of concern, he rushed toward her. "My lady, are you all right? What's happened? I saw you running from the house."

Surprised, delighted, then worried about what he would say when he learned of her confrontation with his father, she immediately got to her feet.

She hesitated to answer, but decided there was no point dissembling. "I had an argument with your father."

"Ah," he sighed as if he wasn't at all surprised. "Please sit down and I'll make some tea."

She didn't want tea, but she couldn't think of a good reason to refuse.

"You mustn't be upset about that," he said as he filled the kettle from a pitcher of water near the hearth. "He's a stubborn, opinionated man, but whatever you quarrelled about, he'll be swift to forgive a duke's daughter."

Perhaps so, but she wasn't a duke's daughter.

And worse than that, she'd been far too tempted to accept the earl's bribe and try to win his son's hand in marriage without worrying about the consequences.

"What did you quarrel about?" Lord Bromwell asked as he sat opposite.

He might as well know, in case his father tried to bribe another young lady. "My lord, are you aware of how far your father is willing to go to see you married?"

"I'm aware that is one of the goals of his life and that he's willing to do a great deal to bring it about, with or without my cooperation," Lord Bromwell replied grimly. "How much is he selling me for these days? I believe my price was up to five thousand pounds before I sailed. I expect he's dropped it some, now that I'm famous. Or maybe he hopes for a quick sale so he could announce our engagement at the ball."

"How can he do such a thing?" she asked, relieved that he knew his father's schemes, but upset for him nonetheless. "How can he have so little grasp of his son's merits that he thinks he must pay a woman to marry you?"

"He's a man of fixed notions and I was a disappointment to him as a child. He still sees me as a weak, sickly lad with odd fascinations, likely to die at any moment."

"That doesn't excuse his treatment of you."

"No," Lord Bromwell replied without bitterness. "It does, however, explain it."

She flushed, more sorry than ever that she had lost her temper. Obviously, Lord Bromwell didn't feel the need for anyone to champion him. "I'm afraid I berated him quite thoroughly before I left the room without waiting to be excused."

Lord Bromwell's eyes widened and he ignored the steaming kettle. "You walked out on him?"

"Yes. I suppose now he'll demand that I leave."

Lord Bromwell's amazement turned to reflection. "Perhaps not. He tends to fly into a rage easily, then calm down just as swiftly. It means he doesn't brood and is rarely sullen, but that also makes it difficult to know what to expect from him sometimes. Fortunately, since you're a duke's daughter, I believe he'll be inclined to act as if nothing at all untoward has happened between you."

He gave her a companionable smile as he finally lifted the kettle from the crane and began to make the tea with the same deliberate care he likely brought to the studies that made him famous.

He paused when he saw the books on the sideboard, Diana Westover's on top.

"Have you read much of Diana's book? It's quite exciting," he said as he poured the water from the kettle into the teapot.

"I started it, but I found another I prefer," she said, rising and putting *The Castle of Count Korlovsky* to one side, revealing the book beneath.

He flushed and smiled and then busied himself with the tea.

"Your father kept a copy after all," she said, returning to her seat.

"So I see."

"You're a wonderful writer, my lord. I feel as if I'm there with you, through the good and the bad. And I had no idea spiders came in such variety until I met you."

His smile grew, although he still didn't look at her. "That is why I wrote my book—so more people could appreciate not just spiders, but all the wonderful plants, animals and insects of the world, as well as the different peoples. The variety is really quite astonishing."

Lord Bromwell handed her a teacup and, taking the chipped one again, settled back in his chair.

"I have good news for you," he said, not aware that

everything he did for her made her feel more like a criminal and less worthy of his good opinion. "I spoke to my friend the attorney, who described your case—without naming you specifically—to one of the best solicitors in London. There may be a way to either make your parents see reason, or be deprived of their control over you."

Feeling like the worst, most ungrateful sinner on earth, Nell gazed down at the cup in her lap.

What would happen if people learned he'd been tricked, duped into thinking that he was helping the daughter of the Duke of Wymerton instead of the poor offspring of a clerk and his wife?

What would he think of her then, and after she was gone, or if Lord Sturmpole found her and had her arrested?

"I thought you would be pleased," Lord Bromwell said with puzzlement. "Or are you still upset about my father? Don't be. I'm quite used to his machinations."

"It's not that," she said, raising despondent eyes. Whatever happened, she couldn't bear deceiving Lord Bromwell another moment. Every deed he did, every word he said, was like a sword in her side, or another step on the road to damnation. The time had come to be honest with this man who was so honorable, so good and so generous. "I'm not a duke's daughter. I'm not Lady Eleanor Springford. My name is Nell Springley, and I'm a thief."

Bromwell heard her words, comprehended their general meaning, and yet it was as if he'd been struck by a poison dart, one that rendered its victim inert.

She wasn't Lady Eleanor, daughter of the Duke of Wymerton? She was somebody else entirely—and a *thief?*

"I stole some gowns and money from Lord Sturmpole

of Staynesborough. I didn't do so out of greed, or because I'm a habitual thief," she hurriedly continued. "My father was the younger son of a knight, my mother a merchant's daughter. They raised me well and sent me to a good school, but when they died of a fever within two weeks of each other, I discovered my father had gambled and borrowed too much. I was left penniless. Through friends from school I found employment as a companion to Lady Sturmpole at their estate in Yorkshire.

"Lord Sturmpole was never there, though, and I never received a penny of my pay. When I complained to Lady Sturmpole, she told me to write to her husband. I did, but he only wrote back with excuses and promising to pay the entire amount when he arrived in person. Lady Sturmpole assured me her husband would make all right when he returned from London and since I had no one to turn to, very little money left and nowhere else to live, I stayed.

"Lord Sturmpole finally arrived some five months after I did. I was called into his study to receive my wages, or so I thought. I was also going to give him my notice.

"When I got to the study, he told me he would be glad to pay me all that he owed, and more, if I would…" She blushed and drew a deep, ragged breath. "If I would let him come to my bed."

Bromwell didn't speak. He couldn't. He had never been more outraged and furiously angry in his life, and not even the most colourful epithet seemed appropriate to describe a man who would treat her in such a manner, or make that obscene offer.

"Naturally I refused at once and demanded my wages. Instead of paying me, he…he tried to…"

As she fell silent, her eyes anguished, her throat working,

Bromwell set down his teacup before he shattered it. "There's no need for you to go into details. I can guess what he tried to do. He should thank God he didn't succeed."

Or I would hunt him down and kill him. Painfully.

"No, he didn't," she confirmed. "I fought back and when he tired, he locked me in the room. I called out to the servants to help me, but they wouldn't. He's the only employer for miles and they wouldn't risk his displeasure, I suppose. I finally managed to get the lock open with a letter opener. The house was quiet—no doubt Lord Sturmpole thought I'd see sense in the morning.

"So I got a few of my clothes and what money I had, and then I went to his wife's dressing room and took three gowns and the pin money she kept in a drawer. It wasn't much—not nearly enough to cover my wages. And then I ran. The stagecoach went by not far from the estate and I managed to meet it just in time."

By now, the worst of Bromwell's fury was subsiding, to be replaced by a cold anger and firm purpose. He would see that Lord Sturmpole regretted what he'd done, and what he'd tried to do.

However, all he said to the anguished woman before him was, "What you did seems perfectly justifiable to me."

"And to me, or I wouldn't have done it. Unfortunately, I'm sure he wouldn't hesitate to have me charged with theft if he finds me. That's why I was travelling alone and told you I was Lady Eleanor. Until the coach overturned, I was planning to take ship to Ireland, or America, where he couldn't find me."

The knuckles of her clasped hands whitened as she leaned forward and regarded Bromwell beseechingly, as if he were a judge at the Old Bailey with the power of life and death over her. "I promise you, my lord, I did *nothing* to encourage Lord Sturmpole or make him think I would welcome his advances. You must believe me in spite of what I've done. I've never broken the law before."

It wasn't difficult for him to answer her heartfelt plea. "I do believe you. The man cheated you, so you took goods in compensation. He did something far worse than robbery. He attempted to rape you."

She flinched when he said "rape," reminding him that while she was courageous and strong, she had been through a terrible ordeal.

"Forgive me if my choice of terms distresses you," he said in a gentler tone. "I'm trying to think in legal terms, because I believe his is by far the greater crime. He should be imprisoned, if not hanged."

"He is a powerful man," Nell noted warily.

"Who must and will be stopped," Bromwell said firmly as he got to his feet.

Although she was relieved that Lord Bromwell believed her, he was as angry and upset as if he were the one who'd been attacked.

"I doubt you're the first women in his employ he's treated in this manner and I fear you won't be the last unless he's imprisoned and convicted."

She had been so worried about her own fate, she hadn't stopped to consider if anyone else had been the victim of Lord Sturmpole's lust. "Yes, I see."

Lord Bromwell began to pace, just as his father had. "I'll speak to my friend Drury. He's the best barrister in England. He'll know how to proceed in a way that will lead to Sturmpole's conviction and your safety." He stopped and faced her squarely. "You must promise me that you'll stay here and continue to be Lady Eleanor until we've done so."

Lord Bromwell spoke softly, but there was resolve beneath his words and a sternly determined expression in his stormy eyes. Now she was looking not at a well-educated, civilized viscount, but the heir of Celt, Saxon, Norman, Viking, Roman—every warrior race that had ever set foot and fought in Britain.

"Leave my father to me," he continued. "I'll ensure that you're welcome to remain at Granshire Hall until I can return from London."

She nodded, sure he would. But his plan also meant he would be leaving her here again, without him.

His visage softened a little, making him more like the Lord Bromwell she knew. "I can appreciate why you felt driven to lie to me and I bear you no grudge or ill will. I only wish you had felt confident enough in my compassion to tell me sooner."

"I wanted to," she truthfully replied, regretting that she hadn't. "I was afraid to trust anyone."

"And now?" he prompted.

"Now I can."

She thought he might embrace her then, or kiss her, but he didn't. He held out his arm with as much formality as if he were about to present her to the Prince Regent. "We should return to the house. I'll find my father and smooth things over with him, then leave for London at once."

"But you've only just returned."

"The sooner I see Drury, the sooner Sturmpole can be stopped."

She could not argue with that, so she took his arm,

gathered up the books from the sideboard and together they went back to Granshire Hall.

Dena, her cap and apron white as snow, her serge dress clean as it could be and her expression grim as death, was dusting the bedroom when Nell returned, her lips pursed as if the presence of dust was a personal insult.

The dour maid was one of the last people she wanted to see after the events of the morning, or to have to speak to; however, she supposed she had no choice but to accept her presence.

"I found Lord Bromwell's book in the library," she said, setting the pair of volumes on the table by the bed. "And *The Castle of Count Korlovsky,* too. I hear it's very good."

Dena merely sniffed and continued to dust.

"I gather it's rather frightening."

Dena frowned. "I wouldn't know, my lady. I don't read novels."

She would have used just that tone if she'd said, *I don't like novels. Bunch of nonsense.*

Nell sat on the end of the bed. "Don't you ever feel you want a bit of nonsense?" she asked. "Something to distract you from the cares of the day?"

"Some of us don't have that kind of time, my lady, and would find better uses if we did."

Nell's nerves were already stretched taut, and the maid's disrespectful manner grated. "I don't know to whom you think you're speaking, Dena, but I suggest you address me with more respect."

Dena stopped dusting and her face grew red. "Respect?" she repeated. "You expect me to respect a woman trying to seduce Lady Granshire's son?"

Nell could scarcely believe she'd heard aright—except for the look on Dena's face. "I am not trying to seduce Lord Bromwell!"

If there was any seduction here, it was mutual—but she would not enlighten Dena on that point.

"Say what you like, Lord Bromwell will never marry you. He'll see through your snares," Dena retorted, shaking her dust rag at Nell with every word. "Lady Granshire's son may be odd, but he's no fool."

"I am *not* trying to trap Lord Bromwell into marriage, or into my bed!"

Dena's expression revealed exactly what she thought of Nell's protest. "You won't be the first who's tried and you won't be the last," she said firmly. "Batting your eyes and looking at him like that."

"I do not bat my eyes at him! I admire and respect him."

"I wasn't born yesterday, my lady."

"Neither was he," Nell shot back before she remembered she was supposed to be a lady, and therefore a servant's superior. "How dare you speak to me in this fashion? Who are you to say whom Lord Bromwell should or should not marry?"

The maid balled her dust rag in her work-worn hands. "I'm sorry, my lady, but I'm worried about the countess. She's always been good to me, and she's not strong. Even though the viscount doesn't think she's really sick, she's not really well, either. If Lord Bromwell makes a bad marriage, that'll be as bad as him going on another voyage. I fear either one'll be the death of her."

Dena might not be the most pleasant of women, but clearly, a fiercely loyal heart beat within that narrow chest.

"Then you may rest easy, Dena, and stay for another

twenty, for I assure you, I wouldn't marry Lord Bromwell even if he asked me."

The maid's eyes widened as if she couldn't believe a woman would ever refuse the viscount's hand. "Why not?"

"I have no desire to marry a man who will leave me for months and even years at a time to go chasing after spiders," Nell lied.

"But I thought—"

"What you thought was obviously wrong."

Her anger diminishing, Nell spoke sincerely. "Even if I wouldn't marry the viscount, I do like him, so there will be one more woman who'll be worried about him when he sails. We shall all have to pray for his safe return."

"Aye, my lady."

Nell took a few conciliatory steps toward her. "Perhaps if you don't have any pressing responsibilities, you could stay and help me alter the gown the countess gave me for the ball? I fear it's a bit too long."

Dena's thin lips twitched up in a smile for a fraction of a second. "I'll be happy to, my lady."

Then, to Nell's further surprise, her expression grew curious and conspiratorial. "Is it true what they're saying in the servants' hall? Did you really take Lord Granshire to task about his son?"

Nell nodded. "I did, so now I'm also worried he'll send me away."

"Oh, I wouldn't be concerned about that, my lady," Dena said with unexpected confidence as she went to the wardrobe and got out the Nile-green silk gown with rounded neck and puffed sleeves. "He may bluster and bellow, but if the countess wants you to stay, you'll stay."

* * *

Bromwell strode into his father's study, where Fallingbrook had said he could find the earl. It was a room that Bromwell always entered with trepidation even now, having been forced to endure parental cross-examinations and lectures in this chamber for as long as he could remember.

It didn't help that his father had had the room decorated like some sort of hunting lodge of the damned, with the heads of stags and boars, as well as swords, pikes and crossbows on the panelled walls. A portrait of his grandfather, stern and disapproving, or perhaps suffering from chronic indigestion, gazed down from above the limestone mantel. There were smaller, equally frowning faces of his other ancestors there, too, as if they sat in judgment of the heirs of Granshire and found them all lacking.

A similar expression was on his father's face as he stood by the windows surveying the gardens. Plans for the massive waterworks he was planning to build were spread out on the desk nearby.

"Father, I must speak with you," Bromwell announced, doing his best to control his tumultuous feelings.

The earl turned to face him, his expression strangely enigmatic. Normally his father's mood and emotions were as easy to read as a book produced with a very large font. "Ah, Justinian. I had heard you were come home. So, she has already complained to you, has she?"

"If you're referring to Lady Eleanor, she's told me what happened between you."

"Then you are aware that she dared to upbraid me. She

told me, and in no uncertain terms, that I do not sufficiently respect your work and your dedication to it."

Bromwell still couldn't decipher his father's mood, but his voice was oddly calm, considering what he was describing.

His father's next words took him completely by surprise, making Bromwell feel as disoriented as when the coach had overturned.

"She's right. I don't. I don't understand why a grown man of good breeding and fortune would want to spend his time on a cramped, stinking ship looking for bugs."

Bromwell subdued a sigh. He should never have entertained any hope that his father would ever appreciate his son's chosen life's work—but at least he'd kept a copy of his book.

It was better, too, that he was annoyed with his son, not Lady…Miss Springley. "I have long since given up expecting you to."

The earl cleared his throat. "However, she's wrong to think I don't believe you're a fine man and that I'm not pleased with you. I'm proud of your behavior in dire circumstances during your voyage. I respect the fame you've justly earned with your book. You've brought honor to our family's name, Justinian."

Bromwell hadn't felt this rattled in years, not since he'd realized the ship was going down, so it took a moment for him to be able to speak and he seemed to have developed a lump in his throat.

"Thank you, Father," he said at last. "That means a great deal to me."

His father walked toward the desk and began to roll up the plans. "I've always been proud of you," he said, without looking directly as his son, "and if you'd gone into politics or even the law like that friend of yours…"

He glanced sharply up at his son, then cleared his throat again and looked back at his plans. "Never mind. You didn't, and you could have done worse—and I didn't need Lady Eleanor to point that out."

Bromwell refrained from noting that apparently he did.

His father set the plans aside and sat behind his desk, gesturing for Bromwell to sit as well, in the sort of over-stuffed chair his father preferred.

When he had, the earl looked him straight in the eye. "Lady Eleanor's a remarkable young woman."

It didn't sound as if his father was angry at her or, he thought with relief, intending to ask her to leave. "Yes, she is."

"A bit high-spirited, but there's nothing wrong with that in a young woman, especially if she's pretty. She's clever, too, I think."

Bromwell suddenly realized where this train of thought was heading.

"A man could do a lot worse for a wife," his father noted, proving that Bromwell had guessed correctly, and it was not a welcome conclusion.

"Lady Eleanor told me about your offer regarding marriage," Bromwell replied. "I thought I had made it quite clear the last time we spoke on that subject that while I'm not averse to the notion of marriage, I won't take a wife until *I* decide the time has come. Besides, no woman of sense would wish to marry a man who was planning to leave home for several months, if not years."

Which was another example of Miss Springley's intelligence and good sense.

"Wives of soldiers and sailors put up with such separations all the time," his father countered.

"Yes, but at least they can expect to have letters and other news."

"Your voyage depends on getting the money you require. What if you can't?"

"I shall, just as I did before."

His father crossed his arms. "Since you are so set upon sailing, *I* will pay."

Bromwell couldn't have been more surprised if his father had declared a wish to accompany him.

"On one condition."

Chapter Twelve

Creatures in the natural world have many ways of hiding. Some keep to the shadows and dark places. Others have developed hides or fur that make them difficult to spot in foliage, such as the tiger or leopard. Others resemble inanimate objects, so that although they are in plain view, they are as good as invisible to their pursuer.

—from *The Spider's Web,* by Lord Bromwell

Bromwell realized he should have known the offer would come with a catch.

"You must marry before you sail," his father declared. "If you do, not only will I pay the expenses of your expedition, I'll provide your wife with an establishment in London, or anywhere else she chooses, servants, a carriage and an income of five thousand pounds per annum for the rest of her life."

As shocked as Bromwell was by his father's proposal, it hadn't escaped his notice that his father hadn't stipulated whom he must marry. The earl would surely feel quite differently if he knew the truth about Miss Springley.

And yet to have such an offer…it was as tempting as Miss Springley. And if he married Miss Springley, that would solve her problems as well as his own.

Except that she had said she wouldn't want to be married to a man who then abandoned her for years, and he still believed it would be wrong to desert a wife so soon after marriage. "Do you have any particular bride in mind?"

His father looked as startled as he had been. "Why, Lady Eleanor, of course. If I am any judge of women, you have only to ask her. Her defence of you was most impressive and impassioned."

Bromwell got to his feet. "I regret to disappoint you yet again, Father, but in spite of your offer, I will not ask her, or any woman, to marry me before I sail."

That unfortunately familiar look of exasperation came to his father's features.

"What the devil is wrong with you, Justinian?" he demanded as he, too, rose, so they stood eye to eye. "You want your expedition. Very well. I give it to you—and all you have to do is marry a beautiful woman who cares for you, a woman who will be well taken care of while you're gone." His father spread his hands. "What more can you want?"

His father would never understand. Never. "I won't be bribed into marriage, Father, and neither will she. I managed to finance my previous expedition without your aid, and I will do so again. If and when I marry, it will be for love, not money, or even to further my work."

His father sat heavily in his chair. "God save me from foolish young men and their romantic notions!"

Bromwell tilted his head to regard the man who had

sired him and with whom he seemed to have so little in common, except for some physical features like hair and eye color. And yet… "If I am stubborn and romantic in my notions, it's probably because my father is both, as well."

Lord Granshire couldn't have looked more shocked if Bromwell had struck him. "Romantic? Are you mad?"

Seeing his father with new eyes, Bromwell smiled and gestured at the plans now curling at the edges. "The fountain you're having built—Venus and Adonis are in the center of it, are they not? Only a romantic would choose two lovers for such a centrepiece.

"I think there are other qualities I owe to my parents as well, such as my persistence. My mother continues to hope I can be dissuaded from sailing. And many another father would have thrown up his hands at my refusal to marry years ago. Mine, however, still tries to persuade me."

His father had apparently been struck speechless, so Bromwell continued without waiting for a response. "I'm going back to London today, Father, and I hope you'll allow Lady Eleanor to remain here until the ball."

The earl found his voice as he put his hands on his desk and hoisted himself to his feet. "Yes, of course she may stay. I had no intention of asking the daughter of the Duke of Wymerton to leave."

He regarded his son with a most unusual expression, as if he were still considering what Bromwell had said and attempting to decide if he agreed.

A decision apparently made, he cleared his throat and said, "I have to go into Bath later today. Why don't you join me for that part of your journey? You can tell me all about the paper you're presenting to the Linnean Society."

That was another surprise that took Bromwell aback. He

glanced at the portrait over the fireplace, half-expecting to see that the mouth of his grandfather's portrait had fallen open with equal shock. "You know about that?"

"I'm not completely in the dark about your activities, my son, even if I don't know the exact subject. Some spider, no doubt. I trust it's an exotic one."

"The most dangerous specimen yet discovered, the Brazilian wandering spider," Bromwell replied.

"That should keep 'em all awake. Now come along, Justinian," his father ordered as he started to the door. "We'd best take our leave of your mother and that young lady whose heart you're going to break."

Bromwell came to a dead halt. "Do you really think I could do that?"

His father raised a brow. "If I am any judge of women," he said before continuing out the door.

As Bromwell dutifully followed, his brow wrinkled as he considered a possible—and unwelcome—outcome he had not foreseen.

Dena had long since stopped tidying. She now sat by the hearth with Nell, telling stories about Lord Bromwell when he was a boy.

Nell wasn't surprised to learn that he'd always been kindhearted and generous, warm and loving. Unfortunately, he hadn't been a robust child and had spent many days ill in bed with various ailments. Dena told her how it had pained his mother to send him away to school; she'd insisted on getting the opinions of three different doctors before she'd allow it. But not only had Lord Bromwell survived, he'd thrived. He'd even flourished away from his father's overbearing hand and, Nell surmised, his mother's watchful, worried eye. He'd made good friends, too, "even if they all seemed like rowdy rascals the first time they came to visit. That Smythe-Medway, for instance. Now there was a boy needed a good thrashing! He put a snake in cook's bed and nearly scared the life out of her."

How she wished she could have seen Lord Bromwell as a boy, with big bluish gray eyes and tousled hair, studiously staring at a spider's web, or the other boys whose good opinion had meant so much to him.

A knock at the door ended their friendly tête-à-tête. "Oh, dear, I've been here too long!" Dena quietly declared as she hurried to open it.

A footman stood on the threshold. "If you please, my lady," he said, looking past Dena, "the countess wishes you to join her in her sitting room."

Nell rose, suddenly tense. What if the countess didn't want her to stay?

She managed to sound calm, however, as she answered. "Of course."

"Don't worry," Dena said in a confidential whisper as Nell went past her into the hall. "She likes you."

Somewhat encouraged but still full of trepidation, Nell followed the footman to the countess's sitting room.

She wasn't sure what to expect when she entered, but she hadn't anticipated finding Lord Bromwell and the earl. The viscount stood by the window, his hands behind his back, while his father was in the same attitude near the hearth.

Then Lord Bromwell smiled, and she immediately felt all would be well—or that at least she was going to be able to stay.

"Ah, my lady, here you are. I need to go to Bath to make the final arrangements for the orchestra for the ball," the earl announced as if they hadn't met earlier that day. "Since my son's off to London again, we're going to Bath in my coach and have to take our leave."

"You're welcome to stay here as our guest," Lord Bromwell confirmed. "My mother is pleased to have your company."

"Indeed, I am," Lady Granshire said with a smile, although her eyes were on her son, as if she was afraid she'd forget what he looked like all too soon.

"I shall only be away for a few days," the earl declared, obviously thinking he would be missed as much, and by both of them. "And my son assures us he'll return in time for the ball."

"Drury's going to bring me back," Lord Bromwell supplied, "and you mustn't have any fears for my safety, Mother. Drury hasn't tried to drive since he returned from the war, and I won't, either."

"Come, Justinian," the earl said. "We had best be on our way if we're to have a decent supper in Bath tonight."

The viscount approached his mother and kissed her cheek as she grasped his hand. "Goodbye, Mother. I'll be back before the ball. I promise."

"Then I know you will be," she said, dabbing at her eyes with a scented lace handkerchief.

He regarded Nell steadily as he bowed. "I look forward to seeing you again, Lady Eleanor."

"And I, you, my lord."

The viscount went to the door while the earl kissed his wife's hand. "Adieu, ladies," he said, bowing with a flourish before he followed his son out of the room.

After the door had closed, Lady Granshire sniffled into her handkerchief, while Nell stifled a sigh.

At least the countess had the claim of love and family on Lord Bromwell, Nell thought as she walked toward the window that overlooked the drive. *She* could only be grateful that he didn't despise her for her deception, and she admired him all the more for offering to help her in spite of it.

The earl's coach was already waiting, as were the liveried driver and footmen. In a very few moments, the earl and his son appeared. The earl entered first and as the footman waited, Lord Bromwell put his foot on the step, then paused and looked back over his shoulder and upward. He must have seen her, for he gave a brief wave before embarking. The footman put up the step, closed the door and took his place at the back of the coach.

With the crack of the driver's whip, the four well-matched black horses leapt into motion, taking Lord Bromwell and his father away and leaving her alone with his quietly weeping mother.

"Perhaps you'd rather be alone," Nell said as she turned back into the room, "or would you like me to send for Dena?"

The countess wiped her eyes. "No, please stay. It's a comfort being with someone who shares my distress."

Nell wondered if she should say she didn't, or at least not to the same degree, but feared the countess would think she was making light of her dismay.

"He won't be gone for very long," she said, sitting across from Lady Granshire.

"This time," the countess added mournfully.

What could she say to that? She couldn't promise that her son would always return. "I must thank you again for your kind hospitality."

The countess waved a listless hand. "It's nothing, and I do like having a young lady nearby, especially one my son so obviously cares for."

Nell shifted uncomfortably. Clearly she was not doing enough to hide her growing regard for Lord Bromwell if everyone here could see it. She would have to be more careful when he returned. "I hope it doesn't cause you any trouble."

"Who last protected you, my dear?"

Nell glanced sharply at the countess, unsure how to answer that, or even what she meant exactly. A woman who was a man's mistress was said to be under his protection.

"My parents, of course," she said after a moment, "but I hope my godfather will come to my aid."

"And who might he be?"

"Why, Lord Ruttles," Nell answered, baffled by the question. Had Lady Granshire forgotten what she'd told them? Perhaps she really was ill…

The countess's expression didn't change as she regarded Nell with her son's eyes. "No, he is not, just as you are not Lady Eleanor Springford."

The breath fled Nell's lungs and her heart started to pound as if she were before a firing squad.

How did the countess know? Or had she guessed? Was it because of something she had said or done? And what should she do now?

Before she could decide, the countess leaned forward and put her hand on Nell's arm.

"Does my son think you're Lady Eleanor, or is he in on the ruse, too?" she asked. She didn't sound angry; she sounded merely curious, which confused Nell even more.

Yet one thing seemed clear—whatever she did and

whatever happened next, there was no need to lie anymore. "He knows who I really am."

Now.

The countess nodded, as if this was the answer she'd been expecting. "No doubt my son thought it best to pretend you were a titled woman to ensure that you could stay. Whatever the reason for that deception, however, I'm grateful you've come and have cause to hope I could be more grateful to you yet."

How could she possibly be grateful after Nell had tried to trick them?

"How long have you been my son's mistress?"

"I am not his mistress!" Nell cried, aghast and determined to make that clear.

"Please, my dear, there's no need to deny it if you are," Lady Granshire said with that same unexpected equanimity. "My son is comely, well educated and titled. What woman of sense *wouldn't* want him? And I've read my son's book, so I'm well aware that he's a grown man and an experienced one at that. No doubt you aren't his first lover."

She was probably right, and that gave Nell a different sort of pain.

"However, my dear, you *are* the first he's ever cared enough about to bring here, in any guise, which tells me his feelings for you must be beyond anything he's ever felt for his other mistresses."

"We aren't lovers," she helplessly replied. "It's just as he said—he came to my aid when the coach overturned and offered to help me."

Nell rose again, determined to leave this painful interview. The room. The house. Despite her promise to Lord Bromwell, she couldn't stay here. "I should go."

"Stay."

Lady Granshire shared something else with her son—a tone of command that was rare, yet thus all the more impressive when utilized.

Nell obediently perched on the edge of the sofa.

"I'm sorry if I've insulted and upset you," the countess said in a conciliatory tone. "I meant no harm or insult to you. Any woman who has earned my son's love is no common woman, and if there is a man's judgment I trust, it is his. So I'm predisposed to love you, too, and do all I can for you. Can you believe that, my dear?"

A few moments ago, she might not have, but as she regarded Lady Granshire now and saw her sincerity, she could. And did. "Yes."

The countess smiled and looked at her with hope. "So as you've been honest with my son, won't you trust me and be honest with me, too?"

It wasn't an easy request for her to answer, until she realized that Lady Granshire could have summoned the magistrate the day she first arrived and had her arrested for impersonating a duke's daughter. She had not.

Nevertheless, she still hesitated, until Lady Granshire leaned forward, took her hand and regarded her with a searching gaze that was also very like the viscount's. "If my son loves you, that's all I need to know."

After hearing the countess's heartfelt words, Nell's defences crumbled. She told Lady Granshire everything, just as she had told Lord Bromwell. Except for the kisses and other intimate moments they'd shared. Some things weren't meant to be shared, especially with a man's mother.

"So your son has offered to help me," she finished,

"and he goes to London in part to consult with his friend, the attorney."

"What a terrible situation! So much worse than the other!" the countess cried, patting Nell's hand and making her feel that it hadn't been a mistake to trust her.

"Rest assured, we'll see that Lord Sturmpole makes no more trouble for you," Lady Granshire continued. "My husband is not without some influence, too—and you mustn't even think of leaving until your situation can be sorted out."

"Thank you, my lady," Nell replied with gratitude. "You've all been so kind and generous to me, I don't know how I shall ever repay you."

Lady Granshire's eyes suddenly gleamed with a greedy, desperate light. "There *is* a way."

Chapter Thirteen

At this time, the method by which spiders avoid being trapped in their own webs remains one of nature's great mysteries. Is there something about the composition of their bodies, or is the immunity something to do with the strands themselves? This is only one of the questions regarding these fascinating creatures that has kept me watching them at work for hours at a time.

—from *The Spider's Web,* by Lord Bromwell

"I know the power certain feelings can exert over a person, how they cause them to make decisions that they wouldn't consider otherwise," Lady Granshire said. "I believe you can wield such power over my son. You can succeed where my husband and I fail. You can convince my son to stay in England, where he will be safe."

Nell immediately and vehemently shook her head. "No, I couldn't. I wouldn't. Please, don't ask such a thing of me!"

"Think of the dangers he will face if he goes on another expedition," the countess pleaded. "After all our kindness to you, and especially after his, is this how you would repay him? By not doing everything in your power to keep him here?"

"Even if I had such power as you think I possess, I wouldn't try to persuade him to give up his life's work."

"Instead you would let him risk his life wandering the world looking for bugs?"

Nell's heart broke to think of him so far away, or dead, but she would not put her fears before his aspirations. "Because it is his heart's desire, yes, I would."

The countess's face flushed and her knuckles whitened as she clutched her crumpled, damp handkerchief. "There are plenty of spiders in England he could study. If you could get him to stay in England, I will see to it that, whatever happens, you will want for nothing for the rest of your life."

How far was the woman prepared to go, what would she offer, to keep her son in England? "I notice you don't propose marriage."

"Since you aren't really a lady, my husband would never agree to a marriage," the countess grimly replied, "no matter what Justinian or I could say. And unfortunately, while the estate itself is entailed to Justinian, the income is not. My husband could cut Justinian off without a cent. If he marries a woman the earl considers unsuitable, he would."

"Even if your husband did as you say, do you doubt your son's capacity to earn a living?"

"Don't you?" Lady Granshire countered. "How much do you think his passion for spiders will pay? Consider what he will lose if he marries against his father's will."

"You do realize what it would make me if I accepted your offer?"

The countess drew herself up, reminding Nell that she

was a wealthy, titled lady. "Since you've lied so effectively to so many, you must forgive me if I thought your scruples might not be so lofty."

"Whatever I am, I am not a whore, my lady," Nell replied, stung by Lady Granshire's words and more by their truth.

The countess pushed herself up from the sofa, her whole body shaking, her lawn cap askew, the silken folds of her black gown quivering, as she upbraided Nell. "Have you no pity? No sympathy for a mother's love? You have not sat up all night praying for your baby's safety, fearing he will die at the dawn. You have not waited by that same bed listening to every breath, your own matching, as if you were breathing for him. You've never lain alone in the dark, unable to sleep, wondering where your child was. If he was alive or dead. Or ill in some godforsaken place calling out for you."

Nell *did* appreciate the countess's feelings, and her heart filled with pity for the woman's worried misery. "I do sympathize, my lady," she said, her voice gentle and quiet, although she was still firm in her resolve. "But your son is not a boy anymore. He is a man, and he has made a man's decision."

She took the older woman's thin hands in hers and looked into Lady Granshire's eyes that were the same cloud-gray as her son's. "When he sails, yours will not be the only heart breaking, nor you the only one anxiously praying for his safe return. But because I care, I *must* let him go. To hold him here, even if I could, would be to break his heart."

The countess leaned forward, her gaze intense. "What if you could be married to him? What if we could do away with his father's objections?"

"It would be no true marriage if I used a false name."

"No, I meant under your own." The woman leaned closer still, her eyes burning with fierce determination. "My husband wants one thing above all—a grandson, so that he can be sure his family name will continue. If you were to get with child, he might be willing to overlook your lack of family."

This was the most outrageous offer yet. Outrageous and impertinent and impossible and…tempting.

Very tempting.

"It would have to be a clandestine marriage," Lady Granshire continued in a rush as Nell fought the appeal of her suggestion, "but eventually, and especially if you provide the heir he so desperately wants, I think he would come 'round and forgive you."

Forgive *her?* That hadn't been her proposal, her scheme.

Yet more important than the countess's offer, or her own desire, was the viscount's happiness. Nothing else could take precedence over that, or the fulfilment of her own desire would have come at too high a price.

So Nell shook her head. "Knowing how much he cares about his work and his feelings about leaving a wife behind, I wouldn't marry him even if I could, just as I won't try to persuade him to stay in England. I wouldn't want to be responsible for the bitter resentment that would surely follow if I did."

Even then, the countess wasn't yet ready to surrender. "If he had a wife he loved, and children, surely they would be ample compensation for the loss of an expedition. After all, he's already been on one."

Nell refused to agree. "While he'd surely be an excellent husband and father, that lost opportunity would still be there, like a canker in his heart, so I won't ask him not to sail even if I never have a good night's sleep again."

When she finally realized Nell was adamant, the countess put her face in her hands, sank onto the couch and started to sob. "He won't come back if he sails again. I know he won't!"

Nell sat beside the older woman who loved her son so dearly and put her arm around her, trying to be strong, although she, too, could easily envision shipwreck or illness or some other disaster taking Lord Bromwell's life. "We shall have to hope and pray that he'll return as he did before, and remember that whatever difficulties he may face, he's a strong, brave, clever man."

Lady Granshire raised her tear-streaked face to look at Nell. "Will you stay here with me even after he's gone? My husband has little patience for my fears and even when he tries, he cannot comfort me. Nor the servants, although Dena has been with me so long. They try, but they don't love Justinian as we do."

Nell had never allowed herself to call what she felt for Lord Bromwell "love." But that was what it was. She knew it, felt it in the core of her heart. She loved him as she had never loved another, and likely never would.

"Or do you have family or friends with whom you'd rather reside?" Lady Granshire asked.

No, she did not, and if she stayed here, as his mother's companion, she would hear news of him as soon as she.

Yet there was another impediment to this plan. "The earl would surely object to my presence if he learns the truth about me."

A resolute gleam came to Lady Granshire's eyes. "Then we shall not tell him unless and until he needs to know, and

I shall also see that you have an income befitting a lady's companion out of my own funds."

The countess sank down on her knees and held out her hands. "I beg you to forgive me and forget the things I said today. Please accept my offer and stay here with me. We can comfort each other when he's gone because, like me, you love him."

Her own eyes filling with tears, Nell quickly stood, then reached down to help the countess to her feet. "I'm very grateful for your offer, my lady, and while I'd like to stay, I don't think I should make any more plans or promises until your son returns."

And then…?

She would not think about "and then" until she had to.

"Lord Bromwell to see you, Sir Douglas," Edgar Minor announced from the door of the study of Drury's town house.

After arriving in London, Bromwell had come directly to Drury's. He hadn't even stopped to change his clothes at his father's town house, and it looked like it.

"Good God, what's happened? Has somebody died?" the barrister demanded as he rose from behind his solid oak desk that was as large as a dining table for eight.

Unlike his father's study, Drury's was intended to be a place for work, not impressing other men, and the furnishings and decor reflected that. In addition to the massive desk, a comfortable chair was behind it for the barrister, as well as three other wing chairs for his guests or clients. Shelves of law books lined the walls, and a cabinet for papers stood near the desk. Two well-trimmed oil lamps, a silver inkpot, sand shaker and quill pens were also on the table, although the latter were rarely used.

Even if Drury was now able to write with more ease, he still preferred to prepare most of his cross-examinations in his head.

"No," Bromwell said as he handed his hat to the waiting butler, then closed the door so that they were alone in the room a short distance from the drawing room. "Where's Juliette?"

"Shopping with Fanny for fabric," Drury replied, his voice calm but his eyes full of concern. "Is it something to do with Lady Eleanor? Have her parents returned from Italy?"

Being an old friend, Bromwell didn't wait for an invitation, but threw himself into the nearest chair. "No, because she's not really Lady Eleanor."

For once in his life, Drury's reaction was unmasked and plainly visible, so great was his shock as he slowly lowered himself back into his chair. "She's not? Who the devil is she then?"

"Her name is Nell Springley and she was using a false identity to avoid being charged with a crime she didn't commit."

His composure apparently restored, although Bromwell could still see it was not by the set of his jaw, Drury folded his hands in his lap and regarded Bromwell steadily. "I await the details."

Bromwell was suddenly unsure how to begin, where to start and how much to say. He rose and walked to the window hung with dark green draperies, then back again.

"We aren't talking murder, are we?" Drury inquired.

"Gad, no!" Bromwell replied. "She is the victim of a crime."

He returned to the chair, sat and took a deep breath. Then he told Drury everything about Nell Springley, up to and including his decision to maintain the ruse that she was Lady Eleanor for the time being.

Drury would understand that. He and Juliette had pretended to be cousins so they could stay in the earl's town house not so very long ago, and Juliette had pretended that her maid had stolen her baggage and absconded, which was where Bromwell got the idea for the excuse they'd given his father.

Bromwell decided to leave out the full extent of his intimacy with Nell, for that could have no bearing on Drury's opinion of her legal predicament.

"What will the law say?" Bromwell asked when he was finished. "Could she be arrested and brought to trial for theft?"

The barrister nodded. "Unfortunately, yes. Her employer could bring charges—although he would have to prove them. However, under the circumstances, Miss Springley could also accuse him of attempted rape. It could be that the possibility of such a charge and ensuing scandal would be sufficient motive for Sturmpole to keep silent—or he may think the jury will take his word over Miss Springley's. In that case, he would likely accuse her of lying to cover up the theft."

Drury frowned ever so slightly. "It would have been better if Miss Springley had gone straight to the local magistrate after escaping Sturmpole's house."

Bromwell couldn't disagree, but he spoke in her defence regardless. "I think she wanted to put as much distance between herself and Sturmpole as she could and as quickly as she could."

Drury steepled his crooked fingers. "As understandable as that may be, it does make things more difficult. However, if Sturmpole was in arrears for her wages, he is hardly in a position to complain if she took a comparable sum. As such, it becomes a matter more for a solicitor than a barrister.

"Perhaps a letter from James St. Claire pointing that out and threatening him with a criminal prosecution for his attack and the confinement of Miss Springley will be enough to keep Sturmpole from pursuing the matter further."

"What if that doesn't work?" Bromwell asked. "What if Sturmpole wants her arrested?"

"If neither Jamie nor I can make him see why he should let the matter drop," Drury said, "he'll still have to find her. In the meantime, I'll have my men see what else they can find out about Sturmpole. He's likely the sort who delights in preying upon his servants, and if so, he will have done so before. And he should be in jail."

"As much as I find capital punishment barbaric, I believe that is one man I'd like to see hanged," Bromwell muttered as he got to his feet and stared, unseeing, out the window.

What he did not say, but felt, was that he might even have been able to put the noose around the scoundrel's neck himself. Never in his life had he been more enraged than when Miss Springley had told him what had happened to her.

And if the man had succeeded in his disgusting assault, the bite of a *Phoneutria nigriventer* would have been too easy a death for him.

"If Miss Springley goes with you when you sail, that will give me more time to find evidence against him," Drury remarked.

Bromwell started as if he'd been hit by a blow dart, then wheeled around to face his friend. "That is quite impossible."

Although the rest of him remained motionless, Drury's

expression flickered with surprise for the briefest of moments. "Why?"

"First, because my voyage is a scientific expedition, not a pleasure cruise," Bromwell retorted as he approached the massive desk. "Second, the accommodations aboard ship are primitive at best. Third, it would be most improper. No unmarried woman would dare risk her reputation in such a manner—nor should she."

"Forgive me for leaping to conclusions," Drury said, his eyes, like the rest of his face, inscrutable. "I was under the impression that you cared a great deal for her. Or do you intend to make her wait for your return for the wedding to take place?"

Bromwell stared at his friend as if he'd said the world was flat and he could prove it. His agitation as great as it had ever been in his parents' presence, he splayed his hands on Drury's desk and spoke firmly and decisively. "Gad, Drury, now that you've fallen in love and married, do you think everybody else is teetering on the brink? I have no intention of proposing marriage to Miss Springley—or anyone—before I sail. I would never ask a woman to wait for me, not even with the hope of marriage at my return."

Not even if it broke her heart. Better that than be the death of her.

He pushed himself away from the desk and walked to the window, trying to regain his self-control before he faced his friend again. "How many times must I say I won't marry before I sail and I won't ask a woman to wait for me before people believe me? Why can't anyone understand that it could be years before I return and there's always a chance I never will? It wouldn't be kind or fair to ask a woman to wait for me."

Drury leaned back in his chair, calmly regarding his indignant, dismayed friend. "You know, Buggy, I don't think I've ever seen you so upset."

"Because despite my excellent reasons for not marrying or proposing before I sail, everybody seems to think I should marry Miss Springley, preferably the sooner the better!"

"Everybody?"

"My parents are very keen—but then," he noted, "they don't know who she really is."

His father would surely rescind his offer if he did, and their newfound rapprochement would likely be destroyed, as well.

"So tell them."

Bromwell made no effort to hide his disdain for that ludicrous notion. "I can easily imagine my father's response. It would *not* be favorable."

"You've never let his disapproval dissuade you before."

"This is different."

"How?"

Bromwell realized he had no choice. As distressing as it was, he would have to tell Drury.

He slumped into the chair. "Because Miss Springley has already given me to understand that she would not be amenable to marriage to me."

Drury again raised an inquiring brow. "Is that all?"

Chapter Fourteen

For centuries, the spider has been the subject of fear and misunderstanding. Even one of their earliest admirers, the Reverend Topsel, in his History of Four-footed Beasts and Serpents, *considered them born of some sort of seeds arising from filth and decay, simply because they may be found in even the newest of houses, apparently neglecting to take into account that there will be a lapse of time between the framing of a structure and the final white-washing of walls.*
    —from *The Spider's Web,* by Lord Bromwell

"All?" Bromwell repeated, dumbfounded. "Is that not enough? If she doesn't want to marry me, there's the end of it."

"For a man who can be stubbornly determined," Drury calmly replied, "I'm surprised you're giving up so easily. You didn't give up planning your first expedition when your father refused to fund it, did you? Or when the next five wealthy men laughed in your face? Yet you're willing to reject—"

"You aren't listening," Bromwell interrupted as he got to his feet again. *"She doesn't want me."*

Drury gave him a remarkably sympathetic smile. "I fear we men are not always the best interpreters of the feelings of women. You may recall my own road to domestic bliss was hardly a smooth one."

Yes, Bromwell did know that.

How easy it had seemed to solve all his friends' troubles when he'd been a dispassionate observer of their romantic dilemmas: Edmond and Diana Westover were two of a kind and had only to be made to see it; Brix had loved Fanny for years and only had to fear losing her to realize it; Drury had been attracted to Juliette from the day she saved his life with a basket of potatoes, even if he'd tried to deny it because she was French.

Now Bromwell knew better. When it came to affairs of the heart, things were not necessarily simple.

"Whatever I feel for Miss Springley," he said, "and I do not call it love, my road does not include marriage before I sail. I would never ask a woman to marry me, then wait patiently ashore for years, like Penelope pining for Odysseus, just as I'd never expect a woman to wait for me to return and then marry. It wouldn't be fair to her. And Miss Springley agrees with me."

"So you have discussed marriage with her?"

"I had to," he admitted. "My parents left me little choice. My father made her a most outrageous offer dependent upon marrying me. She refused, but it meant I found out how she felt.

"Besides, you know what this voyage means to me," he continued wearily. "How I've worked and planned and sought the necessary funds. I can't give it up now."

That, too, sounded simple—and it had been, until he'd met Nell Springley.

"I suppose not," Drury agreed, "especially now that Charlie will be able to captain your vessel. I had a letter from him today. He wrote to you at Granshire Hall, I expect, to tell you the news. He's resigned his commission and hopes to sail with you, whether as captain, or your assistant, or a bosun's mate or even a cabin boy."

Bromwell's dismay momentarily fled in the face of this good and welcome news. "That's marvelous! I was wondering whom I could get to captain the ship and now I have the perfect man! If only I could get the rest of the money as easily!"

"Your father still won't help?"

Bromwell flushed. "Miss Springley wasn't the only one he tried to bribe into marriage. He offered to fund the whole expedition if I married her before I sailed—although I'm sure he'd feel quite differently if he knew the truth about her. But there are others I can still solicit. However, that can wait for a little while. I'd rather consult with Jamie St. Claire immediately."

"Very well," Drury said as he rose and strode to the door. "We'll both go to his office, and then we can visit some other associates who inhabit the areas around Fleet Street. They can find out everything we need to know about the lascivious Lord Sturmpole."

"Good God, is that you, Titus?" the Earl of Granshire bellowed across the Pump Room in Bath.

Several people in the large room illuminated by tall windows turned. Curious whispers began as the nobleman headed toward the water dispenser and the tall, beefy, well-dressed, weak-chinned fellow leaning against the bar. The man addressed thus smiled, put down the cup of supposedly curative water, and straightened as the earl reached him and vigorously shook his hand.

"Titus, you old stick, why didn't you write and tell me you were coming to Bath?" the earl demanded. "It's been…what? Ten years since you last set foot here? How is your wife? Has she come to take the waters, too?"

"Alas, my wife is still too unwell to leave Staynesborough," Lord Sturmpole replied, straightening his waistcoat that was a rather bilious green.

"What brings you to Bath, then? You look healthy as a horse."

"A little matter of business," Sturmpole replied. "How is your charming wife? And your illustrious son? I congratulate you on his great success."

"Thank you," the earl replied. "The boy's done very well for himself, although I don't deny I would have preferred he chose another field in which to distinguish himself. But long gone are the days children heeded their parents, eh?"

"Indeed," Sturmpole agreed. "I fear too many young people today don't respect their elders, or their betters."

"Or do their duty," Lord Granshire charged. "In *our* day, a nobleman's son took his duties seriously. Married, had an heir, looked after the estate, respected his parents. Now they either indulge in gaming or wenching, or wander around the world discovering things nobody else much cares about."

As Lord Sturmpole chuckled and nodded his agreement, the earl seemed to mentally shake himself. "Of course, my son has our unqualified support, and his book was a great success, as is he. We're very proud of him, very proud. How long are you in Bath, Titus? My hunt ball is in a fortnight, and you would be welcome to attend."

"I had intended to stay in Bath for several days, so I would be delighted, if it's not too much trouble."

"Oh, no trouble at all! Where are you staying?"

"The Fox and Hound."

"Ah, yes, the good old Fox and Hound. Remember that maid—what was her name? With the large breasts?"

"Bessie."

"Ah, yes. Dead now, I think."

"In some sort of accident, I believe," Sturmpole concurred.

The earl slid his companion a sly smile. "Very friendly girl, poor Bessie was."

"For the right price. I gather your son has had a few adventures of that sort on his travels."

The earl flushed and looked around to see if anybody was listening, although whether he wanted them to be or not was open to conjecture. "Apparently. You've heard about his tattoo? It's a badge of prowess, although he doesn't say so."

"It's no wonder, perhaps, that he's not yet married," Lord Sturmpole replied.

"He's not married because he insists on going on another expedition first. But I'm not without hope," the earl added with a wink.

"Oh? Is there a young lady who's caught his eye?"

"Come to the ball and see for yourself. It only remains for me to get my son to see sense and propose. After all, he's had one expedition—what does he need another for, especially when he's got a pretty young lady from a most illustrious family who seems amenable to marriage just waiting for him to ask? I won't live forever and I need an heir, by God!"

The earl lowered his voice after several people had turned to look at them, albeit with the well-mannered pretence that they were not. "I'm sure Lady Eleanor will get him up to the post better than a father could."

"Lady Eleanor?"

The earl lowered his voice even more. "Springford. Remember her father, the Duke of Wymerton? Horrid bore even at ten and with a harelip, too, but his wife must be a beauty, for his daughter's quite lovely—which only goes to show how stubborn my son can be. He gets *that* from his mother. He met Lady Eleanor in a mail coach, of all places. Thank God it overturned, or he probably wouldn't even have introduced himself.

"I agree it's shocking they were in a mail coach," he said when he saw Lord Sturmpole's startled expression. "My son has some plebeian notions and she…Well, I suppose I shouldn't say any more about her family situation until matters are settled between them, but you remember her father? The fellow always was a dictator, telling us all what to do and making up ridiculous rules when he was prefect."

"Will Lady Eleanor be at your ball?"

"Yes. She's staying at Granshire Hall."

Lord Sturmpole drew his lips back in what was supposed to be a smile. "Excellent! I should very much like to meet her and hear how her father is these days."

Bromwell trotted up the steps to his father's town house. A few hours ago, he had read his paper about the *Phoneutria nigriventer* to the gentlemen of the Linnean Society. As always, they had listened with interest, and yet he had felt no excitement or pleasure in detailing the attributes of that dangerous arachnid. He hadn't experienced the usual delight, that spark of fascination, that desire to explain and illuminate.

It was as if he'd been waiting for Christmas, only to discover it had been indefinitely postponed.

He could guess why.

Despite Drury's offer of assistance and his belief that Miss Springley's difficulties with Lord Sturmpole could be resolved without too much trouble, he couldn't stop thinking about her. Memories of their time together, her face, her kiss, the feel of her in his arms, lingered on the edges of his mind when he was awake, and more than lingered when he was asleep.

During the last week, he'd had the same recurring dream, of Miss Springley dancing the *hura,* the sensual, erotic dance exclusive to the women of Tahiti, her hips swinging, her arms moving in graceful, wavelike motions, her breasts full and round and perfect above a flat stomach, her legs long and lithe.

And she'd been naked, save for a bridal veil and pantelettes.

He'd been thinking time and distance would make such thoughts and dreams recede. Unfortunately, he was forced to conclude that the old adage about distance making the heart grow fonder had some basis in fact.

"Thank you, Millstone," he said as the butler opened the door for him.

"You have a visitor, my lord, awaiting your return in the drawing room," the butler gravely replied as Bromwell handed him his hat, which was very like the one he'd been wearing in the mail coach that had wound up squashed flat beneath him, killing the spider. How surprised Miss Springley had looked when he told her where he'd put it! As if he'd announced he'd eaten it.

He brought his attention back to Millstone and the unexpected visitor. Perhaps it was someone he'd asked to sponsor the expedition, come in person to reply, and if so, that was a hopeful sign. "Who is it?"

Before Millstone answered, Drury appeared on the threshold.

One look, and Bromwell's heart beat faster, and not with joy. They were supposed to meet with Jamie St. Claire tomorrow. This early advent, and Drury's grim visage, probably didn't herald good news.

Drury, however, was his usual composed self as he addressed the butler. "Millstone, please tell the cook I'll be staying for dinner, if his lordship doesn't mind."

Bromwell was too anxious to find out why Drury was there to do more than nod his acquiescence before he grabbed Drury's arm and pulled him into the drawing room.

"There's no need to panic," Drury said before closing the door of the well-appointed room.

Lord Granshire rarely came there, but the earl was not one to live in anything less than the style and luxury his wealth afforded.

"I'm not panicking," Bromwell replied, although if he wasn't, he was very close to it. "What's happened? Miss Springley…?"

"Is safe in Granshire Hall, as far as I know."

Bromwell's relief was intense, but short-lived, as he frowned. "Juliette's not…?"

"She's fine."

"Is it Charlie, then, or Brix or Edmond?"

"No, all our friends and their families are fine," Drury assured him. "It's just that there have been some…developments. Tell me, Buggy, how much do you know about Miss Springley's family?"

Bromwell's brows drew together at the unexpected query. "As far as I know, she has none, or she would have sought their help," he replied. "She never spoke of brothers or sisters, her parents are dead and—"

"I think you'd better sit down, Buggy."

Bromwell was too taken aback by his friend's suggestion to heed it. "What? She has family after all?"

"Yes," Drury confirmed, growing grimmer. "Sit down, Buggy."

This time, the viscount obeyed, being too stunned to disobey. "Where are they?"

"Her mother is dead, just as Miss Springley said. She died of gaol fever in Newgate while awaiting trial. Her father was convicted on a charge of theft and sent to Botany Bay. Records show he was alive when the ship landed, and as far as I can ascertain, he's still there, serving out his sentence."

Bromwell felt curiously light-headed, as if he was again trying to drive the mail coach, only it was going much too fast. "She said they were dead. She didn't tell me they'd been arrested and charged with a crime."

More lies, in addition to the ones she'd already told him.

"Unfortunately, the evidence is incontrovertible, and if Sturmpole finds out about her family history, it will make his case stronger and ours weaker, provided things happened the way Miss Springley said."

Bromwell put his head in his hands and tried to think clearly, dispassionately, although he felt sick. How much could he trust anything she said? "Why would she tell me about Lord Sturmpole at all if she were guilty? She could have kept pretending she was Lady Eleanor. I didn't doubt her story, and neither did anyone else at Granshire Hall."

"That puzzles me, too," Drury admitted. "I can think of only one possible explanation. She confessed the truth— or part of it—because she didn't want to deceive you anymore and she truly felt justified in robbing Lord Sturmpole. However, if you knew about her parents' crime, you would be less likely to believe her version of events—and rightly so."

Bromwell got to his feet, too agitated to sit. "I should go home. I have to find out the truth."

"I thought you might feel that way," Drury said. "I've sent word to Juliette to be ready to leave first thing in the morning." He put his hand on his friend's shoulder and regarded him with sympathy. "Do nothing hasty, Buggy. Wait until we're sure we have all the facts."

Chapter Fifteen

There appears to be two primary responses to danger among all creatures—the urge to run or the resolve to stand and fight. I would say the first is the most natural, provided there is the opportunity to flee. The second impulse can be extremely strong among mothers, however, if they have offspring to protect.

Is this urge to save their children at all costs merely instinct, or is it love?

—from *The Spider's Web,* by Lord Bromwell

Nell smiled at Billings as he and Brutus walked beside her through the woods towards Lord Bromwell's laboratory. The countess was napping, and the day was fine, if cool, making Nell yearn for the fresh air and freedom of the forest. It was by pleasant coincidence that she met Billings and Brutus shortly after she entered the dim confines of the trees, or so he'd implied, although she seemed to encounter him every time she left the formal gardens to walk in the woods.

She enjoyed his company, especially when he told her some of Lord Bromwell's boyhood adventures, and she suspected he liked telling the tales as much as she liked to hear them.

Today was no different, for they hadn't gone very far before he said, "Did you know young Bromwell taught himself to swim?"

"No," she replied, although it seemed logical to assume he possessed that ability, or he might have gone down with his ship.

"Well, he did, when he about ten years old and home for the summer. He was sure his mother wouldn't want him to try, so he didn't tell anybody his plan. Then one day, I'm walking toward the pond and I hear this splashing. Odd sound it was, I thought, so I went to see if there was a wounded duck or sommat like that in the water.

"Instead, I seen him in the pond, his head bobbing along, as he's going from one side t'other.

"Well, my lady, you could have blown me down with a fa…feather," he amended. "And then I run over to where he'd end up.

"'What the devil are you doing?' I asked him. He climbs out of the pond buck naked, smiling like he's just found a pot of gold and says, 'Swimming.'

"'Where'd you learn to do that?' says I. 'School?'

"'No, Billings,' he says pulling on his trousers, 'I watched the frogs. It's quite simple, really.'

"Ain't he a wonder?" Billings concluded with that shy yet proud smile that often came to his face when he spoke of the viscount.

"I suppose his parents never found out about that?" Nell asked.

"Lord no! Although he told the countess he could swim before he sailed."

"His parents probably thought, as you did, that he was taught at school."

Billings sniffed. "If you ask me, he didn't learn anything useful there, just Latin and Greek—and a lot o' good that done 'im during his voyage."

"In his book he gives you credit for many of the practical skills that helped them after the shipwreck," Nell noted, shivering as she contemplated what might have happened if Lord Bromwell hadn't had such a friend in his childhood.

"Aye, he did," Billings said, blushing like a bashful girl at her first ball, "but he would have managed regardless. I never knew a boy so clever and at home in the woods, even if he is a viscount."

When they reached a fork in the path, one way leading to the laboratory, the other off between the shading beeches, ashes and oaks, Billings tugged his forelock. "Well, I'd best be getting over to the pasture. Set some traps there the other day, or rabbits'd be eating the earl's flowers. G'day, my lady."

"Good day, Billings," she replied as the man walked away, the dog trotting beside him.

The more she heard of the viscount, Nell reflected as she continued toward the laboratory, the more there was to admire. To be sure, he wasn't perfect—he could be stubborn and perhaps too preoccupied with spiders—but on the whole, he was one of the finest, bravest, kindest men she'd ever met.

She reached the stone building and, as she entered, thought again that it really should have a lock of some description. Rumors and the fear of large and poisonous spiders would be some deterrent and there wasn't anything of value to anyone but a naturalist or scholar within, but she would feel terrible if anything happened to his collection and he would surely feel worse.

Once inside, she strolled along the shelves, studying the jars and their contents. To be sure, she would hate to come upon some of those preserved specimens alive, but they were becoming like familiar faces and she no longer felt abhorrence when she looked at them. Indeed, she'd taken to studying the various living spiders in the building, noting when there was a new web and, as Lord Bromwell had done in his youth, marvelling at the delicate structures. How was it that they didn't become entangled themselves? And how did they manage to make the threads so evenly spaced?

She paused near the end of the shelves and for the first time noticed something behind two of the jars. Sliding the jars out of the way, she realized it was a dart or tiny, pointed arrow with feathers at one end. She put out her hand to bring it closer—

"Don't touch that!"

She whirled around at Lord Bromwell's command, nearly knocking one of the jars from the shelf. "You're back!"

He strode into the laboratory, looking like a vengeful god. "As you can see. What are you doing here?"

Why had he returned early? Why was he looking at her like that? Why was he speaking so harshly? "I sometimes come here to be alone and look at your collection."

She clasped her hands as her anxious gaze searched his face. "Has something happened, my lord? We weren't expecting you to return so soon."

She thought of his mother, with whom he might have already spoken, and an explanation for his altered behavior came to her. "Your mother told you, didn't she?"

"Told me what?" he replied with a frown.

He was going to find out sooner or later, so there was no reason not to tell him. "Your mother's met the real

Lady Eleanor. She knew I was an impostor from the start and thought you were lying because I'm your mistress."

His eyes flared with surprise, although it was quickly gone, replaced by an analytical expression devoid of emotion, as if she were one of his specimens. "Why didn't she tell me, or my father?"

"She thought you already knew and that we were both hiding the truth from them so that I could stay at Granshire Hall. I told her the truth, about what had happened with Lord Sturmpole, and that I was most certainly not your mistress."

In the stern line of his lips she saw Lord Bromwell's iron will, the same force that had kept him on his chosen path despite those who tried to stop him. What brought that to the fore when he looked at her now? "Since she already knew I wasn't Lady Eleanor, I thought it best to be honest."

Instead of relaxing, his expression grew even more stern and judgmental. "Tell only what is necessary when it's necessary, is that your theory? When were you planning to be completely honest with me?"

"I have been!" she protested.

Except on one point, her conscience chided—the depth and extent of her feelings for him.

"No, you have not."

She stared at him, aghast. What did he think she had kept back? "I told you everything that happened with Lord Sturmpole, exactly as it happened."

"I don't refer to the events with Lord Sturmpole, although what I've learned may have a bearing on that, as well," he said. He nodded at the sofa, addressing her as if he were her employer inquiring about her qualifications. "Please sit down."

"I prefer to stand," she said, straightening her shoulders as she faced him squarely. "I don't know what you've been told, my lord, but I *have* been completely honest with you."

"Everything you've told me about yourself and your history is true?"

"Yes!" she insisted. "I swear it!"

"Including what you said about your parents? That they died of a fever when you were at school?"

"Yes!" Was that the trouble? "I also told you my father gambled and died penniless. Did you learn something of his debts or his creditors?"

A horrible notion came to her. "Was Lord Sturmpole one of his creditors? Is that why he thought he could—?"

Lord Bromwell immediately shook his head. "No…at least, I don't think so." He reached into his jacket pocket and pulled out some papers. "Drury's men—and they are very good at ferreting out information that can be relied upon to be accurate—have discovered certain information regarding your parents that differs from that you've told me."

She sat heavily on the bench beside his worktable. "What information?"

"It is true that your mother died of fever." His manner softened slightly. "Gaol fever, in Newgate Prison."

"Prison?" she gasped. "What was she doing in prison?"

His visage relaxed even more, becoming less angry and more sympathetic. "She was facing the same charges of theft as your father, who is apparently alive and serving out his sentence in Botany Bay."

As Nell stared at him, too stunned to speak, not willing to believe she'd heard aright, he handed her the papers. "These are copies of the court record of his trial, conviction and sentence, the manifest of the ship he sailed on and a list of the convicts who survived the voyage."

As she looked down at the documents, the words on the pages swam before her eyes. Blinking, she looked up at Lord Bromwell. The spiders in their jars behind him began to shift and waver. Then the sheets of paper fell from her lap and spilled onto the floor, and everything around her went black.

Nell slowly became aware of a cool, damp cloth grazing her cheeks and forehead. Then she felt lips where the cloth had been, while Lord Bromwell's deep voice softly called her name and said he was sorry.

She opened her eyes and discovered she wasn't dreaming. Covered by a blanket, she was lying on the sofa in his laboratory, and he was seated beside her. A basin of water was on a low stool beside him.

"I'm so sorry. I shouldn't have blindly assumed you'd lied. I should have allowed for the possibility that you had told me what you believed to be true," he said, lifting the cool, damp cloth from her forehead.

About her parents. Who were not both dead, although she'd been told that they were.

"Are you certain that what you've told me is the truth?" she whispered, grasping his hand as if she'd been washed overboard and he was the lifeline.

Lord Bromwell nodded his head. "Drury's sources are always accurate and there is documentation. According to what was discovered, it's possible your mother might have been found innocent, but the evidence against your father was damning. Perhaps that's why he preferred to let you think he was dead."

"Perhaps," she murmured, wondering if that was true.

And no wonder Lord Bromwell had looked at her as he had when he'd appeared at the laboratory that day, believing that she'd lied. "Did he steal because of his debts?"

"That seems the logical explanation. Who told you he was dead?"

"I got a letter from a vicar in Bristol—or at least someone who claimed to be a vicar," she amended. How could she believe anyone or anything when it came to her parents now? "He said both my parents died of a contagious fever so they were buried right away. He regretted there was no money for a gravestone. I intended to purchase one after I'd earned the money from Lord Sturmpole, so I put off going there.

"I had no reason to believe what he wrote wasn't true. I didn't know my parents were even suspected of a crime, let alone arrested."

"Do you remember the vicar's name?"

"Smith."

Lord Bromwell frowned. "A common name, but we should be able to find out if there was a vicar by that name in Bristol at that time. It could be, however, that your father wrote the letter or had a friend do it."

To spare her pain and shame. "That could be," she allowed, remembering her jovial father and pretty mother.

Had they known arrest was imminent when they'd sent her off to school?

"I had no reason not to believe the letter," she said softly. "My mother, who had been a faithful correspondent, never wrote to me after I received it. Neither of them ever contacted me at all. If they had, I would have gone to them, no matter what they'd done. I would have tried to see them. To think of my mother dying in that awful place—"

She turned away to face the back of the sofa, choking back a sob.

"Cry if you like, Miss Springley," he said gently. "I certainly won't hold it against you. You've had a terrible shock, and my manner of telling you was inexcusably bad."

She turned back, wiping her eyes with the back of her hand. "I don't think it would have mattered how you told me. And I'm grateful to know my father is alive, however I heard it. If not for you and your friend, I might never have known."

"He's over half finished his sentence," Lord Bromwell noted. "He has only about three years left, and then he can return."

As if he were coming back from the dead.

How would her father find her if she was living under another assumed name? How could she find *him* if she wanted to seek him out in three years' time?

Lord Bromwell rose, taking the basin to the table. "So, my mother realized from the start you weren't Lady Eleanor," he said, clearly determined to talk of something else, "and she truly believed I would bring my lover home to meet my parents under an assumed name?"

She must put her father's possible return out of her mind for now and concentrate on the present situation. "Because she *hoped* I was your mistress and would have the power to persuade you to stay in England."

His eyes widened, and as if even his hair was surprised, that lock tumbled over his forehead again. "What did you say to that?"

"That I was not, and even if I thought I could convince you to stay in England, which I surely couldn't, I wouldn't."

"I see," he replied as he reached for the kettle and shook

it to see if there was water within, his expression as grave as if he were making medicine. "How did she respond?"

"She asked me to stay here as her companion. I fear your father is not the most comforting of men."

"No," he agreed as he added more water to the kettle from the pitcher on the sideboard, "and certainly not where I'm concerned."

He spoke calmly, matter-of-factly, telling her—if she had any doubt—just how little power she had over him, regardless of any tender feelings he might have for her.

Which was just as well. "I won't be able to stay now, of course."

He glanced at her before he put the kettle on the crane and pushed it over the fire he must have kindled. "Why?"

"My father is a convicted felon, and I'm in danger of being arrested, too," she reminded him.

"I don't think you need fear for your own fate. Drury and his solicitor friend are quite optimistic about your circumstances. They think Sturmpole can be persuaded to forgo any charges against you to avoid exposure of his own crimes. They're not going to leave it at that, though. They both believe we should be able to find other employees who've suffered the same experience. We're all determined to put a stop to the fellow."

Although she felt some relief, she couldn't be happy. She doubted she could ever be truly happy again. "I still think it would be better if I leave Granshire Hall as soon as possible, to spare you any difficulties that might ensue from your involvement with me."

"If that is what you'd prefer."

Prefer? She had no other choice. "I'm sure your mother can find another, more suitable companion."

"Perhaps," he murmured as the kettle began to whistle. "Where will you go?"

Somewhere. Anywhere. It didn't matter because he would not be there. "Ireland, perhaps. Or America."

"So far?"

"This from a man who plans to sail around the world again?" she asked, trying to hide her anguish even as she went toward him.

"I suppose it's different when you're the one sailing," he said, turning toward her as if they were connected by a strong, if slender, thread.

Their gazes met and held until he put up his hand as if to keep her away.

"I've been planning this expedition for months," he said, desperation in his voice, despair and determination warring in his eyes, "ever since I returned, getting the best crew and raising the funds to buy the ship. I've got the ship and the men I want, and it's only a matter of paying for provisions and setting sail. I've worked and planned for too long to abandon my expedition now. It's not just about the spiders. We could find new plants that will provide medicines and new foods that can help feed the starving. I *want* to go, Nell. I *need* to go."

"I know," she said softly. "That's why I would never hold you back, no matter how much I wished I could. Otherwise, you would surely come to hate me."

"*Hate* you?" He shook his head. "I could never hate you."

"Oh, yes, you could," she countered, putting her hands on his arms and gripping them tightly, feeling the strength of him, the power, the pure masculinity beneath the fine fabrics and expertly tailored clothes. "If you believed I'd kept you from your work, you'd eventually come to resent it, and me. As other men made discoveries, you would wonder what you might have found, if not for me. And who can say what achievements and discoveries my selfishness would have prevented? I won't have that on my conscience, not for all the world."

Or even your love.

She closed her eyes as he reached up to caress her cheek, his touch sending sparks of desire, slivers of need, along her limbs.

"You understand me better than anyone, Nell Springley. Better even than myself. Thank you for letting me go, because of all the women in the world, you are the only one who could have held me here."

His words broke her heart and filled her with pain. To know that she had that power, and that to use it would destroy him.

Yet they were together here, now. Alone. In this paradise of his.

She would make it hers, if only for a little while. She would not think of the future, or the world beyond the door. She would be with him here, now, as she yearned to be.

"Until you leave, until you sail, until then, let me be with you. Let me be your lover," she pleaded softly yet intensely, for she had a will of iron, too, and even though he must and should leave her, she would take what joy she could while she could, if he would agree.

He shook his head. "As much as I would like that, as much as I wish it, that would make our parting all the more difficult. And I would not want to leave you with child."

She wasn't willing to give up. Not yet. "The parting will be difficult whether we make love or not. As for children… There are ways to prevent that, are there not?"

"Theoretically," he replied roughly, his breathing harsh and heavy, as if he fought against an unseen opponent. "I cannot speak to their effectiveness personally."

"I'll take that risk, and if those methods fail, couldn't I go to your friends for help?"

Passion, desire, hope flared in his blue-gray eyes. "Yes—but as a gentleman, I should still say no."

In spite of his words, he didn't move, and she needed no more assurance than that.

"No, my lord, you should be quiet and kiss me," she murmured as she raised herself on her toes and kissed him.

Chapter Sixteen

Never have I known such unmitigated, overwhelming joy, such complete relief and happiness, as when we saw that the vessel making its way toward us. We were grateful to realize it was a British ship, but such was our condition by that time, we would have welcomed a garbage scow, French frigate, pirate ship, or even a well-made raft.

—from *The Spider's Web*, by Lord Bromwell

Bromwell was no fool. His teachers had told him he had a brilliant intellect and praised him for his ability to think clearly and rationally.

Today, rationally, clearly, the honorable thing, the best thing, would be to stop kissing Nell, to let her go and tell her to leave him. That he meant every word he'd ever said about his goals and plans for the future, and nothing she could say or do would change that.

But as always when he was with her, his rational mind was no match for his heart, or his burning desire. He was helpless to set aside his emotions and concentrate on anything except Nell and the feel of her in his arms, her lips on his.

It was so right, so perfect, so good, so meant to be.

Of all the women he had ever met, she was perfect for him. She understood his goals, his needs, his wants. She didn't think him eccentric or a fool because he like spiders and wanted to learn more about them. She was brave, independent, loyal, loving and strong…all the things he would want in a wife.

But most important of all, she understood why he wouldn't marry until he'd been on his expedition. She would give him the freedom to be about the work that meant so much to him.

Even so, a part of him ached to think she could let him go, even as the other part—that rational, scientific part—felt a vast and grateful relief that she would.

Yet whatever the future held, she was here now, kissing him with all the passion any man could ever hope for, and he discovered he was powerless to refuse what she so willingly offered.

His hands slid up her back, holding her closer, the sensation of her breasts against him exciting and arousing. He had seen women unclothed and doing the most heart-stoppingly sensual dances any man had ever witnessed. He had been there to see the feet-pounding, hip-swinging motions, the thrust of hips and breasts. He had been aroused and enticed, but never had he been so passionately excited, so full of desire and yearning and need, as he was now.

Surrendering to that need, and hers, he swept her into his arms and laid her on the sofa. Joining her, he covered her body with his, his hands and mouth seeking, tasting, stroking, caressing. She shoved at his jacket and he shrugged it off. She tore off his cravat as she arched, her breasts against him, her slender throat exposed to his eager, anxious lips and tongue.

Her fingers went to his shirt. After she got his buttons undone, he ripped it from his body. Then her hands were on his naked skin, while he kissed and licked the rounded tops of her breasts above her bodice.

She raised her knees, her skirts bunching about her hips, and he stroked her leg as he propped himself on his elbow and ran his hand through her hair while he kissed her ear, her cheek, her chin.

His erection strained against his trousers, and he wanted nothing more than to tear them off, too, and make love to her as if they were two wild animals in heat.

Except that they were not.

Did she not deserve better than some hasty rutting on the worn sofa of his lab? And what if he did get her with child before he left England? That was, after all, the natural outcome of what they were about to do, the reality rising up like a spectre to haunt him and douse his desire.

With a ragged sigh, he pulled back and got to his feet. "I won't do this, Nell," he said hoarsely, reaching for his shirt. "It isn't right, or fair to you."

She moved to sit up as he put on his shirt, then splayed her hands on his heaving chest. "You're an honorable man, my lord," she said, her voice low and husky. "I'm well aware of the consequences, and I accept them."

She inched forward on the sofa and ran her palms lightly over his nipples before moving toward the buttons of his trousers. "If you won't make love with me, we can still do…things. I've read your book."

His book? For a moment, he could scarcely remember writing one.

"The practices of some of the natives in the islands sounded very intriguing," she said as she finished undoing the buttons. He jumped when she slipped her hand inside. "Although you were not at all specific."

He closed his eyes as her hand encircled him. He knew precisely what passages she was referring to, the memories of what had happened on certain moonlit nights leaping vividly into his mind.

Only to disappear the moment Nell slipped from the sofa to her knees and took him into her mouth.

He groaned softly, cupping the back of her head, as she sucked and licked him, her tongue swirling around the tip until he thought he would burst. He'd never expected... dreamed....

All too soon, she stopped. He opened his eyes, to see her looking up at him with a shy smile. If she wanted to stop, he wouldn't...

And then her hand was around him, moving up and down along his shaft, grazing lightly. Faster and faster she stroked, the urge within him building, building and building until he was over the edge.

Gasping, jerking, he spilled his seed.

"I must have done that right," she said softly, a hint of triumph in her voice, as well as the heat of desire.

"Perfect," he murmured, blushing like a naughty schoolboy as he adjusted his trousers and did up the buttons, although his hands seemed inordinately clumsy. "I had no idea I'd been so...descriptive."

"You weren't. I guessed," Nell said, smiling, flushed with happiness and satisfaction. She had never even imagined doing anything like that, but it had seemed a natural way to give him pleasure, and since she had, she could only be pleased herself.

She rose as he reached into his trouser pocket and handed her his handkerchief.

"You are, without doubt, the most incredible woman in the world—and you have to stop calling me my lord. Especially after…after *this*. My name's Justinian, although that's quite a mouth…"

He blushed and began again, looking like the bashful schoolboy he must have been as he put on his shirt. "My father thought such a name impressive, especially if I became a politician. My friends call me Buggy. They didn't appreciate the difference between spiders and insects when they gave it to me."

She brushed that stray lock of hair off his forehead. "That sounds like something boys would call a schoolmate, but I don't think I could call you that. You're very much a man to me."

"Since you put it that way, I don't think I'd like you to call me that, either. I suppose my name will have to do and I'm suddenly reconciled to it," he said, taking her in his arms and pressing a kiss upon her soft lips. "But I can't continue to call you Miss Springley. Will 'my darling' do?"

"*My* friends call me Nell."

He sat on the sofa and drew her down onto his lap. "Well, Nell, this is familiar. I seem to recall a young lady in precisely this position not so long ago, resulting in a most interesting experience."

She loved it when he spoke with such apparent seriousness and answered him with the same grave tone. "It wouldn't surprise me in the least to discover that you deliberately put that spider in the coach in a crude attempt to seduce unsuspecting young women."

"If I'd had an inkling of your reaction, I might have, although upon further consideration, it occurs to me that there is no other woman in England I would care to have sitting on my lap."

"So you say now."

The merriment disappeared from his eyes. "So I truly believe, with all my heart."

She toyed with one of the buttons on his shirt, not meeting his steadfast gaze. "I'm flattered."

"It's the truth, and now, since I am a firm believer in fair play, I do believe we have something more to do."

"Such as, my lord?"

"You were going to call me Justinian," he reminded her as his hand began a slow glide up her arm.

"Such as, Justinian?"

"Such as…this," he replied, brushing his lips across hers lightly, as he had that first time. "And this." His lips continued to slide over her mouth.

"And this, too," he murmured as his hand grazed her bodice.

She wound her arms about his neck. "You are teasing me, my lord."

"Justinian. And I intend to do much more than that."

"Promise?"

"Oh, yes," he replied as he shifted and moved her down onto the sofa. "Much more."

Nell's heart raced and her body warmed as if he were sending out rays of light and heat like the sun. He shifted them so that he was again above her, his hips on hers, his weight on his knees between her legs and leaning on one elbow, while his other hand explored her.

His kiss deepened, and she responded with fervent excitement, pulling him closer as her palms slid over his back, feeling the muscles bunching and moving beneath the surface of his skin as he stroked and aroused her.

His mouth moved slowly down her neck, and below, to the soft roundness of her breasts and their pebbled peaks. Regardless of her gown, he kissed her there, too, and sucked and nibbled, the sensations incredibly arousing. The pressure of his hips increased slightly as he raised himself to slip one hand into her bodice to cup her. She sighed and gasped and squirmed with a growing craving as the pad of his thumb brushed over the sensitive tip.

His mouth caught hers again, but more aggressively this time, with more need, more longing, more urgency. She responded at once, rising to meet him, running her hands along his heated flesh.

His hand went to her stockinged shin, curling around her and moving upward in an excruciatingly slow progress toward her knee. He reached the garter holding her stocking and pulled the bow until it came undone and fell away. He pushed down the fabric with a caress that made her writhe with expectation. She would never have guessed so simple a thing—a thing she did every day—could be so exciting.

When he inched backward, she began to sit up, ready to help him remove her stocking or anything else he wanted, until he whispered for her to lie back and let him satisfy her as she had satisfied him.

Panting, heart leaping with expectation, she did as he asked and when she felt him untie the drawstring of her pantelettes and lower them, she raised her hips to help, sure she knew what he was going to do. What she would let him do. What she hoped he would do.

She gasped with both surprise and the unexpected thrill of his lips grazing her inner thigh. She had never even imagined being kissed there…or *there!* Or that he would do *that* with his tongue, licking her so intimately, making forays where his fingers had before.

She clutched her skirts, bunching the fabric as she parted her legs more, giving him room, writhing with the growing tension.

And then his hand was on her breast, stroking and touching, arousing her still more.

"Make love with me," she pleaded. "I want you. Oh, please!"

He didn't answer, but in the next moment, his finger glided inside her. She was slick and hot and so ready, the tension snapped almost at once. With a low, guttural cry, she half rose as her muscles pulsed and her toes curled, carried along on waves of blissful release.

When her body relaxed and she lay back, he pressed warm, soft kisses to her neck and the curve of her shoulder.

"*That* was not in your book," she said, wrapping a lock of his hair around her finger.

"Because I didn't learn that on my voyage," he replied as he moved back and got to his feet.

Some of her happiness dissipated, although of course she couldn't expect him to be inexperienced even before he sailed. He was a young, titled gentleman; he would have had plenty of opportunity to learn about women.

"Not every book I've read has been a classic or scientific one," he said as she pulled up her stocking and tied her garter. "You would be shocked if you knew what sort of books one can find in the less reputable bookstores, many of which are read by men who have no compunction about condemning other people for their licentious ways.

"Nor have I actually done that before," he admitted. "That was another experiment and I believe I can consider it a success."

"Very much so," she replied, wondering what else had been in those books.

He began to button his shirt. "We had best get back to the hall. Drury and his wife—who returned with me—will be worried, and my mother anxious. I fear Juliette and Drury half expect you to return in tears. I confess I was rather indignant when I thought you'd lied to me about your parents."

"Another man would have been far more than indignant," she replied, rising to kiss him again. "That's another reason I'm…"

She hesitated for a fraction of a moment, afraid to use that stronger word. "Why I care for you as I do."

"Do you really mean that?" he asked, his expression as studious as if he were taking an examination.

She had to kiss him again when he looked like that, before she wrapped her arms around him and regarded him just as gravely.

"I do. And I've never been happier in my life," she said, meaning it in spite of the undercurrent of sorrow she suspected she'd feel for the rest of her life. "Whatever happens in the future, I'm happier than I've ever been, because you make me so."

"I don't understand how," he ruminated aloud, his brows furrowed. "I am not handsome, or charming. Granted, the pleasure of sexual activity is certainly important, but—"

"You *are* handsome, and charming, and kind, as well as exciting. But more than that, you treat me as your equal, even though I'm so ignorant."

He looked at her with obvious bafflement. "You may not be as well educated—although that is the fault of a society that treats female offspring as incapable of comprehending as well as any male of the species and despite ample evidence to the contrary—but you are as intelligent as anyone I've ever met, male or female, as well as brave and resourceful."

He gave her a rueful smile. "And I might as well admit everything. You don't make me feel like I'm some sort of oddity because I'm so fascinated by spiders. Although…" He put his hands loosely about her waist and smiled. "I must say I find you infinitely more interesting than spiders."

She'd never had a more thrilling compliment. "You do?"

"Indeed," he murmured, leaning down to kiss her again.

The door to the laboratory burst open.

"Bonjour!" cried a merry, well-dressed young woman in a frilly, frothy pink gown and pink velvet spencer, as well as a delightful bonnet with a wide pink ribbon and fabric roses around the brim. "Are we interrupting? Should we leave?"

At the sound of Juliette's voice, knowing Drury must not be far behind, Bromwell quickly stepped away from Nell. Meanwhile, the heat of a blush travelled up his face, as if a description of their recent activity had been tattooed on his forehead.

"Sorry for barging in, Buggy," Drury said as he entered the laboratory behind his wife, who was smiling as genially as if she'd merely intruded on a tea party. "Juliette—"

"I thought you had been chastising and interrogating the

poor girl long enough," his wife interrupted with a smile, "although I see I was quite wrong. *Bonjour,* Miss Springley. I am Juliette, the wife of Sir Douglas Drury, who has not the manners to introduce me."

The dark-haired barrister scowled, although his equally dark eyes were far from angry. "Forgive me, Miss Springley. I am Sir Douglas Drury, and this is my charming and headstrong wife, Juliette."

"He calls me headstrong because I don't obey his every command," Juliette laughingly confided, "and while I am sorry to have interrupted, it is getting late in the day and unless you want the servants to gossip, we had better go back to the hall.

"Not that I care about gossip," Juliette said, slipping her arm through Nell's. "I am quite used to it, but dear Buggy is not, and neither, I think, are you."

As Juliette steered her out the door, Nell didn't even have time to look back as they left the two friends alone.

Chapter Seventeen

And then—oh woe!
The intruder comes
And all my hopes are dashed,
My desire thwarted,
My love denied,
I am again
Alone.

    —found among Lord Bromwell's private papers

Drury turned to Bromwell the moment the women were out the door. "I'm truly sorry we barged in like that, but Juliette was so worried about what you might be saying to Miss Springley, she wouldn't listen. She's a very stubborn woman when she thinks she's right."

"And yet you love her anyway," Bromwell noted as he went to his worktable and leaned against it.

"Can't help it," Drury replied with a smile as he sat in one of the chairs near the hearth. "And I think I'm not the only man here who's in love."

Bromwell didn't reply directly to that statement as he

ran his fingertips, which had so recently skimmed Nell's warm, soft flesh, over a long scar in the tabletop made when his knife slipped as he was attempting to carve a whistle several years ago. "Miss Springley didn't know her father was alive. She truly believed he was dead."

Drury's tone was noncommittal when he replied. "And you believed her, so you couldn't be angry with her."

"You would have believed her, too, if you'd seen her," Bromwell said, crossing his arms. "It was quite obvious she was shocked, so taken aback she fainted—and it was no false swoon, I assure you.

"I've had plenty of experience with those," he added, recalling certain episodes with his mother.

"That doesn't, unfortunately, erase the fact that her father is a convicted felon and she's been impersonating Lady Eleanor Springford."

"Whatever Miss Springley did, she was still attacked and held against her will," Bromwell replied as he reached for his jacket. "Sturmpole was more guilty of a crime than she. As for impersonating Lady Eleanor, I colluded with her in that, so if she's guilty of a crime, so am I. But there's been no harm done. Nobody knows save my family, and you and Juliette."

"I fear it may not be so simple. Did I not hear your father's in Bath? Don't you think he'll mention that there's the daughter of a duke visiting his estate?"

Bromwell felt for the bench beside the table and sat heavily. "Oh, God."

That truly hadn't occurred to him—and it should have.

"I don't want to upset you, Buggy, but we should be prepared. However, since your motive wasn't criminal or malicious and neither was Miss Springley's, it could be that Lady Eleanor won't prosecute, especially if she remains in Italy."

"If Lady Eleanor does prosecute, can we count on your representation?" Bromwell asked, trying to think clearly and plan for any eventuality.

"Of course."

"Thank you."

"As for Sturmpole," Drury said, "from what we've learned of the man, I'm fairly confident he can be persuaded not to press charges, so it's not Sturmpole I'm worried about. It's you. Are you still not willing to marry Miss Springley?"

Bromwell tried to mask the pain his question caused. "She must be free when I sail in case I don't come back. I don't have to tell you, Drury, that sometimes when ships go down, it can be years before the crew is considered lost for good. I won't put her through that."

"So you will break her heart before you sail, and for her own good?"

"If you wish to put it that way, yes," Bromwell said, heading for the door. "There's no point discussing that particular subject again, Drury. I won't, and that's the end of it."

Sighing softly, Drury rose and followed him.

Nell wished she was alone, or with Justinian, as she walked back to the hall, instead of in the company of a woman she'd only just met and in such a fashion.

"You are very fortunate to have won Buggy's heart," Lady Drury remarked as she walked beside Nell. "If I had not my Drury, I am sure I would be jealous."

Nell could hardly deny that there was something of an amorous nature between herself and Lord Bromwell when she'd been discovered in his passionate embrace, but she wasn't willing to encourage any discussion of the subject, either.

"I liked him much better than Drury when I first met them," Lady Drury confessed.

That got Nell's full attention.

"Buggy was kind and polite, even though I was only a seamstress and obviously French—both of which made it quite impossible for Drury to even like me, let alone love me, or so we both thought. Our hearts, however, would not listen."

Nell knew exactly what she meant. If her head could rule her heart, she wouldn't still be here, and she certainly wouldn't ever be alone with Justinian.

"You saw my husband's hands, I'm sure."

Nell had indeed noticed her husband's gnarled, twisted fingers. "Yes."

"He was tortured when he was captured in France during the war. By my brother."

Nell came to an abrupt halt. "Your brother?" she repeated incredulously.

"*Oui,* although it pains me to confess it. After the war, Drury found my brother and killed him for what he had done, not just to him, but others, too."

Her husband had killed her own brother? "And you still married him?"

"Because I love him more than I could ever hate him, and I could understand why he did what he did. But there was a time I was sure we could never be together, until we realized we loved each other enough to overcome what threatened to keep us apart."

Nell wondered why Lady Drury was being so forthcoming to a stranger, but it hardly seemed like a question one could ask. Nor did she wish to speak of her feelings for Justinian, or tell her that her father was a convict in Australia.

"You think I am forward, to tell you these things," Lady Drury said, answering Nell's silent query as they reached the terrace. "I tell you because I know who you are and what your father did. My husband has no secrets from me. And I speak to you this way, as if we are old and dear friends, because I want Buggy to be happy. I fear you might think your father and your rank mean you are not worthy to be his wife."

Lady Drury stopped and looked Nell steadily in the eye. "Buggy is not the sort of man who toys with a woman's affections, or makes love with them for sport. If I am any judge, he loves you very much. If he asks you to be his wife and you love him, you should accept him."

Nell didn't want to hear this. She didn't want to believe Justinian loved her, not when he was going to leave her. When he must leave her.

She turned toward the house. "Thank you for your advice, my lady. I will bear it in mind if he ever asks."

And for his sake, I will refuse.

Clad in her dressing gown and nightgown, her feet in simple slippers she had knit herself, Nell stood by the window of her bedchamber in Granshire Hall.

Her thoughts were not on the view of the formal gardens below, or the beauty of the clear night sky liberally sprinkled with stars. In her mind's eye, she was seeing her mother at their final farewell, when Nell had not known it would be their last.

Had her mother guessed it might be so? At the time, she had thought her mother's strained expression and tears were evidence that she would miss her daughter and because their next meeting was likely weeks away. She had even— to her intense regret—been ashamed of her sobbing mother at the main door of the manor house that had become a school, and prouder of her father's cheery manner.

He had always been a jovial, easy-going man. Never had the cares of earning a living seemed to weigh on him as managing the household did to her mother. She had supposed that her mother was simply a more sombre, serious character. It had never occurred to her that perhaps her father ignored their troubles, while her mother could not.

Had it been his idea to find a solution through thievery, a solution that had cost her mother her life, him his freedom and bestowed the stain and shame of their crime on their daughter?

If only she could see him again, to ask him about that, or even just be with him once more.

What might have happened if her mother had lived? Might she have been found innocent? If so, her daughter might not have had to accept employment with Lady Sturmpole and thus find herself deep in a mire of her own.

And yet, Nell mused as the moon rose full and bright over the wood beyond the garden, if she had not taken employment with Lady Sturmpole and been attacked by her husband, if she had not fled, she would never have met Justinian.

That was the one good thing that had happened to her in the past six months—except that the happiness she had experienced would bring her an equal, if not greater, measure of sorrow when it was time for them to part.

But not yet. Not yet.

She lowered her gaze to the dark garden. No light shone upon the terrace. No sound disturbed the silence, save for the occasional cry of a night bird or an owl swooping down in the darkness to catch a mouse.

Now she could go to him. He might think being together here too great a risk, too likely to cause gossip and scandal. If so, she would leave him, but if not…

Her eyes were already accustomed to the dark, so she needed no candle as she cautiously opened her bedroom door and looked into the empty corridor. Moving quietly, carefully, for old floors could creak—and loudly—she closed her door and made her way to his, easing it open.

She had never been in Justinian's bedroom before. It was a large chamber suited to the heir of a great house, with a huge, curtained bed with a set of bed stairs beside it at the far end. Those curtains were open, as were the draperies and shutters over the two tall, narrow windows that faced the front of the house and the long sweeping drive— the opposite view to hers, and away from his laboratory. Wondering if that was deliberate on the part of his parents, and if he liked to be awakened by the sun, she ventured closer to the bed.

Justinian lay sprawled diagonally on his back, his naked chest visible above the satin coverlet. He had one leanly muscular arm over his chest, the other slung out to the side. The rest of his body was hidden beneath the covers.

As she tiptoed nearer, she noted how Spartan the chamber was. Apart from the bed and a table beside it holding a lamp, there was a wardrobe by the wall to the left. A pedestal table with papers and ink and quills upon it, as well as a Chippendale chair, stood near the window, and a plain washstand and dressing table were half-hidden behind a folding screen. There was no looking glass of any kind, and the dressing table was bare of anything save a brush and shaving items.

Three more steps and she was beside the bed.

How young Justinian looked when he slept, with that lock of hair falling on his forehead! How sweet and innocent and boyish. If this was the way his mother always thought of him, no wonder she was so upset that he would leave England for unknown, dangerous parts of the world.

Yet he was no innocent, naive youth. He was a virile, experienced man who was showing her what true intimacy between a man and a woman could be.

And she wanted to learn more.

Untying her robe, she let it fall open as she took another step closer.

He moved and she froze. Still asleep, he sighed, muttered something and rolled away from her, the coverlet coming with him, but leaving his back exposed.

Three thin, parallel black lines in a pattern of slightly angular concentric circles had been drawn on his back. The majority of the design was still hidden below the coverlet; nevertheless, she could see enough to guess that she was looking at his tattoo and that it was a spider's web.

She should have known.

How low did it go on his body? Was there a spider, too?

Going to the other side of the bed, she took off her robe and laid it on the foot of the bed. Hiking up her nightgown of thin white linen, she climbed onto the high bed, which dipped so much she expected him to wake.

He didn't, so she leaned toward him and slowly pulled the coverlet down, until she could see the whole tattoo. It *was* a web and in the center was a small black spider.

She reached out to trace it, but as she put her fingertip

on his skin, he immediately turned over and she found herself beneath him, with her arms over her head, her wrists held in his vicelike grip. It happened so swiftly, she didn't even have time to suck in her breath.

"Nell!" he gasped, his eyes wide and vibrantly alert.

He let go at once, but didn't move from atop her as he ran his gaze over her. "What are you…?"

He paused when he realized she was wearing only her nightgown, then spoke with measured calm, although he didn't move. "Forgive my extreme reaction. As a result of my voyage and the situations I encountered, I tend to sleep lightly. You must have been very quiet."

Her breathing quickened when passionate warmth kindled in his eyes as his gaze moved slowly down her body in what was like a leisurely caress. "Or did you come here in a state of undress to alert me to some emergency? Perchance the house is afire?"

"The house is not ablaze, although I am rather… heated," she whispered in response.

He ran his fingertip around the neckline of her nightgown. "No thieves or poachers afoot?"

"None of which I am aware," she replied, sliding her hands up his lean arms to his broad shoulders.

Feeling bold and mischievous, very aware of his body above hers, she smiled. "Perhaps I came to see your tattoo."

"Ah, and did you?"

"Yes, so I could win the bet at White's, if I were a member."

He laughed softly as he leaned down to kiss the tip of her nose. "No one will ever win that wager, because the proof would require me to expose a portion of my anatomy to those I would rather not."

She reached down to the approximate location of the tattoo.

"Perhaps you would have been wiser to have it on your arm or chest, like a seaman."

"It was all I could do to get them to stop when they did. Among the Tahitians it's a sign of adulthood for the men to have that portion of their body covered completely by a tattoo."

She tried to imagine that. "Is it painful?"

"Less painful than having to sit so far from you at supper," he murmured, gliding his mouth over hers. "And only slightly more painful than having to make polite conversation afterward, when all I really wanted to do was this…." He kissed her lips. "And this." He kissed her neck. "And this…"

His lips slid downward toward her breasts as he undid the drawstring at the neck of her nightgown. "I suppose I should suggest that your presence here is highly improper and likely to cause a scandal should we be discovered *in flagrante delicto*. However, I find I am much too pleased and delighted to protest."

"Good," she said, brushing her fingertips along the dark T of hair between his nipples and down toward his navel, where she felt the growing evidence of his arousal.

He kissed her again, with more urgent need and she responded in kind. Bending her knees, she shifted so that she could feel all of him, while his hand slid inside the neck of her nightgown to her breast. As he gently kneaded the soft weight, she reached down to bring him closer, aware that her legs were bare, and her gown bunched about her hips.

His breathing heavy, he moved slightly to the side, so that he could caress her where she was moist, and ready.

She felt him hesitate. Knew what he feared and, for a moment, thought he meant to stop.

Whatever happened, she wanted him to love her fully, completely, as she would never love another. She didn't want to wait. She wanted to be with him now.

She reached for the neck of her nightgown. The fabric was old and thin, and with her own hands she tore it, until she lay beneath him naked and willing.

Chapter Eighteen

As in other cultures, the peoples of the South Seas
have many rituals and beliefs about food, including
the notion of tapu, or forbidden foods. For instance,
bananas are forbidden to women, and the punishment, should a woman be seen eating one, is to be
immediately clubbed to death.
—from *The Spider's Web*, by Lord Bromwell

Even then, Justinian hesitated as his heated gaze swept
over her body.

Impatient, as determined as he could be, she seized his
face between her hands and captured his mouth with fierce
and hungry need. As she did, she wiggled closer and
reached down, guiding him where she wanted him to go.

"Please," she pleaded, panting, her voice a harsh
whisper. "Please. There are ways to prevent…aren't there?
The girls at school said so. If you stop…"

"Yes, there are ways," he rasped even as he finally gave
her what she craved and pushed inside. There was a pain,
a moment's anguish, gone as soon as he began to thrust.

She felt the same tightening, the urgency, stronger than before. Anticipating that wonderful release, she arched against him, bare flesh to bare flesh.

His thrusts quickened and became more urgent, more powerful. The sinews in his neck grew more visible and his rough panting sounded in her ears.

Gasping encouragement or moaning softly, she wrapped her legs around him, instinctively locking her ankles to hold him close.

The sweet pressure, the glorious tension, grew. Muscles tightened. Toes curled. She clenched her teeth to keep from crying out…

And then—

And then, release, like a star shooting across the sky in the darkest part of night and she panted like an animal as her body rose of its own accord.

With an answering groan, he pulled back, head bowed, jerking as his seed spilled onto her naked stomach.

She caught her breath as he slowly sat on his haunches, bracing himself with his arms on either side of her while he drew in great gulps of air.

"My God, I've never…" He paused, then shook his head. "I've never felt anything like that."

"Because I was a virgin?" she asked, even more jealous of the other woman who had been in his arms.

He smiled and shook his head. "Because I've never cared more for a woman."

"Nor I for any man," she assured him.

She watched him as he climbed off the bed and went to fetch water in a Wedgwood basin and a towel of fine, soft linen.

"You've ruined your nightgown," he noted. "That may be difficult to explain."

"I have another just the same," she said as he returned. "Now I'm glad they're so plain. No one will be able to tell the difference. I'll hide this one beneath my other undergarments."

"I should have realized you'd have a plan," he said, sitting beside her.

He dipped the towel in the water. She held out her hand, but again he shook his head. "Let me," he said as he began to wash her stomach, and then between her thighs. "This provides more opportunity to observe your naked body— and a particularly fine naked body it is, too."

In spite of what they'd done together, she blushed as he washed her. "I feel like one of your spiders."

"You are even more lovely than an *Argiope bruennichi*."

"Is that intended to be a compliment?"

"Oh, yes. It's a very beautiful spider."

"Then I thank you, sir."

"As I thank you."

Finished his ministrations, he turned to set the basin on the table beside the bed. "Do you know, I don't think I've ever enjoyed a visit to the ancestral acres more."

She sat up, then reluctantly rose and picked up the remnants of her nightgown.

"Are you leaving?" he asked, his brow furrowing as, still magnificently naked, he got up from the bed. "You've had your way with me so now you'll rush off?"

"I would rather stay, but if I'm found here, my lord—"

He took her in his arms and silenced her with a kiss. "There is a little time yet before that becomes a concern."

Taking her hand, he sat on the bed, then drew her down beside him. "But what is this *my lord?*"

"Habit, I suppose," she said, nestling beside him as they lay back on the soft pillows.

Habit, and because she couldn't ever really forget the gulf of rank, title and fortune that lay between them. Not even here. Not even now.

She ran her fingertip up and down the line of dark brown hairs from his navel to his chest. "I wish I could sail with you. We went to the Isle of Man once, in very rough weather, and I didn't get seasick."

Her tone was teasing, but she spoke only half in jest. She would gladly go with him to the ends of the earth, if he would ask her. "Perhaps I should stow away."

"You've never been in a ship's hold, have you?" he asked gravely. "There's scarcely room for a rat to run and the stench from the bilge would knock you flat."

Not willing to abandon that proposal just yet, and despite his grim tone, she said, "I could disguise myself as a boy and sign on with the crew."

"That would be even less likely to succeed. You are much too pretty and your figure would give you away."

"I could bind my breasts, cut off my hair and dirty my face."

"Which just goes to show how little you know of life at sea. There is no privacy on a ship the size we will have."

His chest rose and fell with a deep sigh. "I'm not happy to be leaving you and the thought of having you with me is very tempting," he said softly as he caressed her cheek, "but it's not just life on the ship that's difficult. There are storms and wrecks, islanders who may welcome you or decide you'd make a nice addition to the pot, and you don't know which until you land. And pirates aren't the merry brigands some ballads suggest. They are terrible brutes and a swift death would be a mercy if we were ever captured, especially if you're a woman. I've seen…" He drew in a ragged breath. "I would kill you myself before I'd let you fall into a pirate's hands."

"You make it sound terrible indeed," she whispered, her fears for him increasing, and she was tempted as she'd never been before to do what Lady Granshire had asked her to do, to use whatever means she could to keep him in England.

But what then? They could never marry and she would be the destroyer of his dreams.

She moved away. "It's time for me to go."

He laid a hand on her bare arm. "If I were going to the Mediterranean, or even the coast of Africa or the West Indies, I would take you, but not where I'm going. It would be far too much of a risk, and while I'm willing to take that gamble with my own life, I won't with yours."

She nodded and got out of the bed, the air making her shiver as she reached for her dressing gown.

"There's no need for you to get out of a warm bed to see me to the door," she said, trying to sound happy. "I can manage on my own."

"I want to see you to the door," he said, climbing off the bed.

"If the noblewomen of England had any inkling of the body beneath your clothes," she said as he pulled on a pair of trousers, "they would be even more eager to meet you."

He laughed, then pulled a face. "They torment me enough as it is. I certainly wouldn't want to encourage them."

Her torn gown over her arm, Nell went to the door. He met her there, and smiled down at her. "You're the most

wonderful, remarkable woman I've ever met, Nell Springley, and if ever I were to ask a woman to wait for me, it
would be you."

Ask me! she silently pleaded. *Ask me and I will.*

He took her hand and brought it to his lips, kissing the
back of her hand. "Good night, Miss Springley."

"Good night, my lord," she replied.

And as she slipped into the corridor, she was sure of one
thing:

Even if he didn't ask her, she would wait for him.

"You wished to see me, Mother?" Bromwell asked as
he entered his mother's sitting room a few days later.

As usual, she was reclining on her chaise, and this
morning, she looked pale, with dark circles under her eyes.

Remorse nipped at him. He hadn't yet spoken with Dr.
Heathfield about her treatment and he should have, regardless of his desire to spend every moment he could
with Nell. "Have you been drinking chocolate in the
evenings again?"

Although he had no scientific basis for his query, he suspected there was something in chocolate that affected
sleep, for he'd often noticed that his mother would become
more energized after drinking it, then complain that she
hadn't been able to fall asleep later.

Not unexpectedly, however, she always ascribed her
sleeplessness to a different cause, as she did today. "How
can I sleep peacefully when you're leaving England again?"

He had no answer to that, so he made none as he sat
across from her on a well-upholstered chair. He had to hide
a wince, for he'd pulled a muscle last night when demonstrating the *upa upa* for Nell. He'd been telling her about

the dances of the Tahitians, and she'd confessed to seeing him dance by the pond. Once he'd gotten over his initial embarrassment, he'd explained that he danced because it was excellent exercise.

She'd begged a demonstration, he'd complied, and somewhere between the dance, her attempts to imitate it and what had followed, he'd pulled a muscle in his side. It was a slight strain, and only hurt if he moved a certain way, but he didn't want to have to explain the source of that twinge to his mother.

He also sincerely hoped she hadn't summoned him here because his intimate encounters with Nell had been discovered.

"I've had a letter from your father. He requests that you join him in Bath as soon as possible. Apparently he requires your assistance with a financial matter."

His relief that her summons had nothing to do with Nell was swiftly overcome by baffled curiosity.

His father wished to consult with *him* on a financial matter? Despite his coming of age, his father had never shared information about his financial affairs or estate business before. "What sort of financial matter?"

"He doesn't say. Only that it's important, and he expects you to join him at The King's Arms this afternoon."

That was typical of his father—no explanation or opportunity to refuse, simply an order and the expectation of obedience.

However, he had no other pressing demands upon his time, except for wanting to be with Nell every available opportunity, and the request was so unusual he nodded his agreement. "Very well, Mother. I'll stay the night in Bath and return in the morning."

"I've already ordered a horse saddled for you."

Bromwell didn't think riding would aggravate his slight injury and so, dutifully, rose. "If you'll excuse me then."

"And would you stop in at the apothecary's? I need some more of my medicine."

"I'll visit Dr. Heathfield while I'm there. I'm concerned this latest medication is not as effective as it should be, considering your continuing sleeplessness."

"I feel quite wonderful after my morning dose."

Her comment led Bromwell to suspect the main ingredient in Dr. Heathfield's latest medication was some kind of narcotic that induced euphoria, possibly an opiate that could be dangerous if taken too long, or in too high a dosage.

"Nevertheless, Mother, I want to be sure it's not doing more harm than good." He gave her a loving smile. "After all, you aren't the only one who worries."

She reached out for his hand and pressed it to her cool cheek before she wordlessly let him go.

Bromwell found Nell in the garden, looking like a nymph in a gown of soft green, her overtunic dotted with small embroidered roses. Unfortunately, she wasn't alone, as he would have preferred even for this temporary and short-lived parting. Drury and Juliette were with her.

"Ah, Buggy, here you are!" Juliette cried when she saw him walking toward them on the gravel path.

"I hope your mother isn't unwell?" Nell said, blushing when their gazes met, as if recalling certain portions of the *upa upa* done while he was naked.

He found himself blushing, too, as he replied. "She's a little tired, but otherwise well. She's received a letter from my father asking me to meet him in Bath this afternoon. Apparently he has some business he wishes to discuss with me."

Drury, who was well acquainted with the earl, was as surprised as Bromwell by the request. "He's never discussed such things with you before, has he?"

Bromwell shook his head and, when he answered, spoke as much to Nell as to his oldest friend. "Not once, so I think I should go, and unfortunately it must be right away. I won't be back until tomorrow."

"Of course you must go if your father requests your help," Nell said quietly.

"It wasn't exactly a request," Bromwell replied with a wry smile. "A command, more like."

"Perhaps he has reconsidered and will sponsor your expedition," Juliette said hopefully.

Bromwell glanced at Nell before shaking his head. "I highly doubt it. It's probably something about the ball."

He started to bow in farewell, until Juliette grabbed her husband's arm and started to pull him toward the terrace. "Come along, my love. Let us leave them to say goodbye alone."

"As you see, Buggy, you aren't the only one who gets ordered about," the barrister remarked as he allowed his wife to lead him away.

With Bromwell's silent gratitude. He would much prefer to say goodbye to Nell in private.

"Since time is short, let's walk to the stables together," Nell proposed.

Bromwell nodded his acquiescence, remembering a part of the garden in that vicinity where they could take their leave without being seen.

"Is it really true that Lady Drury was a seamstress?" Nell asked as Drury and his wife disappeared behind a yew hedge.

"Yes, and living in deplorable conditions the first time we

met," Bromwell replied. "She saved Drury's life by hurling a basketful of potatoes at men who were attacking him."

"I can believe she's not afraid of anything."

"Like everyone, she has her moments of doubt and fear, although she hides them very well. She certainly did the first time we met, after Drury sent her to fetch me. She had to come get me at Sir Joseph Banks's house, and I'm sure that wasn't easy for her, and then Drury was remarkably rude to her." He smiled at Nell. "Afterward, I realized he'd been rude because he was so intrigued by her."

"He didn't do anything so insolent as kiss her, did he?" she asked archly, with the sparkle of mischief that he adored in her eyes.

"No," Bromwell said softly as they reached the little nook in the shrubbery. "Even though he hated the French, he wasn't *that* impolite, whereas I…" He gathered her in his arms and kissed her gently. "Find I have no memory…" She wrapped her arms around him and sighed as he kissed the lobe of her ear. "Of rules of etiquette and proper deportment…" Then her neck. "When I am with you."

"Clearly, my lord," she murmured as she relaxed against him, her body leaning into his, "I forget how a young woman ought to act with a gentleman when I'm with you."

He caught her mouth with his, and kissed her deeply. "I don't want to go," he whispered as he slid his mouth to her soft cheek, "not even for a single night."

"I don't want you to go," she murmured as he caressed her. "Not even for an hour."

They kissed again, deeply, passionately, as desperately as if this were their final parting, until he broke the embrace and stepped back, flushed and breathless. "If we don't stop now, I'm going to make love with you right here."

Exhilaration took hold of Nell as she spotted the back of the stables out of the corner of her eye, a place sheltered from the yard and the rest of the garden.

"Not here—there," she whispered.

Yearning to be with him intimately today if she couldn't be with him that night, she took his hand to lead him. He resisted a little, but not for long, as she pulled him toward the shadowed, sheltered spot.

Her back to the wall, she turned, to be engulfed in his embrace. "I'll miss you," she gasped as he spread kisses over her face and neck.

He regarded her with primitive, primal greed. "Promise me you'll wait. Promise me you'll wait for me to come back."

Was he speaking of this brief sojourn, or his longer voyage? Whichever one he meant, her answer was the same. "Yes!"

As if that single word released him from all restraint, he pushed her back against the wall and kissed her with fervent, heated ardour. As his hands boldly caressed her, he spread her knees with his. She thrilled to the pressure of his limb and leaned against it as she slid her tongue into his hot mouth.

With a low growl, he reached down to lift her gown and soon he was stroking her most private place with growing need as he kissed her, making her moist and ready while she ran her hands beneath his vest and shirt. The drawstring of her pantelettes snapped, then his hand slipped within.

All too soon he withdrew and she whimpered with the loss, until he cupped her buttocks and lifted her, so that she could hold him around the waist with her legs.

She wanted him with every fiber, every particle, of her body and her heart. "Yes, oh, yes," she hissed as she worked at the buttons of his trousers with one hand, the other around his neck, until he was free.

Holding him, she shifted, while he positioned himself. Then he was inside her.

This was no gentle lovemaking, no tender contact. He took her with primal, swift and hungry need as she responded, until he groaned and filled her, while she pressed her lips together to stifle her own triumphant cries of release.

Sated, panting, his head in the crook of her neck, he leaned against her. She slowly lowered her legs, only now aware of the rough brick behind her and that her pantelettes were that pile of white linen on the ground.

"Oh, God," he muttered as he moved back and his head bowed as he buttoned his trousers, raising remorseful eyes to look at her. "We shouldn't…" He shook his head. "I was too overwhelmed to stop."

She was as aware of that as he as she picked up her undergarment. "I've heard a woman can't get pregnant the first time," she said, hoping to lessen his obvious remorse because she felt none, except for his sake. To bear his child, whatever happened, no longer seemed a fate to be avoided.

"I fear that's an old wives' tale," he said as he tucked in his shirt.

"Sometimes those old wives were right, weren't they?"

"Perhaps. Let us hope so. But now I have to go. The groom will be looking for me."

"Justinian, I meant what I said," she replied, wanting him to know how she felt, needing him to, whatever happened. "I'll wait for you, wherever you go and however long it may be."

He simply nodded once and left her.

Chapter Nineteen

The loss was a severe one, and may set back the study of arachnology for years to come.
　　　　　　　　　　　　—The *Bath Crier*

"Ah, Bromwell, here you are at last!" his father cried from an upper window of The King's Arms when his son rode into the yard beneath the high arched gate. "Hurry! The banker has been waiting for over an hour."

Bromwell did as his father bid and soon entered a wainscoted, comfortably appointed upper room where the remains of a large luncheon sat upon the table. A man who looked every inch the prosperous, if somewhat unfashionably attired, middle-aged man of finance and who'd been seated by the fireplace, rose when Bromwell entered. His father, meanwhile, assumed his usual commanding pose by the fireplace, one arm draped over the mantel.

"This is Mr. Denby, my banker," the earl announced.

"I'm honored to meet you, my lord," Mr. Denby said, bowing. "Your book was wonderful, quite wonderful!"

"Thank you."

"Sit down, Mr. Denby, and you, too, Justinian," the earl commanded.

Bromwell obeyed, and when he did, he saw a copy of the *Bath Crier* near the bucket of coals on the tiled hearth, obviously intended to be used to help light the fire. It was open to the society column.

Then it was as if the bottom had fallen out of Bromwell's chair, for there, in the bottom paragraph, he read, *"Lately returned to London and reputed to be coming soon to our fair city, the Duke of Wymerton and his family. His musical daughters are sure to be a welcome addition to social gatherings in the weeks to come."*

Had his father seen that?

He couldn't have, or he surely would have said something at once, Bromwell realized with relief. He immediately and surreptitiously shoved the paper beneath the bucket with his foot. His father would never stoop to lighting a fire, so as long as the paper was beneath the bucket, he wouldn't see it…although his father was going to have to learn the truth about Nell soon. After all, she was going to be his daughter-in-law.

Of course he must and would marry her now. He had asked her to wait and she had agreed. How could he expect her to do that unless they wed? And she must have the protection of his name and rank if she got with child. He would never leave her here to bear his child out of wedlock.

And yet leave her in England he must. He couldn't take her with him, no matter how much he loved her. A voyage such as he planned might be the death of her, and he would die himself before he would put her in such danger.

"Well, Denby, give my son the documents," his father impatiently ordered.

The earl gestured at the table beside the hearth. In addition to several papers of legal size, there was a jar of ink, a quill pen, and some sand for blotting. Clearly his father had been signing papers of some sort, or preparing to.

"If you will be so good as to sign here, my lord," Mr. Denby said, presenting Bromwell with a raft of papers and pointing to the bottommost line, beside the current date.

"What is this?" Bromwell asked, flipping the pages held together with ribbon.

"Your father is giving you ten thousand pounds for your expedition, on the understanding that you will avail yourself of certain expertise I possess. I deal with many merchants who ship goods all over the world."

Bromwell couldn't quite believe what he was hearing. He turned his questioning gaze to his father. "You're giving me ten thousand pounds for my expedition? And all I have to do is avail myself of your banker's experience?"

"I'd rather be spending it purchasing a London establishment for you and a wife," his father growled, "but since you seem resolved to sail off again, you might as well go as soon as possible, so you'll be back all the quicker."

Bromwell put down the papers and faced his father. "Thank you," he said, overwhelmed and grateful—but not as happy as he thought he'd be.

As he would have been before he met Nell.

"However, no matter what reason you give for your generosity," he continued, determined to remind himself of the reason he had to leave her, "you aren't just helping me, you're contributing to the understanding of—"

"I'm upsetting your mother, that's what I'm doing," the earl declared, scowling. "She's going to faint when she hears what I've done."

"I'll try again to make her appreciate why I must go," Bromwell vowed, "and I'll send letters home whenever I can."

"Just come back safe and healthy," his father said gruffly. "And when you do, for God's sake, get married and make us grandparents."

"I will," Bromwell promised with every intention of fulfilling that vow. "Thank you."

Even as he said it, the vocal expression of his gratitude seemed far too cold and formal, so Bromwell did something he'd never done in his life.

He went to his father and embraced him.

Even more surprising, his father hugged him back.

After a moment, Bromwell pulled away and cleared the lump from his throat while, swiping at his eyes, his father strode to the window.

"I'd like to ask Mr. Denby to make an addition to the papers, if I may," Bromwell said.

His father, once more composed, turned to look at him.

"I want the funds to be a loan, not a gift, and one that I'll gladly repay." He addressed the banker. "Can we not set up a system whereby some of the royalties from my book can go to my father as repayment?"

Bromwell held up his hand when his father looked about to protest. "I insist, Father. And don't think it's going to be so very much. I daresay it won't even be enough to pay for the new fountain you want to put by the terrace."

He thought of something else Mr. Denby could do with another portion of the income from his royalties.

But that must wait until later, after he'd asked Nell to marry him.

And provided she said yes.

* * *

The next day, in her pelisse and with her shawl wrapped around her for extra warmth, Nell walked briskly along the fern-bordered path from the garden to Justinian's laboratory. Overhead, a wren flitted amid the branches of a lichen-coated ash surrounded by birch and alder trees. The day was cool, but no clouds threatened rain and the air was still, unlike her tumultuous mind. She wanted to be alone, away even from Sir Douglas Drury and his wife.

It was not that they were unpleasant, and it had been tempting to ask all sorts of questions about Justinian, but she found their mutual happiness and obvious love difficult to endure. It was too much a reminder of what she couldn't have with Justinian.

She wouldn't think about that, she told herself. She would think of something else. His father's summons, for instance. Justinian had clearly been taken aback by the earl's request for consultation.

She still couldn't understand how his father could have had so little regard for his son's intelligence in the past. On the other hand, she had never known Justinian as a child, and it might be difficult for some parents to see their child as an adult.

Her parents had only ever known her as a child. What would they think of the woman she'd become? What would they say if they knew she'd been so intimate with a man who was not, and never would be, her husband?

She'd accepted that as part of the price for being with him, and while she'd been thrilled he'd asked her to wait for him and she had every intention of doing so, there had been no talk of marriage.

They would be apart for so long, and there would be

many days she would never know how he was, or if he was well, or if he was even still alive. More and more she was sympathizing with the countess, and more and more she was tempted to beg him to stay.

"Well, well, well, who have we here?"

Nell's breath froze in her lungs as she spun around, to see Lord Sturmpole standing on the path.

How had he come there? Why had she not heard or seen…?

"You don't look happy to see me, my dear."

"I'm not," she retorted, backing away toward the laboratory. "What do you want?"

"Why, you, of course. It wasn't very sporting of you to run away like that."

"Sporting? You attacked me and then locked me in a room."

"Attacked? Ye gods, that's a bit strong for the demonstration of my affections."

She desperately wondered where Billings and Brutus were, and if they were within call. The gardeners wouldn't be so very far away, either. "If you don't leave, I'll scream!"

"I don't think so, not unless you wish to appear before the magistrate in Bath. There is the matter of the money and clothes you stole, not to mention impersonating Lady Eleanor Springford."

Of course if he knew where she was, he must have learned who she was pretending to be.

"So unless you wish to be arrested, you will do exactly as I say."

"How did you find me?"

"I was approaching the house on horseback to see if my suspicions were correct when I saw you cross the garden and come this way. You certainly didn't waste any time enticing another man after you left me, did you?"

His lips curved up in that familiar, terrible leer. "You can stop staring at me like that, milady. I wouldn't dream of preventing you from playing whatever game it is you're playing with that fool of an earl and his no doubt equally foolish son."

"Then what *do* you want?"

"What you wouldn't give me before, that's all. Just once, and I'll be satisfied, and we can call what you took payment for services rendered."

"That's...?" She couldn't call it *all;* to let him do what he would with her was very far from nothing.

His thick lips curved up. "Yes, my dear, that's all. Just once, and then I'll be on my way back to Staynesborough."

"Why?" she cried. "Why do you want me? What am I to you?"

"You're the little whore who dared to say no—to *me!*"

"But there are other women!"

"You underestimate your appeal."

"Or is it because I wounded your pride? I got away, so your arrogant conceit demands you come after me."

"Who do you think you are, to refuse me?" he retorted. "You are nothing—little better than a servant!"

Yet she was enough for Lord Bromwell to love, and that gave her confidence and the determination to stop Sturmpole from ever attacking another woman in his employ.

"Have me arrested if you will, but if you do, I shall charge you with attempted rape and assault."

His eyes flared with anger even as he laughed with scorn. "Who do you think the authorities will believe?"

She put on a smile as false as his laugh. "Me, because

I shall have Sir Douglas Drury as my advocate, and he never loses."

To her surprise and growing dread, Sturmpole didn't look impressed. "You speak as if I would have the case tried in London. It would, of course, be heard in Staynesborough, and there I *own* the magistrate."

It was possible that he did, at least in a sense.

Her throat dry, Nell could think of only one thing to do—she had to get help. Find Billings or Brutus, or run back to Granshire Hall.

Shouting for the gamekeeper and his dog, she broke into a run, heading for the garden.

But Sturmpole had anticipated her flight and he caught the back of her pelisse, then jerked her back to him.

"I don't think so," he growled as he roughly grabbed her arms and spun her around to face him, his breath reeking of stale wine. "One way or another, I'll have you. I didn't come all the way from Staynesborough for nothing."

"You did, you disgusting degenerate!" Nell cried, hitting him.

Holding her tight, he started dragging her toward the laboratory. "No woman says no to me. No woman refuses and robs *me!*"

"Billings! Brutus!" she shouted as she dug in her heels.

His face contorted with rage, Sturmpole struck her hard across the mouth, knocking her to the ground. Regardless of the pain, she scrambled to her feet, trying to run, but the ground was damp and muddy and she slipped.

"Shut your mouth!" Sturmpole ordered as he pulled her to her feet. "If you're calling the gamekeeper, he's on the far side of the estate. I saw him."

"You didn't—you're lying!" Nell retorted, hoping she

was right, her cut lip throbbing as blood trickled down her chin and onto her torn and muddy pelisse. "Lord Bromwell will kill you if you hurt me!"

"When he finds out the trick you've played, he'll be calling for your head," Sturmpole charged as he shoved open the door of the laboratory with his shoulder.

She grabbed the door frame with both hands. He pulled hard, forcing her to let go. Holding her with one hand, he raised the other to strike—then stopped and stared as he caught sight of the jars upon the shelves.

For that brief instant, his hold relaxed. She pulled away and grabbed one of the heavy glass jars. He realized what she was going to do and knocked it from her hand. The jar shattered on the floor, spilling its contents.

Nell tried to rush past him to the door, but Sturmpole grabbed her shoulders and threw her toward the sofa. She slipped on the wet floor and fell hard on her knees. Ignoring the pain and broken glass, she scrambled to her feet, aiming for the table and the candleholder there.

Again he saw what she intended and stepped in front of her to block her.

She moved sideways and grabbed another jar. She threw it at him, hitting him on the shoulder. She grasped another and threw it, too, narrowly missing him but making him duck before it, too, shattered. Another hit the side of his face before breaking on the floor.

The air reeked of alcohol, her eyes watered and her lip still bled; nevertheless, Nell kept throwing jars of preserved spiders, aiming for Sturmpole's head or chest, making him keep his distance as she worked her way back toward the hearth and the cupboard where Justinian kept the cutlery, including all the knives.

Chapter Twenty

My dear Buggy, what are you trying to do? Give your old friends attacks of apoplexy? Drive us to early graves? Is it not enough that we have to live in fear you'll be bitten by some exotic insect and die in fearful agonies, or that you'll be the main item on a cannibal's menu, that you must put yourself in harm's way in England, too?

—from a letter to Lord Bromwell, written by the
Honorable Brixton Smythe-Medway

It was breaking glass, Bromwell realized as he broke into a run along the wooded path. Breaking glass in the woods, where his lab was, and his spiders.

And Nell? God help him, was Nell there, too?

She hadn't been in the garden when he'd returned with the news of his father's unexpected generosity; he'd sought her out at once, while his father went to speak to his mother, as they'd decided in the carriage on their return from Bath. When he'd asked Fallingbrook where he could find Lady Eleanor, he'd said she'd gone out for a walk.

His heartbeat quickening at the louder and undeniable sounds of a struggle, Bromwell rushed into the building. He nearly slipped on the floor slick with alcohol and crushed specimens, and crunching with broken glass. A man he'd never seen before stood in front of Nell, who was by the hearth. Her lip was cut and bleeding, her gown torn and splattered with mud, and she held an upraised knife to protect herself from that lout who was obviously attacking her.

With a roar of pure animal rage, he launched himself at the attacker and tackled him to the ground, regardless of the broken glass. Straddling the man who did his best to buck him off, Bromwell got his hands around the brigand's throat and squeezed.

He was no chivalrous gentleman now. He was a primitive warrior prepared to kill to protect the woman he loved.

"Stop, stop!" Nell cried. "You'll kill him!"

The man's face was purple, his eyes bulging, as Nell's shouts brought Bromwell back to civilization—but only just. Spotting something lying on the ground amidst the ruin of his collection, he let go of the ruffian's throat with one hand and reached for it.

"This is a blow dart coated in the venom of a *Phoneutria nigriventer,* the most lethal spider yet discovered," he said, his voice hoarse with his barely suppressed rage. "I have only to break your skin with it to see you die in agony or, if you do not die, be painfully rendered impotent for life—a more fitting punishment, perhaps, for the likes of you."

Drawing in great rasping breaths, his eyes wide with terror, the man finally went still.

"Do you know who is this, Nell?" Bromwell demanded, glancing sharply at her.

Her face was palely aghast, the knife still clutched in her trembling hand. "Sturmpole," she breathlessly replied.

Bromwell moved the dart a little closer to Sturmpole's mottled skin.

"He came upon me in the woods," she continued. "He… he wanted me to…."

"I can guess what he wanted," Bromwell said, his voice slightly calmer, although he was even more tempted to put an end to this rogue's life. Or at least prick him with the dart so priapism would set in. "He's going to be arrested and charged with attempted murder."

"I wasn't trying to kill her!" Sturmpole protested, spittle on his lips.

"Whatever you were trying to do, you struck her and could have killed her. The evidence is there on her face. And there's the attempted rape at Staynesborough. You had better reconcile yourself to a long stay in a cold, damp prison, my lord."

Still holding the dart near Sturmpole's neck, Bromwell got up and pulled him to his feet. "Nell, perhaps you'd be so good as to tie his hands with that length of rope near the door. Be careful. The floor is slippery." He scowled at the nobleman, who kept his frightened, sidelong glance on the dart. "I'm going to charge you with destruction of property, too."

"I'm sorry about your specimens, Justinian," Nell said as she took hold of Sturmpole's hands to tie them. "I threw the jars at him to keep him away."

"Then the specimens are well lost," Bromwell replied, not regretting their destruction if it had helped her. "Nell, you hold the dart while I tie the knot. All those hours at sea have made me quite proficient in that art."

Nell did as he asked, gingerly taking hold of the weapon.

"It's not really poison," he said, his ire once more under control, and giving her the ghost of a smile when he saw her expression. "The only danger is its sharp point—which I would gladly have shoved into his neck," he finished truthfully, "if he'd succeeded in his disgusting quest."

Sturmpole emitted a moan, which Bromwell ignored as he started to frog march his prisoner outside. He halted when Drury appeared on the threshold.

The attorney couldn't have looked more surprised if he'd been told Nell was the Queen of England. "Good God, what's happened?"

"This oaf attacked Nell. I want him arrested and charged with attempted murder."

Drury's shock was swiftly mastered, replaced with his usual cool composure. "Of course."

Drury started to come inside, then realized what was on the floor. "Bring him here and I'll take him back to the hall." He turned to address Juliette, who had arrived behind him. "Juliette, would you help Miss Springley?"

"I'll do that," Bromwell said at once while wiping his hands on his trousers. Miraculously, he wasn't badly cut. "Juliette, perhaps you wouldn't mind going ahead and alerting the servants that we'll require assistance? And the apothecary should be sent for."

Juliette immediately hurried away, while Drury took charge of the damp, scowling Sturmpole, holding him firmly by the arm.

"Don't get any ideas about trying to get away, my lord," Drury said as he pulled him out the door. "My hands may not look strong, but I assure you, I am quite capable of incapacitating you and that prospect is far from disturbing."

When they were gone, Bromwell closed the door, went to Nell and took her in his arms.

"If you hadn't come…" she murmured, leaning against him.

He held her close, all too aware of what might have happened. "I'm so sorry I wasn't here sooner."

"You came before it was too late," she said, choking back her tears. "I was so afraid!"

"But not too frightened to defend yourself—and very well, too," he said, stroking her damp, matted hair, cherishing her, relieved beyond measure that she was safe. "You truly are the most remarkable woman."

Her body began to tremble, a natural reaction to the attack and the shock and the vital energy she'd summoned to fight Sturmpole off.

"We had best get you to the hall and see to that cut. Have you any others?"

"I don't think so…but Justinian, I've destroyed your collection!"

"Never mind that," he said, truly not caring as long as she was safe. "I'll get others. My father's agreed to fund the rest of my expedition—and I suspect his change of heart is due to a most remarkable young woman who championed me."

"Oh, Justinian!" she cried. "That's wonderful!"

And then she began to sob in earnest. Loving her, adoring her, cherishing her, he gathered her up in his arms to carry her to the hall, holding her close to his heart.

Where she belonged.

Where she would always belong.

Justinian carried Nell back to the hall and up to her bedroom, calling for the servants as he went and issuing orders like the aristocrat he was. She was too exhausted to protest, although he must be tired, and she didn't care what the servants thought. Dena came rushing up the stairs after them, all but ordering Justinian to let her take care of her.

Bromwell didn't stop until he set her gently on the bed. Ignoring the anxiously hovering Dena, he quickly looked at Nell's bruised, cut hands and even lifted her alcohol-scented, muddy skirts to look at her knees.

"I'll have to clean these abrasions later," he said, turning her hands over and kissing the back of them. "Fortunately, they aren't deep and there's no glass embedded that I can see. I'll use my magnifying glass to be certain, though."

"My lord, leave her to me," Dena said. "I'll look after her. She needs a bath and a hot cup of tea and some clean clothes. You can tend to her wounds later."

"I shall," he promised as he stepped back and Dena quickly ordered another maid waiting by the door to bring a bath and plenty of hot water.

"I'm going to make sure Sturmpole's under lock and key," he said, "then I'll return."

His pointed gaze silenced whatever protests Nell or Dena might have made.

When he was gone, Nell wrapped her arms around herself. He was going to leave her soon, for much longer. Now he would have even more reason to go, because she'd destroyed his collection.

"Let me help you out of those clothes," Dena said. "We'll get you washed and then you'll feel better."

Having no strength to refuse, Nell silently submitted until she was naked beneath a dressing gown and the bath was ready by the hearth. Another maid had carried in enough clean linen for the entire household, some of which now cushioned the tub, and Mrs. Fallingbrook herself had brought in two pitchers of water for rinsing her hair.

At Nell's request, only Dena still remained to help her.

"Thank you, Dena," she said wearily, more tired than she'd ever been in her life.

She let the robe fall and stepped gingerly into the bath. Her knees were bruised, and she smelled terrible, of alcohol and blood and sweat, so she was glad of the chance to get clean. With a sigh, she laid her head upon her knees.

How close she had come to what she'd prevented before! What might have happened if Justinian hadn't arrived when he did and her strength was failing?

"You may leave, Dena."

Nell's eyes flew open at the sound of Justinian's voice. He was standing by the door, looking marvellous and healthy, slightly damp hair brushing his shirt collar. Although she was happy to see him, she could unfortunately guess what Dena would make of this.

Yet she didn't ask him to go, or Dena to stay. Instead she watched as he closed the door behind the reluctantly departing maid and started toward the bath.

"Feeling better?" he asked.

"Now that my hero is here."

He stopped a few feet away. "You're going to give me an exaggerated sense of my own worth using such terms."

"Impossible," she replied.

He once again began to approach the tub.

"You might wish to reconsider," she warned, although her heartbeat quickened and that familiar yearning invaded her body. "I smell terrible."

"I'm quite used to the smell of that particular type of alcohol," he said. "It's like perfume to me."

Every ache caused by the attack began to diminish, while another sort grew. Well aware that he was watching her with the same intensity with which he studied his spiders, she reached for the lump of lavender-scented soap on the stool Dena had set nearby for that purpose, moving with slow deliberation. The warm water washed over her breasts and droplets fell from her outstretched arm. "I should wash my hair. Would you like to help?"

Justinian was immediately beside the tub, stripping off his jacket and rolling up his sleeves. "I hope your knees aren't too sore," he said as his gaze swept over her.

"Only a little," she said, looking up at him and smiling at the thought that if the tub were larger, he could join her.

He paused as he finished rolling up the second sleeve. "What are you thinking about with that devilishly sly look on your face?"

"That is for me to know, my lord, but I will say that it involves a tub. A larger one."

His eyes widened, making him look delightfully shy. "I see."

He knelt beside the tub. "Unfortunately, we shall have to make do with this," he said as he began to unpin her hair.

"Bend over, please," he said when he was done, reaching for the pitcher that was on the towel-covered floor beside the tub.

She did, gripping the sides of the tub, then gave a little yelp as cool water cascaded over her head.

"I'm sorry," he said as he began to soap her hair, massaging her scalp with his long slender fingers. "The other pitcher is likely to be just as cold."

"It's all right, as long as my hair gets clean," she said, leaning back with a sigh. She would put up with worse than that to have him wash her hair.

After what seemed a very little while, he picked up the other pitcher to rinse her hair. "Brace yourself," he warned before the cold water descended this time.

Spluttering and shivering, she put out her arm. "Towel, please."

He gave it to her, kissing her hand as he did. Smiling, she swiftly dried her face and rubbed her hair, then wrapped her head in the towel.

"You look nice in a turban," he remarked when she was finished. "But then, I'd think you looked nice in anything... and especially in nothing."

The water in the tub was much cooler; nevertheless, her body warmed. "Perhaps you should leave and let me finish my toilette in peace, before I do something that will really make the servants talk."

"That sounds promising," he remarked as he got to his feet and held open a large towel. "What did you have in mind?"

She gave him a wicked, wanton smile as she rose, naked as Venus, from the tub. "Come closer, my lord, and I'll show you."

"That cut on your lip might start bleeding again," he warned.

"I wasn't intending to use my mouth."

"My lord," Fallingbrook called from the other side of Nell's bedroom door sometime later, "supper will be served in half an hour."

"We'll be downstairs shortly," Bromwell answered as he

finished buttoning his trousers. He gave the blissfully sated Nell a rueful smile. "I wonder how he knew I was here?"

"A fortunate guess?" she suggested from where she lay naked beneath the rumpled sheets of the bed. What had started as one thing, intended only to satisfy him, had soon enough become another, although they were more careful than they'd been by the stables. "Or perhaps a logical conclusion."

Justinian pulled his shirt over his head. "I believe my feelings for you had not escaped the servants' notice prior to this, and I suppose Dena told him where I was."

Nell sat up and brushed her dishevelled hair from her face. "Dena once thought I was trying to seduce you into marriage. I hope she won't think she was right—although of course she's quite wrong."

He frowned as he walked over to her dressing table and ran her brush through his hair, and she instantly regretted mentioning marriage.

She got out of the bed and hurried to put on her chemise. "How soon before the magistrate's men can come from Bath, do you think?"

"They should be here before dark, but only just, even if they come at a gallop, and I'm sure Drury would make sure they did. They'll have to stay the night and keep Sturmpole under guard in the stable, then take him to Bath in the morning."

She went to the wardrobe and selected a gown, a simple one of light blue wool trimmed with brown piping. She stepped into it and pulled it up, then hurried to put her hair up in some semblance of a style. "Will you lace me, please?"

"Gladly, now and every chance I get," he replied,

coming behind her and doing as she asked, his deft fingers swiftly tying the knot.

She rose and turned toward him when he finished.

He reached out to take her hands gently in his. "Nell, you must know I love you," he said softly, the truth of that even more apparent in his eyes than in his voice and words. "So much so, I can scarcely believe it. For so long, and especially after my friends fell in love, I've feared something was missing in me, some capacity to feel deeply. That I was incapable of experiencing love and desire as they so obviously did.

"I told myself it was no great matter, because I had my work and that was more than enough to content me. Even so, I planned to marry someday. I believed I would simply select a woman whose temperament was the most compatible with mine, and one who wouldn't be jealous of my devotion to my work."

His grip tightened ever so slightly. "And then I met you, and discovered that it wasn't that something had been lacking within me. I simply hadn't met the right woman. Now I have, and I believe you love me, too, because I don't think you would ever have come to my bed otherwise."

"No, I would not," she whispered in confirmation.

He went down on one knee. "Then, Nell, would you do me the very great honor of marrying me?"

Chapter Twenty-One

There is much fluttering among the petticoats as the time draws near for the Earl of Granshire's hunt ball, especially as it has been confirmed by the earl that his son, the notable naturalist and author, will be attending.

—from the Social Circle column of the *Bath Crier*

A host of emotions ran through Nell at his softly, intently spoken request—joy, hope, fear, dismay, concern—while she gazed into his questioning face.

There was no doubt, no hesitation, in the eyes that regarded her so steadily. No worry, no concern, only love. Sincere, deep-seated love.

"I know this must come as a shock to you after all I've said about not marrying before I sail," he continued just as ardently and sincerely, "but seeing Sturmpole attacking you, I realized how very much I love you, need you and want you to be my wife. Nobody understands me, or loves me, the way you do. If we hadn't shared the same coach, if it hadn't overturned, I would still be thinking myself incapable of deep, devoted, passionate love. I would still be alone, and lonely."

Oh, how his words stabbed at her and made her long to ignore the world and all its restraints and conventions! If she could think only of herself, if she didn't truly love him, she might have been able to.

Since she did love him, she must think of him, and his future without her, because with her, he would suffer. Not at first, perhaps. But later. And she would not have him resent her for anything.

Not even his hand in marriage.

So she pulled her hands free and did what had to be done, even if it broke both their hearts. "No, Justinian, I won't marry you."

The dismay and disappointment in his eyes nearly weakened her resolve, but as he could be strong for what he believed necessary, so could she.

"I don't doubt that you love me as much as I love you," she said, "but I'm still the penniless daughter of a convicted felon. Such a marriage will make you a pariah to your friends and family, as well as other important, influential people who can aid you in your work."

"If it does, so be it," he returned, desperation furrowing his brow. "I would rather have you. Look at Drury, who married a seamstress—and a French one, at that. His legal career hasn't suffered. Surely to God I can marry—"

"Whoever you like, because you are famous, too? I'd like to think so. I'd like to believe that we may do as we wish with no thought to how it will change our lives, save for the better.

"But we both know that's not so. We aren't marooned on a deserted island, just the two of us.

"There is your work to consider—and we must—as well as your family. We can't ignore them, or pretend they don't exist.

"And there is something else to take into account. You're going to be gone for a long time, Justinian, and as strong as our love is now, I fear it will weaken with time and distance. Or worst of all, that you won't come back at all."

She put her fingertips on his lips to silence his protests. "I don't think it would be wise to bind ourselves in a marriage when you are leaving soon, and for so long."

"What if you're with child?" he protested just as fervently as he'd proposed. "We weren't careful before I went to Bath."

"I would not have you bound in a marriage you no longer wanted even under those circumstances. If that happens, your friends will help me, will they not?"

He nodded mutely, but his eyes were so full of anguish she couldn't look him in the face.

"My lord!" Fallingbrook called out from behind the door again. "Will you please come down? The countess is getting upset."

Still without speaking, his expression cold as stone, immutable as a rock, Justinian held out his arm to escort her from the room. "Since there is no more to be said, we had better go."

As she took his arm, she swallowed hard and choked back her tears, although she really wanted to throw herself on the bed and cry until she could cry no more.

Then run away and never look back.

"Sturmpole! By God, I went to school with him!" the earl was all but shouting as Bromwell and Nell reached the threshold of the drawing room. "He was a fine fellow, so whoever would have guessed...?"

Standing beside the hearth, arms crossed over his chest puffed out like an enraged rooster, Lord Granshire fell silent when he saw Nell and his son. Juliette sat on the Grecian couch beside the countess, and Drury was by the windows, his ruined hands clasped behind his back.

The countess immediately got to her feet. "What is it? What's wrong?" she demanded, glancing uneasily from her son to Nell.

In that instant, in that precise moment, as his mother looked at him with worry, as Nell's grip tightened on his forearm, Bromwell knew what he must do. And in that instant, that precise moment, he was equally certain it was the right, best, only thing to do.

"Be happy, Mother," he said, smiling at her and everyone else gathered there. "I'm not going on another expedition."

"What?" Nell cried, her hand dropping as she turned to stare at him.

"What?" his father roared as if Bromwell had lost his mind.

"What?" his mother gasped, sitting heavily.

"Why?" and *"Pourquoi?"* demanded Drury and Juliette in unison.

Bromwell ignored them, speaking only to Nell as if they were alone, because right then, they might as well have been on that deserted island.

Regarding her with all the love he felt, sure of his decision as he'd never been so sure of anything in his life, not even his desire to study spiders, he said, "I've been a stubborn, selfish fool. If I must choose between my expedition and you, I gladly, happily choose you. And you mustn't fear that I'll come to resent you or regret my choice. How can I regret anything that will make me so happy and so blessed?"

Still doubtful, still unsure, Nell didn't reply as her anxious gaze searched his face.

"I mean it, Nell," he assured her. "I think marriage—provided it's to you—will be even more interesting than any expedition could ever be."

"Not to mention vastly more entertaining and comfortable," Drury said from the sofa, where he now stood behind Juliette.

"But your studies, your plans, the spiders!" Nell protested in astonished, uncertain gasps, as if she still couldn't believe he meant what he said.

"As my mother has noted on more than one occasion, there are plenty of spiders in Britain. I shall devote myself to studying the local arachnids. After all, some things are common to all the species, such as the navigation and construction of their webs and—"

"By God, *now* you see the light?" his father demanded abruptly and loudly, coming out of his shocked stupor. "After refusing to listen to sense all these years?"

"Oh, be quiet, Frederic!" the countess ordered, leaping to her feet and more animated than Bromwell had seen in years. "Miss Springley has not yet accepted his proposal."

"Miss Springley?" the earl cried. "Who the devil is Miss Springley?"

"I am," Nell said quietly. "I'm not Lady Eleanor Springford, but Eleanor Springley, the impoverished daughter of

Edward Springley, who's been convicted of theft and transported to Botany Bay."

"Oh…my…God!" the earl choked, reaching for the mantel to steady himself. "Is that *true?*"

"Yes, but I don't care," Bromwell firmly replied.

"Whereas I do," Nell said, louder and with more confidence, her eyes shining not with unshed tears, but fierce determination. "I'm well aware of what marriage to a woman like me will cost your son, so no, Justinian, I still won't marry you and be the ruin of your career."

"What do you mean, *ruin?*" Juliette exclaimed with disbelief. "Buggy is famous for his work, and justly so—work he can continue to do. And he will always be received by the people who matter. As for those small-minded people who will not because of the woman he loves, he does not need their friendship or support."

"She's right," Drury said calmly. "In fact, those of a romantic bent will likely be even more inclined to buy your books, wondering if they'll be able to see hints of the sentimental lover in the naturalist."

"You're being ridiculous," Bromwell said, too upset by Nell's continuing refusal to be amused.

He turned to Nell and grasped her cold hands. "Except for the part about not being received by fools and idiots. I don't care about that."

"Do you mean to say," his father said as if the point was finally penetrating his gray matter, "that this young woman is not the daughter of the Duke of Wymerton?"

"No, she isn't," his wife affirmed, "but if she makes Justinian happy—"

"And she's got no dowry or property at all, nor likely to?"

"Father, I don't care if she's poor," Bromwell said. He

looked down at Nell, his eyes pleading. "Please, Nell, won't you accept me?"

She shook her head, her eyes bright with unshed tears. "To give up your expedition for me…it's too much, Justinian. I won't have that on my conscience."

Juliette sighed with exasperation. "Why must he give it up? Can he not take his wife on the expedition with him?"

Bromwell shook his head. "I wouldn't subject my wife to the deprivations and dangers."

Drury tilted his head to one side and gave Bromwell his Death Stare. "Do you know, Buggy, there are times you sound remarkably like your father? How many times have you told me that he wouldn't see you as an adult with the capacity to decide your own fate? What are you doing but taking the decision to choose her own fate out of Nell's hands? Are you not treating *her* like a child rather than an adult?"

If someone had shot a cannon at Bromwell's head, it would hardly have been more disturbing. Because Drury was right. He had never seen his urge to protect Nell in that arrogant light.

A sudden vision, previously unimaginable, came to him—of having his work as well as Nell for his wife, of facing the future, whatever it held, with her by his side, to love, to cherish and to comfort all the days of his life.

If she would only say yes.

Nell felt poised on a precipice between hope and dismay, longing and fulfillment. Even if Justinian loved her enough to marry her regardless of what society might think, if she couldn't sail with him, she must hold firm and refuse to marry him in spite of the urgings of her heart. Too much could happen between the time he sailed and when he returned, and she would not have him bound to her under those conditions, no matter how much she loved him.

"The voyage will be dangerous and uncomfortable," he said slowly, regarding her steadily, "and the ship cramped and the food terrible and there is always the threat of illness, but if you would like to marry me and come with me under those circumstances…?"

If she would like it? "Are you sure, Justinian?"

The look in his eyes alone would have been enough, and then he said, with all the conviction of complete truth, "Yes."

"Yes!" she cried, throwing herself into his arms, laughing and crying at the same time, overwhelmed with joy and relief and hope and happiness. "Yes, I'll marry you!"

He drew back and regarded her with his most studious expression. "You truly mean that? You will accept me?"

As if she was the one making concessions! "If you'll really marry me in spite of my father's crime and my lack of fortune and rank."

His answer was a passionate kiss, until his father drew everyone's attention away from the young and happy couple.

"Do you expect me to contribute the necessary funds to your expedition if you marry this…this *woman?*"

Bromwell regarded his father with calm acceptance. He should have realized his father's support would be conditional, capricious and liable to be withdrawn if he was displeased.

However, he no longer cared, because Nell had agreed to marry him.

"If that's how you choose to respond to my happiness, so be it," he said evenly, his arms still around her. "I shall find other sponsors, as I did before. However, since Nell's agreed to be my wife, nothing you or anyone else can say will deter me from marrying her."

The countess rose, hands clasped, her expression desperate, and Bromwell feared he was about to hear more pleas to stay in England, especially if he had a wife.

"Frederic, you *must* provide the funds for his expedition, and especially whatever money they require to make their accommodation aboard ship more comfortable."

Bromwell and everyone else in the room regarded her with incredulity, not just for what she said, but because of the firm tone with which she said it.

Lady Granshire went to her son and, taking his hand in hers, looked at him with tears running down her cheeks. "Naturally I would prefer that you stay in England, but it is finally clear to me how much this voyage means to you, and what it would mean if you didn't sail."

Taking one of Nell's hands, too, she addressed her with a smile, although her lips trembled and her tears still flowed. "I'll be a little less worried, though, knowing he has someone who loves him to look after him."

She drew in a ragged breath, then spoke to her son again with that unexpected resolve. "You must promise me, though, Justinian, that you'll be even more careful, because you'll be responsible for your wife as well as yourself."

"You have my word that I'll protect Nell with my life," he vowed.

"And I shall do the same for him," Nell added, equally sincere.

The countess embraced her, and Bromwell's heart swelled not just with joy because he was going to get to spend the rest of his life married to Nell, but because his mother had come 'round—if not completely, at least to acceptance.

"My dear, surely you cannot countenance such a union!" her husband protested. "She is nothing, a nobody—worse than nobody, if her father—"

The countess whirled around to face her husband. "She is the woman your son loves—the son you've belittled and derided even after his great success."

She walked up to her husband and poked him in the chest as she spoke. "You care more about your precious estate, this house and your blasted garden than you ever have for us. I've put up with that, and you, for thirty years for the sake of our marriage and our son, because I was afraid of gossip and scandal. But no more, Frederic. If you don't accept this marriage, I shall leave you and reveal certain details of your life that will cause a scandal such as you have never even imagined!"

The earl blanched, but haughtily demanded, "What *details?*"

"There are certain books—illegal books—you keep hidden in the library, books of such a lewd nature, you should be ashamed to even touch them!"

Bromwell glanced at Nell, who raised a brow, wondering if this was the reading material he'd been referring to that wasn't of a classical or scientific nature. His answering rueful grin told her that it was.

"You…you…know about…?" the earl spluttered, his face as red as his scarlet waistcoat.

"I believe, my love, that we should retire from this family gathering and await the butler's summons to supper elsewhere," Drury said, taking his wife's hand and leading her, somewhat unwillingly, from the room.

"What sort of books are they talking about?" Juliette whispered as she gained the hall.

"I'll explain when we're alone," Drury murmured as he closed the door behind them.

Chapter Twenty-Two

It has recently been brought to our notice that a certain Lord from the north has been arraigned on a charge of assault, as well as other crimes of such a nature that we shall refrain from disclosing them in their entirety lest we upset our female readers.

—The *Bath Crier*

By the time the door had closed, the earl had managed to recover some of his composure. "My dear wife, no doubt you're overwrought, a condition not unexpected given the startling and shocking events of the day. I'm sure upon further reflection, you'll see that I'm quite right to oppose a marriage that can only humiliate our son and cause him difficulties in the future."

"You certainly ought to be an expert on humiliating our son," his wife retorted. "You've been doing it for years, and heaven only knows how he might have turned out if not for *my* love and comfort."

"For which I'm exceedingly grateful," Bromwell interjected, hoping to end this distressing confrontation. "And if you truly wish to leave Father, Mother, I won't question your decision."

How could he, when her unhappiness, anger and resentment must have been building for years? "However, with regard to his reaction to my marriage and the withdrawal of his financial support, you may set yourself at ease. Nothing he says or does will deter me from marrying Nell, and I'm sure we'll be able to sail with or without his help."

In spite of that determination, he regarded his father with genuine, heartfelt sorrow. "I wish it could be otherwise, Father. I was happy and proud when you offered me the money without conditions, and enjoyed our journey back to Granshire when we talked like friends. I would that we could continue in such a way. But I won't give up Nell because of your fears of what society will say, any more than I gave up going on my first expedition because you thought it the height of lunacy.

"The choice is yours, Father. Accept my wife or not as you will, but we _shall_ marry and we _will_ sail."

Whatever Bromwell had expected his father to do, it wasn't to walk slowly up to his wife and look at her with genuine distress. "You would really do that, Susanna? You would really leave me?"

"I would," she said, her voice wavering a little. "You should be proud of our son and happy that he's found a woman who loves him and isn't after his money, or his title. How many young women do we know would refuse him because she thought it was best for _him?_"

The earl looked from his wife to his son and the woman standing anxiously beside him as if he'd never really seen Nell before. "I do want you to be happy, Justinian."

He turned back to his wife. "I didn't realize how much

I was distressing you, Susanna. I will accept Justinian's choice, and if he wants to sail off to some godforsaken…" He reined in his temper. "Whatever he wants to do, he'll have my full support, both in good wishes and funds."

"I'll stay. Oh, Frederic, I'll stay!" the countess cried, pulling him into her arms. "Although you must also get rid of those books."

"Anything for you, my dear," he replied, kissing her fervently.

Nell grabbed Bromwell's arm and pulled him toward the door. "I think we should leave them alone for a little while."

Fallingbrook, as stunned as Bromwell, was standing in the doorway. "Dinner is served," he whispered as Nell closed the door behind them.

"Tell the cook dinner will have to be delayed a little while," Nell told him. "You'll find us in the garden."

"Congratulate me, Fallingbrook!" Justinian said merrily. "I'm getting married."

"Are you indeed, my lord?" the butler murmured absently, his gaze still on the closed door of the drawing room. "When might we meet the fortunate bride?"

The night of the Earl of Granshire's hunt ball, Granshire Hall was ablaze with light from nearly a thousand candles. Music from the orchestra drifted from the ballroom into the rest of the house, and outside, several carriages lined the drive. Coachmen, footmen and linkboys clustered in small groups, occasionally quaffing mugs of mulled wine and ale brought to them from the kitchen.

Inside the manor, finely dressed men and women milled about, awaiting the start of the dancing. Torches had also been lit in the garden, and the night was warm enough that a few couples drifted to the terrace for a breath of fresh air or more intimate conversation.

Inside, near one of the French doors leading to the terrace, a group of three couples watched as the earl, his wife, his son and his son's fiancée greeted the arriving guests.

Lady Francesca Smythe-Medway wore an evening gown of pale pink taffeta, the bodice trimmed with lace as was the hem, and she had diamonds in her ears and around her throat. Standing beside Fanny and dressed in deep blue satin with tight sleeves and sapphire earrings set in silver was Diana the wife of Viscount Adderley. Next to her was Juliette, in a fashionable concoction of Nile green that she had made herself, the bodice embroidered with golden leaves. Their husbands were much more plainly attired in black formal evening dress, but even so, they were the object of many admiring glances from other women, as their wives were the object of many men's.

All of whom they ignored.

The Honorable Brixton Smythe-Medway, whose straw-colored hair defied the efforts of comb, brush and valet to lie flat, declared, "I've never seen Buggy looking so…so…"

His brow furrowed, Brix turned to his wife with a pleading look. "What's the word I'm looking for?"

"Happy?" Fanny proposed.

"Heroic?" Diana supplied, her eyes twinkling.

"Triumphant?" suggested Edmond, Viscount Adderley.

"Successful in life and in love," Drury said in a tone that implied the matter was settled.

"You're all right," Brix replied with a grin. "Good ol' Buggy. I always knew he'd find the right woman someday. I just never expected it would be in a mail coach."

"I daresay neither did he," Edmond said. "Which goes

to show we never know where we'll be when Cupid aims his arrow."

"Don't go all poetic on us," Brix warned. "I'm glad the earl has seen the light at last about Bromwell's abilities, and his mother's looking very pleased."

"Who could not be pleased with Nell?" Juliette asked. "She's a lovely girl. And see how she looks at Buggy! *That* is love."

"See how every other young woman here is looking at him," Brix said, waggling his brows. "Egad, he was popular before but he looks a very Adonis now. It's a good thing Miss Springley snatched him up when she had the chance."

His wife swatted Brix lightly with her fan. "I wouldn't be speaking of missed opportunities, if I were you," she warned.

Brix rubbed his arm as if she'd hurt him and put on an aggrieved face. "Yes, but I made no claim to being observant. How could I, when I couldn't see the rose right under my nose?"

His wife smiled and stroked his arm with her fan.

"My dears, I tell you, it's really true," a woman noted in an excited whisper as a gaggle of women passed by, her voice audible as the orchestra took a short break to get out new music. "Not of the first rank, or indeed, any rank at all. And her father—"

As one, Bromwell's friends turned to look at the speaker with varying degrees of scorn. The woman flushed and fell silent, then moved swiftly away, trailed by her equally silent companions.

"So it begins," Edmond noted with a sigh.

They all looked serious for a moment, for each had been the subject of rumor, gossip and speculation.

"I find it fascinating that the faces of gossips possess

the same bovine aspect," Brix said, doing a very passable imitation of Buggy at his most studious. "It is easy, if one has a creative cast of mind, to imagine them as cows standing in a field chewing their cud."

The tension eased, and they shared a smile.

"Where's Charlie? I thought he'd be here," Drury said, surveying the ballroom. "Buggy's anxious to talk to him about the ship's provisions."

"There he is now, waiting at the end of the receiving line like a dutiful officer," Edmond said, nodding at the tall, commanding figure in the line moving slowly toward the earl and his family. "Even without his uniform, he's every inch the officer, isn't he?"

"I'll sleep better knowing he's in command of Buggy's ship," Fanny said, earning nods of agreement from her companions.

"He's not the only other late arrival," Diana noted as a beautiful young woman dressed in the height of fashion in a gown of jonquil silk with ruffles from hem to knee, lace around the bodice and a necklace of garnets, appeared at the entrance to the ballroom. Pearls and more garnets were in her ornately dressed hair. The older gentleman with her, however, was dressed in what would have been appropriate for a ball fifty years ago. "Who is that?"

"The Duke of Wymerton and Lady Eleanor Springford!" Fallingbrook announced.

Nell started and Bromwell stared, while his mother smiled and his father cleared his throat.

"Gad, Snouty, how are you? It's been years!" the earl said as he moved toward the older man.

Meanwhile, Lady Eleanor let go of her father's arm

and gracefully approached the countess, who was looking better rested than she had for many months since Bromwell had found out exactly what was in her medicine, which was mostly comprised of caffeine, and put a stop to it.

"I was delighted to receive your invitation," Lady Eleanor said in a musical voice and with a smile which revealed that even her teeth were lovely. "As well as your letter."

Nell stared at the countess, and so did her son. "Letter?" Bromwell murmured.

"Yes," Lady Eleanor said, turning to him. "I understand I've been of great assistance to you both, although I didn't know it."

Nell wondered if she should say something—anything— or just be quiet and let Bromwell, who looked equally lost, speak.

Lady Eleanor solved her problem for her. "I'm not at all upset that you felt it necessary to use my name. Indeed, when the countess told me of your predicament, I was quite happy to oblige."

A hint of merriment sparkled in her bright blue eyes as she ran a swift gaze over Bromwell, then addressed Nell. "I can't say I blame you a bit for wanting to accept his invitation, even if it required pretending to be someone else."

By now, Bromwell's face was scarlet, while Nell was more sorry than ever she'd used Lady Eleanor's name.

The orchestra's leader looked at the earl, who nodded at Bromwell. "It's time."

"I say, Charlie!" Bromwell called to a tall young man with a regal bearing who was standing near the earl, who was still talking to the duke while his wife looked on.

The younger man skirted the older three and hurried to join them. "Aye aye, sir!" he said, saluting as he came to a halt.

"Lady Eleanor, Miss Springley, this is Charles Grendon, late of His Majesty's Navy and my very good friend. He's going to captain our ship when we go on our expedition.

"Charlie, would you be so good as to engage Lady Eleanor for the first dance? He's a most accomplished dancer," he assured her.

"I'd be delighted," Grendon replied with a polite bow.

As grim as if he were about to be executed, Bromwell took Nell's arm. "I wish we didn't have the honor of leading the first dance," he said as they started forward.

"Smile, my lord," she whispered. "It's easier than the *upa upa*."

"I thought I was going to swoon when Lady Eleanor was announced!" Nell said later that evening as she and Justinian strolled on the terrace.

"I was shocked myself," he replied. "To think my mother had written to her and told her everything—and she wasn't angry or upset. Indeed, she's a very agreeable young lady. I note Charlie seems quite taken with her."

"She's very beautiful."

Bromwell laughed softly. "She's pretty, I suppose, and well dressed in a gown that fits, but…" He took her hands and held them out in front of him so he could survey her in the lovely gown of pale blue silk she wore. "Her beauty is nothing compared to yours."

Still holding his hands, Nell leaned back against the balustrade. "I fear your mother's a very sly woman in some ways."

"I suppose she's had to be sometimes, to get around my father. I must say, she seems quite a different woman now that I'm getting married."

"If we were staying in England, she'd be even happier."

"No doubt, but she'll have plenty of time to spend with us when we return."

"And our children, if we are so blessed," Nell said softly, turning so that her back was to him. "Show me again how the women of Tahiti give birth, without the crouching, of course, or you'll crease your breeches."

"We can't have that," he said with a low chuckle as he came close behind and put his arms around her.

With a sigh, she relaxed against him as he ran his hands down her stomach.

"Are you sure about the expedition? What if you get with child on the voyage?"

She turned in his arms so that she was facing him. "There'll be a physician on the ship, won't there?"

"Yes. Dr. Reynolds is a very competent, open-minded fellow who wishes to learn about native medicines."

"And if we're in the islands, there are midwives, are there not?"

"Yes."

"Then since you will be with me, too, what need have I to fear? I will be in the best possible hands, and so will any children we may have."

"You are the most amazing woman I've ever laid eyes on. Such a pity you don't appreciate spiders."

"I don't hate them anymore," she protested. "I'm even beginning to like them."

Bromwell smiled broadly. "I knew you were different from the moment you landed in my lap."

"I knew you were different the moment you told me you'd put that spider in your hat." She caressed his cheek. "I also thought you were the most handsome man I'd ever seen."

In his evening dress, he looked as comely as any man in the ballroom, and given what else he had accomplished, he was superior to most. "I still find it hard to believe such a clever, famous, handsome man wants to marry me."

"Believe it, Nell," he whispered as he pulled her into his arms, "and believe that you are the one blessing me by accepting my hand, for that is the truth."

His lips met hers with the same gentle, wonderful tenderness of their first kiss, and then, as always, desire unfurled within her, fueling the undercurrent of passion between them.

She guided him back into the shadows and the vine-covered walls, out of sight, away from the illuminated windows and the people inside.

He laughed softly. "This is hardly the time or place for an intimate encounter."

"I only want to be alone with you for a few moments," she replied with bogus innocence. "Not so long we'll be missed."

"I may not be able to tear myself away."

"Oh, very well," she said with a disappointed sigh. "After all, we'll have the rest of our…"

He was staring at something over her shoulder and she twisted to see what it was. "What are you looking at?"

"There's an *Araneus diadematus* starting to build a web in the vines," he admitted sheepishly, nodding toward thin white filaments barely visible among the green leaves. "There's the bridge line, and the start of the spokes."

Smiling, happier than she'd ever been, looking forward to the future and the adventures yet to come, she slipped her arm through that of the famous Lord Bromwell and leaned her head on his broad shoulder. "Let's watch it together, shall we?"

Epilogue

The Explorer docked on Wednesday, August 5, the entire crew intact after a successful voyage. The Earl of Granshire has confirmed that his son, the famous naturalist, will be publishing a new book on the venture.
— Bath Crier

Plymouth, 1825

"Make way there! Demme, let me through! I want to see my grandson!" the Earl of Granshire cried as he pushed his way through the crowd of seaman, navvies, families and friends of arriving passengers at the Dover wharf.

His wife, holding a scented handkerchief to her nose to cover the odors of tar, hemp and sweating men, followed in his wake. Despite the crowd and the stench, however, she was no less excited than her husband.

Lord Granshire halted and pointed at the small boy in the bow of an approaching longboat. "There! There he is!"

Shouting hellos, the earl took off his hat and waved. "And there's Justinian!"

He turned to his wife, who was jumping up and down trying to see over his shoulder. "He looks very healthy and so does Nell and—good God! Is that a baby in her arms?"

With an excited cry, Lady Granshire shoved past him, nearly sending the earl over the edge of the wharf into the water below. "It *is* a baby! And look at little Douglas—how sturdy and brown he is!"

"Buggy!" the Honorable Brixton Smythe-Medway shouted from among the crowd a few feet closer to the end of the wharf. "Nell! Charlie!"

"Watch what you're about, Brix," Drury warned as he moved away from his friend and nearly collided with Edmond beside him. "Sorry, Edmond, but our friend is a little overenthused."

Edmond gave Drury a sardonic smile. "Just imagine if our wives were here. It's a fortunate twist of fate that they're all expecting again. Otherwise we'd never have been able to convince them to wait for us at the earl's town house."

"It looks like Buggy hasn't been remiss in that aspect. Did *you* know they'd had another baby?"

Drury shook his head. "They must have wanted to surprise us."

"They've succeeded," Edmond replied.

The longboat reached the wharf and a general hubbub ensued. Charlie, sun-browned and showing some gray at the temples, was the first over the thwarts and onto the wharf. Buggy handed his son over to him, then turned to take the baby from Nell's arms while Charlie helped her onto the wharf. Once Nell was on the wooden platform, Buggy gave her the baby, then climbed out to stand beside them.

The countess got to them first and she threw her arms

around her son. "Oh, my boy! My blessed, blessed boy! You're home and you're never leaving again!"

"No, I'm not," he assured her before turning to another older man in the longboat, his face deeply tanned by the sun, his slender frame and gaunt face hinting at years of deprivation, as if returning from long and weary exile. The old man rarely took his gaze from Nell unless it was to look at her children. "This is Nell's father, Edward Springley."

"Delighted, I'm sure," the countess murmured, barely looking away from her son.

"Hello, young man," the earl said to the little boy standing with his arms crossed, surveying the chaos as if he found it fascinating until the earl interrupted his study. "Can you guess who I am?"

"My other grandfather?" the lad replied warily.

"Other grandfather?" the earl repeated.

"Yes, that's my Mama's papa there. He's been in Australia. It's a marvelous country. I'm going back when I'm older."

"I sincerely hope not," the earl muttered.

"You're also the Earl of Granshire and a very important man, Papa says," the little boy added, which brought a beaming smile back to the earl's face.

"As clever as his father, by God!" the earl proudly exclaimed to everyone within earshot.

"And a fine healthy child he is," Bromwell said as he managed to disengage himself from his mother.

"As is his sister," he finished with a nod and a smile at the baby cradled in Nell's arms.

"A granddaughter! Let me see her!" the countess cried.

Nell gently moved the blanket away from the slumbering infant's face and exchanged happy and proud smiles with her husband and father as the countess and his male friends clustered around.

"My God, she's a beauty!" Brix declared as he studied the slumbering infant with dark brown curling hair and plump cheeks. "I claim her for my Harry."

"If she's anything like her parents, I think my Brom might do well to consider her when the time comes," Drury mused aloud, "but don't any of you tell Juliette I said so."

Edmond leaned close. "Such a charmer will break a lot of hearts," he said gravely, "although being Buggy's daughter, she's bound to be a bluestocking. If so, she'll never do for my rascal D'Arcy, or his brother, either."

Nell laughed heartily. "She's only a baby! Let her grow up and she shall make her own choice—and it may be none of your sons."

"May I hold her?" the countess asked, reaching out eagerly.

"Of course," Nell said. "I haven't got my land legs yet."

"Papa says you have lots of horses," little Douglas said to the earl. "Can I ride one?"

"Certainly!" the earl replied. "And one of my best bitches just had a litter, so you shall have a puppy, too."

"Papa, did you hear!" Douglas cried with delight. "A *Canis lupus familiaris!* He's going to give me a *Canis lupus familiaris!*"

"Yes, Douglas, I hear you, and so can the whole wharf. Now, where's Charlie got to?" Bromwell asked, looking around. "He said something about not coming for dinner and I…oh, isn't that…? Egad, it is!"

They all stared at Charlie, who was over by a stack of barrels kissing Lady Eleanor Springford as passionately as any of them had ever kissed their wives, which was very passionately indeed.

"Yes, well, I suppose we can leave him here," Bromwell said, turning to lead the way from the wharf to the area of the docks where carriages could wait.

"You and the children shall come with us in the barouche," his father announced, taking his grandson by the hand.

He glanced at Nell's father and gave him a smile. "Mr. Springley, too, of course."

"As you wish. And you'll come to call tomorrow?" Bromwell asked his friends.

"On the contrary," Brix merrily replied. "We're following you, for our wives are already there, anxiously waiting and probably complaining about all our faults."

"The children are there, too," Edmond added, "the ones already born and the ones who will be within the next few months."

"Oh, how wonderful!" Nell exclaimed as she gripped her husband's arm to steady herself as she also took her father by the hand. "I have so much to ask them—and tell them, too. I'm thinking of writing a book about our voyage, but unlike Justinian's, mine will be a romantic novel."

"Excellent!" Edmond cried. "Diana will be pleased. She's been saying you should be a writer ever since your first letter arrived. She found it delightful."

Nell beamed with pleasure and Buggy's face shone with pride as they all followed the earl to the waiting carriages, until the countess came to an abrupt halt and turned to her son and his wife. "You haven't told us her name! What is my granddaughter's name?"

"We named her after the woman the goddess Minerva turned into a spider," Nell said.

As the younger men and Mr. Springley smiled, the earl and the countess looked baffled.

Viscount Bromwell, known as Buggy to his friends, grinned from ear to ear. "Her name is Arachne Juliette Diana Francesca."

"Well now," Sir Douglas Drury said gravely, "*that* is what I call a name."

"Here, here!" his friends agreed.

* * * * *

*Celebrate Harlequin's 60th anniversary
with Harlequin® Superromance®
and the DIAMOND LEGACY miniseries!*

*Follow the stories of four cousins as they come to terms
with the complications of love and what it means to be a
family. Discover with them the sixty-year-old secret that
rocks not one but two families in…
A DAUGHTER'S TRUST by Tara Taylor Quinn.*

*Available in September 2009
from Harlequin® Superromance®*

RICK'S APPOINTMENT with his attorney early Wednesday morning went only moderately better than his meeting with social services the day before. The prognosis wasn't great—but at least his attorney was going to file a motion for DNA testing. Just so Rick could petition to see the child…his sister's baby. The sister he didn't know he had until it was too late.

The rest of what his attorney said had been downhill from there.

Cell phone in hand before he'd even reached his Nitro, Rick punched in the speed dial number he'd programmed the day before.

Maybe foster parent Sue Bookman hadn't received his message. Or had lost his number. Maybe she didn't want to talk to him. At this point he didn't much care what she wanted.

"Hello?" She answered before the first ring was complete. And sounded breathless.

Young and breathless.

"Ms. Bookman?"

"Yes. This is Rick Kraynick, right?"

"Yes, ma'am."

"I recognized your number on caller ID," she said, her

voice uneven, as though she was still engaged in whatever physical activity had her so breathless to begin with. "I'm sorry I didn't get back to you. I've been a little…distracted."

The words came in more disjointed spurts. Was she jogging?

"No problem," he said, when, in fact, he'd spent the better part of the night before watching his phone. And fretting. "Did I get you at a bad time?"

"No worse than usual," she said, adding, "Better than some. So, how can I help?"

God, if only this could be so easy. He'd ask. She'd help. And life could go well. At least for one little person in his family.

It would be a first.

"Mr. Kraynick?"

"Yes. Sorry. I was…are you sure there isn't a better time to call?"

"I'm bouncing a baby, Mr. Kraynick. It's what I do."

"Is it Carrie?" he asked quickly, his pulse racing.

"How do you know Carrie?" She sounded defensive, which wouldn't do him any good.

"I'm her uncle," he explained, "her mother's— Christy's—older brother, and I know you have her."

"I can neither confirm nor deny your allegations, Mr. Kraynick. Please call social services." She rattled off the number.

"Wait!" he said, unable to hide his urgency. "Please," he said more calmly. "Just hear me out."

"How did you find me?"

"A friend of Christy's."

"I'm sorry I can't help you, Mr. Kraynick," she said softly. "This conversation is over."

"I grew up in foster care," he said, as though that gave him some special privilege. Some insider's edge.

"Then you know you shouldn't be calling me at all."

"Yes… But Carrie is my niece," he said. "I need to see her. To know that she's okay."

"You'll have to go through social services to arrange that."

"I'm sure you know it's not as easy as it sounds. I'm a single man with no real ties and I've no intention of petitioning for custody. They aren't real eager to give me the time of day. I never even knew Carrie's mother. For all intents and purposes, our mother didn't raise either one of us. All I have going for me is half a set of genes. My lawyer's on it, but it could be weeks—months—before this is sorted out. Carrie could be adopted by then. Which would be fine, great for her, but then I'd have lost my chance. I don't want to take her. I won't hurt her. I just have to see her."

"I'm sorry, Mr. Kraynick, but…"

* * * * *

*Find out if Rick Kraynick will ever have a chance
to meet his niece.
Look for A DAUGHTER'S TRUST
by Tara Taylor Quinn,
available in September 2009.*

**We'll be spotlighting a different series
every month throughout 2009
to celebrate our 60th anniversary.**

**Look for Harlequin® Superromance®
in September!**

*Celebrate with
The Diamond Legacy
miniseries!*

Follow the stories of four cousins as they come to terms
with the complications of love and what it means to
be a family. Discover with them the sixty-year-old secret
that rocks not one but two families.

A DAUGHTER'S TRUST by *Tara Taylor Quinn*
September

FOR THE LOVE OF FAMILY by *Kathleen O'Brien*
October

LIKE FATHER, LIKE SON by *Karina Bliss*
November

A MOTHER'S SECRET by *Janice Kay Johnson*
December

Available wherever books are sold.

You're invited to join our Tell Harlequin Reader Panel!

By joining our new reader panel you will:

- Receive Harlequin® books—they are FREE and yours to keep with no obligation to purchase anything!
- Participate in fun online surveys
- Exchange opinions and ideas with women just like you
- Have a say in our new book ideas and help us publish the best in women's fiction

In addition, you will have a chance to win great prizes and receive special gifts!
See Web site for details. Some conditions apply.
Space is limited.

To join, visit us at
www.TellHarlequin.com.

Tell
HARLEQUIN

REQUEST YOUR FREE BOOKS!

 Harlequin® Historical
Historical Romantic Adventure!

2 FREE NOVELS PLUS 2 FREE GIFTS!

YES! Please send me 2 FREE Harlequin® Historical novels and my 2 FREE gifts (gifts are worth about $10). After receiving them, if I don't wish to receive any more books, I can return the shipping statement marked "cancel". If I don't cancel, I will receive 6 brand-new novels every month and be billed just $4.94 per book in the U.S. or $5.49 per book in Canada. That's a savings of 20% off the cover price! It's quite a bargain! Shipping and handling is just 50¢ per book.* I understand that accepting the 2 free books and gifts places me under no obligation to buy anything. I can always return a shipment and cancel at any time. Even if I never buy another book, the two free books and gifts are mine to keep forever.

246 HDN EYS3 349 HDN EYTF

Name	(PLEASE PRINT)	
Address		Apt. #
City	State/Prov.	Zip/Postal Code

Signature (if under 18, a parent or guardian must sign)

Mail to the **Harlequin Reader Service**:
IN U.S.A.: P.O. Box 1867, Buffalo, NY 14240-1867
IN CANADA: P.O. Box 609, Fort Erie, Ontario L2A 5X3

Not valid to current subscribers of Harlequin Historical books.

Want to try two free books from another line?
Call 1-800-873-8635 or visit www.morefreebooks.com.

* Terms and prices subject to change without notice. Prices do not include applicable taxes. Sales tax applicable in N.Y. Canadian residents will be charged applicable provincial taxes and GST. Offer not valid in Quebec. This offer is limited to one order per household. All orders subject to approval. Credit or debit balances in a customer's account(s) may be offset by any other outstanding balance owed by or to the customer. Please allow 4 to 6 weeks for delivery. Offer available while quantities last.

Your Privacy: Harlequin Books is committed to protecting your privacy. Our Privacy Policy is available online at www.eHarlequin.com or upon request from the Reader Service. From time to time we make our lists of customers available to reputable third parties who may have a product or service of interest to you. If you would prefer we not share your name and address, please check here. ☐

HH09R

COMING NEXT MONTH FROM
HARLEQUIN®
HISTORICAL

Available August 25, 2009

• **THE PIRATICAL MISS RAVENHURST**
by **Louise Allen**
(Regency)
Forced to flee Jamaica disguised as a boy, Clemence Ravenhurst falls
straight into the clutches of one of the most dangerous pirates in the
Caribbean! Nathan Stanier, disgraced undercover naval officer, protects
her on their perilous journey. But who can protect his carefully guarded
heart from her?
The final installment of Louise Allen's Those Scandalous Ravenhursts
miniseries!

• **THE DUKE'S CINDERELLA BRIDE**
by **Carole Mortimer**
(Regency)
The Duke of Stourbridge thought Jane Smith a servant girl, so when
Miss Jane is wrongly turned out of her home for inappropriate behavior
after their encounter, the Duke takes her in as his ward. Jane knows she
cannot fall for his devastating charm. Their marriage would be forbidden—
especially if he were to discover her shameful secret....
The first in Carole Mortimer's The Notorious St. Claires *miniseries*

• **TEXAS WEDDING FOR THEIR BABY'S SAKE**
by **Kathryn Albright**
(Western)
Caroline Benet thought she'd never see soldier Brandon Dumont again—but
the shocking discovery that she is carrying his child forces her to find
him.... Darkly brooding Brandon feels his injuries hinder him from being
the man Caroline deserves, so he will marry her in name only. It takes a
threat on Caroline's life to make him see he could never let her or their
unborn child out of his sight again....
The Soldier and the Socialite

• **IN THE MASTER'S BED**
by **Blythe Gifford**
(Medieval)
To live the life of independence she craves, Jane has to disguise herself as
a young man! She will allow no one to take away her freedom. But she
doesn't foresee her attraction to Duncan—who stirs unknown but delightful
sensations in her highly receptive, very feminine body.
He would teach her the art of sensuality!